THIEV

is a unique experience: an outlaw world of the imagination, where mayhem and skulduggery rule and magic is still potent; brought to life by today's top fantasy writers, who are free to use one another's characters (but not to kill them off ... or at least not too freely!).

The idea for Thieves' World and the colorful city called Sanctuary came to Robert Lynn Asprin in 1978. After many twists and turns (documented in the volumes), the idea took off — and took on its own reality, as the best fantasy worlds have a way of doing. The result is one of F&SF's most unique success stories: a bestseller from the beginning, a series that is a challenge to writers, a delight to readers, and a favorite of fans.

Dramatis Personae

The Townspeople:

Illyra — Half-blood S'danzo seeress with True Sight.
  Dubro — Bazaar blacksmith and husband to Illyra.
Hakiem — Storyteller and confidant extraordinaire.
Jubal — Lynchpin of Sanctuary's organized crime. A magical healing has cost him decades of life. Many believe he is dead.
  Saliman — His aide and only friend.
Lalo the Limner — Artist gifted with magic he does not fully understand.
  Gilla — His indomitable wife.
Lastel; One-Thumb — Uptown merchant and owner of the Vulgar Unicorn. Freed from magic by Cime, he is a confused shadow of his former self.
Mama Becho — Owner of a disreputable Downwind tavern.
Mor-am, Moria — Brother and sister sell-swords. Former hawkmasks cut adrift by Jubal's downfall.
Mradhon Vis — Nisibisi adventurer and sometime spy.
Myrtis — Ageless owner of the Aphrodesia House.
Samlor hil Samt — Trader from the north and sometime resident of Sanctuary.

The Magicians:

Ischade — Necromancer and thief. Her curse is passed to her lovers, who die from it.
  Haught — A slave sent to her by the Stepsons; now free.
Enas Yorl — Shapeshifter cursed with immortality and wisdom.

The Rankans living in Sanctuary:

Cime — Assassin, particularly of magicians. Her involvement with Tempus is both ancient and mysterious.
Prince Kadakithis — Charismatic but naive governor of the town. Exiled to Sanctuary by his half-brother the Rankan Emperor.
Molin Torchholder; Torch — Archpriest of Vashanka. Next to the Prince the highest ranking imperial official in Sanctuary.
Stepsons; Sacred Banders — Members of a mercenary unit.
  Critias — Veteran fighter paired with Straton.
  Nikodemos; Stealth — Particularly skilled in mental and martial arts.
  Straton; Ace — Veteran fighter paired with Critias.
Tempus Thales; the Riddler — Hell-Hound. Nearly immortal mercenary through the power of Vashanka. Commander of the Stepsons.
Walegrin — Rankan army officer in charge of the Sanctuary garrison. Half-brother of Illyra the Seeress.

The Gods:

Heqt — Toad-faced goddess from pre-Ilsigi times.
Shipri — Ilsigi mother goddess.
Vashanka — The Rankan Stormgod. Patron of their conquering armies.

THE FACE OF CHAOS

Edited by
ROBERT LYNN ASPRIN & LYNN ABBEY

ACE FANTASY BOOKS
NEW YORK

"Introduction" copyright © 1983 by Robert Lynn Asprin.
"High Moon" copyright © 1983 by Janet Morris.
"Necromant" copyright © 1983 by C.J. Cherryh.
"The Art of Alliance" copyright © 1983 by Robert Lynn Asprin.
"The Corners of Memory" copyright © 1983 by Lynn Abbey.
"Votary" copyright © 1983 by David Drake.
"Mirror Image" © 1983 by Diana L. Paxson.

THE FACE OF CHAOS

An Ace Fantasy Book / published by arrangement with
the editors

PRINTING HISTORY
Ace Fantasy edition / October 1983
Tenth printing / January 1986
Eleventh printing / May 1986

ISBN: 0-441-80587-6

Ace Fantasy Books are published by The Berkley Publishing Group,
200 Madison Avenue, New York, New York 10016.
PRINTED IN THE UNITED STATES OF AMERICA

CONTENTS

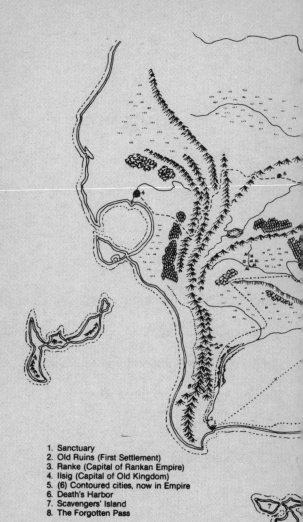

1. Sanctuary
2. Old Ruins (First Settlement)
3. Ranke (Capital of Rankan Empire)
4. Ilsig (Capital of Old Kingdom)
5. (6) Contoured cities, now in Empire
6. Death's Harbor
7. Scavengers' Island
8. The Forgotten Pass

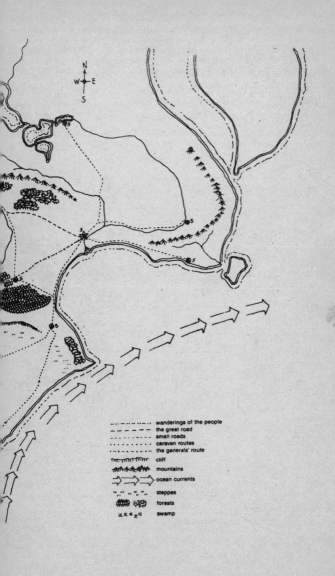

wanderings of the people
the great road
small roads
caravan routes
the generals' route
cliff
mountains
ocean currents
steppes
forests
swamp

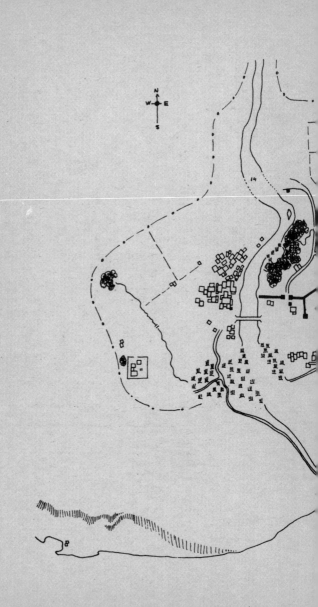

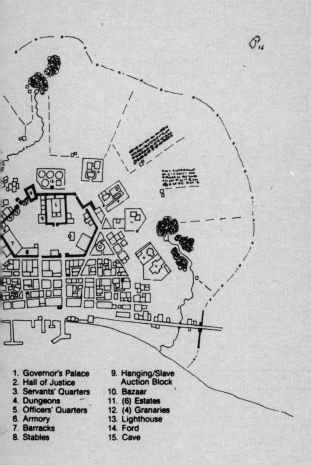

1. Governor's Palace
2. Hall of Justice
3. Servants' Quarters
4. Dungeons
5. Officers' Quarters
6. Armory
7. Barracks
8. Stables

9. Hanging/Slave
   Auction Block
10. Bazaar
11. (6) Estates
12. (4) Granaries
13. Lighthouse
14. Ford
15. Cave

← ~1 mile →

THE FACE OF CHAOS

INTRODUCTION

Robert Lynn Asprin

"The Face of Chaos will laugh at us all before the cycle completes its turn!"

The words were barely audible above the din of the bazaar, but they caught the ear of Illyra, stopping her in her tracks. Ignoring her husband's puzzled glance, she made her way into the crowds in search of the source of the voice. Though only half S'danzo, the cards were still her trade and she owed it to her clan to discover any intruders into their secrets.

A yellow-toothed smile flashed at her out of deep shadow, beside a stand. Peering closely, she recognized Hakiem, Sanctuary's oldest and most noted storyteller, squatting in the shelter, away from the morning sun's bright glare.

"Good morning, old one," she said coolly, "and what does a storyteller know of the cards?"

"Too little to try to earn a living reading them," Hakiem replied, scratching himself idly, "but much for one untrained in interpreting their messages.''

"You spoke of the Face of Chaos. Don't tell me you've finally paid for a reading?''

"Not at my age.'' The storyteller waved. "I'd prefer that the events of the future come as surprises. But I have eyes enough to know that that card means great change and upheaval. It requires no special sight to realize it must be showing often in readings these days, with the newcomers in town. I have ears, Illyra, as I have eyes. An old man listens and watches, enough not to be fooled by one who walks younger than her makeup and dress would lead most to believe.''

Illyra frowned. "Such observations could cost me dearly, old one.''

"Thou art wise, mistress. Wise enough to know the value of silence, as a hungry tongue talks more freely.''

"Very well, Hakiem,'' the fortune-teller laughed, slipping a coin into his outstretched palm. "Dull your ears, eyes *and* tongue with breakfast at my expense . . . and perhaps a cup of wine to toast the Face of Chaos.''

"A moment, mistress,'' the storyteller called as she turned to go. "A mistake! This is silver.''

"Your eyes are as keen as ever, you old devil. Take the extra as a reward for courage. I've heard what you have to do to gather the stories you *can* tell!''

Hakiem slid the coin into the pouch belted within his tunic and heard the satisfying clink as it joined the others secreted there. These days he extorted breakfast money more out of habit than need. Purses were growing fat in Sanctuary with the influx of wealth brought by the newcomers. Even extortion was growing easier, as people became less tightfisted. Some, like Illyra, seemed almost eager to give it away. Already, this morning, he had collected enough for ten breakfasts without exerting the effort hitherto required to obtain enough for one. After decades of decay, Sanctuary was coming to life again with the influx of wealth brought by the Beysib troops. Their military strength was far greater than the Sanctuary garrison could muster, and only the fact that the foreigners had made no claim to the governance of the city itself kept it in the hands of the Prince and his ministers. But the threat was always there, potent, lending a new spice of danger to the customary activities of the people of the city.

Scratching again, the storyteller frowned into the morning brightness, and not all his wrinkles were from squinting. It was almost . . . no, it *was* too good to be true. Hakiem had too many years of anguish behind him *not* to look a gift horse in the mouth. All gifts had a price, no matter how well-hidden or inconsequential it might seem at the time. It only stood to reason that the sudden prosperity brought by the newcomers would exact a price from the hell-hole known as Sanctuary. Exactly how high or terrible a price the storyteller was currently unable to puzzle out. (There were still hawks in Sanctuary, though not so easily brought to hand . . . and one hawkmaster in particular.) Sharper eyes than Hakiem's would be scrutinizing the effects and long-range implications of the new arrivals. Still, it would do him well to keep his ears open and . . .

"Hakiem! Here he is! I found him! Hakiem!"

The storyteller groaned inwardly as a brightly bedecked teenager leapt up and down, flapping his arms to reveal Hakiem's refuge to his comrades. Fame, too, had its price . . . and this particular one was named Mikali, a young fop whose main vocation seemed to be spending his father's wealth on fine clothing. That, and serving as Hakiem's self-proclaimed herald. Though the money from the more fashionable sides of Sanctuary was nice, the storyteller often longed for the days of anonymity when he'd had to rely on his own wits and skills to peddle his stories. Perhaps it was for this reason he clung to some of his old haunts in the Bazaar and the Maze.

"Here he is!" the youth proclaimed to his rapidly assembling audience. "The only man in Sanctuary who didn't run and hide when the Beysib fleet arrived in our harbors."

Hakiem cleared his throat noisily. "Do I know you, young man?"

A rude snicker rippled through the crowd as the youth flushed with embarrassment.

"S . . . Surely you remember. It's me, Mikali. Yesterday. . . ."

"If *you* know *me*," the elder interrupted, "you also know I don't tell stories to preserve my health, nor do I tolerate gawkers who block the view of paying customers."

"Of course." Mikali beamed. In a flash he had produced a handkerchief of fine silk. Cupping it in his hands, he began moving through the assemblage, collecting coins. As might be expected, he was loathe to undertake this chore silently.

"A gift for Sanctuary's greatest storyteller. . . . Hear of the landing from the lips of the one who welcomed them to our shore. . . . Gifts. . . . What's that? Coppers?! For Hakiem? Dig deeper into that purse or move along! That's the bravest man in town sitting there. . . . Thank you. . . . Gifts for the bravest man in Sanctuary. . . ."

In a nonce a double handful of coins had found their way into the handkerchief, and Mikali triumphantly presented it to Hakiem with a flourish. The storyteller weighed the parcel carelessly in his hand for a moment, then nodded and slipped the entire thing into his tunic, secretly enjoying the look of dismay that crossed the youth's face as Mikali realized the fine handkerchief would not be returned.

"Though I took my post on the wharf near midday, it was after dark before the fleet had anchored and the first of the Beysib ventured ashore. It was so dark, I did not even see the small boat being lowered over the side of one of the ships. Not until they lit torches and began pulling for the wharf was I aware of their intent to make contact before first light," Hakiem began.

Indeed, on that night Hakiem had nearly dozed off before he realized a boat was finally on its way from the fleet. Even a storyteller's curiosity had its limits.

"It was a sight to frighten children with; that torchlit craft creeping toward our town like some great spider from a nightmare, stalking its prey across an ink-black mirror. Though I was hailed as brave, it embarrasses me not to admit that I watched from the shadows. The wise know that darkness can shield the weak as easily as it harries the strong."

There were nods of acknowlegment throughout the crowd. This was Sanctuary, and every listener, regardless of social status, had sought refuge in the shadows more than once as the occasion arose, and did it more often than he would care to admit.

"Still, once they were ashore, I could see they were men not greatly different from us, so I stepped forth from my place of concealment and went to meet them."

This brave deed that Hakiem took on himself had been born of a mixture of impatience, curiosity, and drink . . . mostly the latter. While the storyteller had indeed been at his watchpost since midday, he had also been indulging all the while, helping himself to the wines left untended in the wharfside saloons. Thus it was that when the boat tied up at the wharf he was more sheets to the wind than its mother vessel had been.

The party from the boat advanced down the pier to the shore; then, rather than proceed into town, it had simply drawn up in a tight knot and waited. As minutes stretched on and no additional boats were dispatched from the fleet, it became apparent that this vanguard was expecting to be met by a delegation from the town. If that were truly the case, it occurred to Hakiem that they might well still be waiting at sunrise.

"You'll have to go to the palace!" he had called without thinking.

At the sound of his voice, the party had turned their glassy-eyed stares on him.

"Palace! Go Palace!" he repeated, ignoring the prickling at the nape of his neck.

"Hakiem!"

A figure in the group had beckoned him forward.

Of all things he had anticipated or feared about the invaders, the last thing Hakiem had expected was to be hailed by name.

Almost of their own volition, his legs propelled him shakily toward the group.

"The first one I met was the the one I least expected," Hakiem confided to his audience. "None other than our own Hort, whom we all believed to be lost at sea, along with his father. To say the least, I was astonished to find him not only among the living, but accompanying these invaders."

"By now you all have not only seen the Beysib, but have all grown accustomed to their strange appearance. Coming on them for the first time by torchlight on a deserted pier as I did, though, was enough to panic a strong man . . . and I am not a strong man. The hands holding the torches were webbed, as if they had come out of the sea rather than across it. The handles of the warriors' swords jutting up from behind their shoulders I had seen from afar, but what I hadn't noted was their eyes. Those dark, unblinking eyes staring at me with the torchlight reflecting in their depths nearly had me convinced that they would pounce on me like a pack of animals if I showed my fear. Even now, by daylight those eyes can . . ."

"Hakiem!"

The storyteller was pleased to note that he was not the only one who started at the sudden cry. He had not lost his touch for drawing an audience into a story. They had forgotten the morning glare and were standing with him on a torchlit pier.

Fast behind his pride, or perhaps overlapping it, was a wave of anger at having been interrupted in mid-tale. It was not a kindly gaze he turned on the interloper.

It was none other than Hort, flanked by two Beysib warriors. For a moment Hakiem had to fight off a wave of unreality, as if the youth had stepped out of the story to confront him in life.

"Hakiem! You must come at once. The Beysa herself wishes to see you."

"She'll have to wait," the storyteller declared haughtily, ignoring the murmurs that had sprung up among his audience, "I'm in the middle of a story."

"But you don't understand," Hort insisted, "she wants to offer you a position in her court!"

"No, *you* don't understand," Hakiem flared back, swelling in his anger without rising from his seat. "I already *am* employed . . . and will be employed until this story is done. These good people have commissioned me to entertain them and I intend to do just that until they are satisfied. You and your fish-eyed friends there will just have to wait."

With that, Hakiem returned his attention to his audience, ignoring Hort's discomfiture. The fact that he had not really wished to start this particular session was unimportant, as was the fact that service with the leader of the Beysib government-in-exile would undoubtedly be lucrative. Any storyteller, much less Sanctuary's best storyteller, did not shirk his professional duty in the midst of a tale, however tempting the counter-offer might be.

Gone were the days when he would scuttle off as soon as a few coins were tossed his way. The old storyteller's pride had grown along with his wealth, and Hakiem was no more exempt than any other citizen of Sanctuary from the effects of the Face of Chaos.

HIGH MOON

Janet Morris

Just south of Caravan Square and the bridge over the White Foal River, the Nisibisi witch had settled in. She had leased the isolated complex—one three-storied "manor house" and its outbuildings—as much because its grounds extended to the White Foal's edge (rivers covered a multitude of disposal problems) as for its proximity to her business interests in the Wideway warehouse district and its convenience to her caravan master, who must visit the Square at all hours.

The caravan disguised their operations. The drugs they'd smuggled in were no more pertinent to her purposes than the dilapidated manor at the end of the bridge's south-running cart track or the goods her men bought and stored in Wideway's most pilferproof holds, though they lubricated her dealings with the locals and eased her troubled nights. It was all subterfuge, a web of lies, plausible lesser evils to which she could own if the

Rankan army caught her or the palace marshal Tempus's Stepsons (mercenary shock troops and "special agents") rousted her minions and flunkies or even brought her up on charges.

Lately, a pair of Stepsons had been her particular concern. And Jagat—her first lieutenant in espionage —was no less worried. Even their Ilsig contact, the unflappable Lastel who had lived a dozen years in Sanctuary, cesspool of the Rankan empire into which all lesser sewers fed, and managed all that time to keep his dual identity as east-side entrepreneur and Maze-dwelling barman uncompromised, was distressed by the attentions the pair of Stepsons were paying her.

She had thought her allies overcautious at first, when it seemed she would be here only long enough to see to the "death" of the Rankan war god, Vashanka. Discrediting the state-cult's power icon was the purpose for which the Nisibisi witch, Roxane, had come down from Wizardwall's fastness, down from her shrouded keep of black marble on its unscalable peak, down among the mortal and the damned. They were all in this together: the mages of Nisibis; Lacan Ajami (warlord of Mygdon and the known world north of Wizardwall) with whom they had made pact; and the whole Mygdonian Alliance which he controlled.

Or so her lord and love had explained it when he decreed that Roxane must come. She had not argued— one pays one's way among sorcerers; she had not worked hard for a decade nor faced danger in twice as long. And if *one* did not serve Mygdon—*only one*—all would suffer. The Alliance was too strong to thwart. So she was here, drawn here with others fit for better, as if some power more than magical was whipping up a tropical storm to cleanse the land and using them to gild its eye.

She should have been home by now; she would have been, but for the hundred ships from Beysib which had come to port and skewed all plans. Word had come from `Mygdon, capital of Mygdonia, through the Nisibisi network, that she must stay.

And so it had become crucial that the Stepsons who sniffed round her skirts be kept at bay—or ensnared, or bought, or enslaved. Or, if not, destroyed. But carefully, so carefully. For Tempus, who had been her enemy three decades ago when he fought the Defender's Wars on Wizardwall's steppes, was a dozen Storm Gods' avatar; no army he sanctified could know defeat; no war he fought could not be won. Combat was life to him; he fought like the gods themselves, like an entelechy from a higher sphere—and even had friends among those powers not corporeal or vulnerable to sortilege of the quotidian sort a human might employ.

And now it was being decreed in Mygdonia's tents that he must be removed from the field—taken out of play in this southern theater, maneuvered north where the warlocks could neutralize him. Such was the word her lover-lord had sent her: move him north, or make him impotent where he stayed. The god he served here had been easier to rout. But she doubted that would incapacitate him; there were other Storm Gods, and Tempus, who under a score of names had fought in more dimensions than she had ever visited, knew them all. Vashanka's denouement might scare the Rankans and give the Ilsigs hope, but more than rumors and manipulation of theomachy by even the finest witch would be needed to make Tempus fold his hands or bow his head. To make him run, then, was an impossibility. To *lure* him north, she hoped, was not. For this was no place for Roxane. Her nose was offended by the stench which blew east from Downwind and north from Fisherman's Row and west from the Maze and south from either the slaughterhouses or the palace—she'd not decided which.

So she had called a meeting, itself an audacious move,

with her kind where they dwelled on Wizardwall's high peaks. When it was done, she was much weakened—it is no small feat to project one's soul so far—and unsatisfied. But she had submitted her strategy and gotten approval, after a fashion, though it pained her to have to ask.

Having gotten it, she was about to set her plan in motion. To begin it, she had called upon Lastel/One-Thumb and cried foul: "Tempus's sister, Cime the free agent, was part of our bargain, Ilsig. If you cannot produce her, then she cannot aid me, and I am paying you far too much for a third-rate criminal's paltry talents."

The huge wrestler adjusted his deceptively soft gut. His east-side house was commodious; dogs barked in their pens and favorite curs lounged about their feet, under the samovar, upon riotous silk prayer rugs, in the embrace of comely krrf-drugged slaves—not her idea of entertainment, but Lastel's, his sweating forehead and heavy breathing proclaimed as he watched the bestial event a dozen other guests found fetching.

The dusky Ilsigs saw nothing wrong in enslaving their own race. Nisibisi had more pride. It was well that these were comfortable with slavery—they would know it far more intimately, by and by.

But her words had jogged her host, and Lastel came up on one elbow, his cushions suddenly askew. He, too, had been partaking of krrf—not smoking it, as was the Ilsig custom, but mixing it with other drugs which made it sink into the blood directly through the skin. The effects were greater, and less predictable.

As she had hoped, her words had the power of krrf behind them. Fear showed in the jowled mountain's eyes. He knew what she was; the fear was her due. Any of these were helpless before her, should she decide a withered soul or two might amuse her. Their essences could lighten her load as krrf lightened theirs.

The gross man spoke quickly, a whine of excuses: the woman had "disappeared . . . taken by Aškelon, the very lord of dreams. All at the Mageguild's fete where the god was vanquished saw it. You need not take my word—witnesses are legion."

She fixed him with her pale stare. Ilsigs were called Wrigglies, and Lastel's craven self was a good example why. She felt disgust and stared longer.

The man before her dropped his eyes, mumbling that their agreement had not hinged on the mage-killer Cime, that he was doing more than his share as it was, for little enough profit, that the risks were too high.

And to prove to her he was still her creature, he warned her again of the Stepsons: "That pair of Whoresons Tempus sicced on you should concern us, not money—which neither of us will be alive to spend if—" One of the slaves cried out, whether in pleasure or pain Roxane could not be certain; Lastel did not even look up, but continued: ". . . Tempus finds out we've thirty stone of krrf in—"

She interrupted him, not letting him name the hiding place. "Then do this that I ask of you, without question. We will be rid of the problem they cause, thereafter, and have our own sources who'll tell us what Tempus does and does not know."

A slave serving mulled wine approached, and both took electrum goblets. For Roxane, the liquor was an advantage: looking into its depths, she could see what few cogent thoughts ran through the fat drug dealer's mind.

He thought of her, and she saw her own beauty: wizard hair like ebony and wavy; her sanguine skin like velvet: he dreamed her naked, with his dogs. She cast a curse without word or effort, reflexively, giving him a social disease no Sanctuary mage or barber-surgeon could cure, complete with running sores upon lips and member, and a virus in control of it which buried itself in the brainstem and came out when it chose. She hardly took note of it; it was a small show of temper, like for like: let him exhibit the condition of his soul, she had decreed.

To banish her leggy nakedness from the surface of her wine, she said straight out: "You know the other bar owners. The Alekeep's proprietor has a girl about to graduate from school. Arrange to host her party, let it be known that you will sell those children krrf—Tamzen is the child I mean. Then have your flunky lead her down to Shambles Cross. Leave them there—up to half a dozen youngsters, it may be—lost in the drug and the slum."

"*That* will tame two vicious Stepsons? You *do* know the men I mean? Janni? And Stealth? They bugger each other, Stepsons. Girls are beside the point. And Stealth—he's a *fuzz*buster—I've seen him with no woman old enough for breasts. Surely—"

"Surely," she cut in smoothly, "you don't want to know more than that—in case it goes awry. Protection in these matters lies in ignorance." She would not tell him more—not that Stealth, called Nikodemos, had come out of Azehur, where he'd earned his war name and worked his way toward Syr in search of a Trôs horse via Mygdonia, hiring on as a caravan guard and general roustabout, or that a dispute over a consignment lost to mountain bandits had made him bond-servant for a year to a Nisibisi mage—her lover-lord. There was a string on Nikodemos, ready to be pulled.

And when he felt it, it would be too late, and she would be at the end of it.

Tempus had allowed Niko to breed his sorrel mare to his own Trôs stallion to quell mutters among knowledge-able Stepsons that assigning Niko and Janni to hazard-ous duty in the town was their commander's way of punishing the slate-haired fighter who had declined

Tempus's offered pairbond in favor of Janni's and had subsequently quit their ranks.

Now the mare was pregnant and Tempus was curious as to what kind of foal the union might produce, but rumors of foul play still abounded.

Critias, Tempus's second in command, had paused in his dour report and now stirred his posset of cooling wine and barley and goat's cheese with a finger, then wiped the finger on his bossed cuirass, burnished from years of use. They were meeting in the mercenaries' guild hostel, in its common room, dark as congealing blood and safe as a grave, where Tempus had bade the veteran mercenary lodge—an operations officer charged with secret actions could be no part of the Stepsons' barracks cohort. They met covertly, on occasion; most times, coded messages brought by unwitting couriers were enough.

Crit, too, it seemed, thought Tempus wrong in sending Janni, a guileless cavalryman, and Niko, the youngest of the Stepsons, to spy upon the witch: clandestine schemes were Crit's province, and Tempus had usurped, overstepped the bounds of their agreement. Tempus had allowed that Crit might take over management of the fielded team and Crit had grunted wryly, saying he'd run them but not take the blame if they lost both men to the witch's wiles.

Tempus had agreed with the pleasant-looking Syrese agent and they had gone on to other business: Prince/Governor Kadakithis was insistent upon contacting Jubal, the slaver whose estate the Stepsons sacked and made their home. "But when we had the black bastard, you said to let him crawl away."

"Kadakithis expressed no interest." Tempus shrugged. "He has changed his mind, perhaps in light of the appearance of these mysterious death squads your people haven't been able to identify or apprehend. If your teams can't deliver Jubal or turn up a hawkmask who is in contact with him, I'll find another way."

"Ischade, the vampire woman who lives in Shambles Cross, is still our best hope. We've sent slave-bait to her and lost it. Like a canny carp, she takes the bait and leaves the hook." Crit's lips were pursed as if his wine had turned to vinegar; his patrician nose drew down with his frown. He ran a hand through his short, feathery hair. "And our joint venture with the Rankan garrison is impeding rather than aiding success. Army Intelligence is a contradiction in terms, like the Mygdonian Alliance or the Sanctuary pacification program. The cutthroats I've got on our payroll are sure the god is dead and all the Rankans soon to follow. The witch—or *some* witch—floats rumors of Mygdonian liberators and Ilsig freedom and the gullible believe. That snotty thief you befriended is either an enemy agent or a pawn of Nisibisi propaganda—telling everyone that *he's* been told by the Ilsig gods themselves that Vashanka was routed . . . I'd like to silence him permanently." Crit's eyes met Tempus's then, and held.

"No," he replied, to all of it, then added: "Gods don't die; men die. Boys die in multitudes. The thief, Shadowspawn, is no threat to us, just misguided, semi-literate, and vain, like all boys. Bring me a conduit to Jubal, or the slaver himself. Contact Niko and have him report—if the witch needs a lesson, I myself will undertake to teach it. And keep your watch upon the fish-eyed folk from the ships—I'm not sure yet that they're as harmless as they seem."

Having given Crit enough to do to keep his mind off the rumors of the god Vashanka's troubles—and hence, his own—he rose to leave. "Some results, by week's end, would be welcome." The officer toasted him cynically as Tempus walked away.

Outside, his Trôs horse whinnied joyfully. He stroked its mist-dappled neck and felt the sweat there. The weather was close, an early heatwave as unwelcome as the late frosts which had frozen the winter crops a week before their harvest and killed the young sets just planted in anticipation of a bounteous fall.

He mounted up and headed south by the granaries toward the palace's north wall where a gate nowhere as peopled or public as the Gate of the Gods was set into the wall by the cisterns. He would talk to Prince Kittycat, then tour the Maze on his way home to the barracks.

But the prince wasn't receiving, and Tempus's mood was ill—just as well; he had been going to confront the young popinjay, as once or twice a month he was sure he must do, without courtesy or appropriate deference. If Kadakithis was holed up in conference with the blond-haired, fish-eyed folk from the ships and had not called upon him to join them, then it was not surprising: since the gods had battled in the sky above the Mageguild, all things had become confused, worse had come to worst, and Tempus's curse had fallen on him once again with its full force.

Perhaps the god *was* dead—certainly, Vashanka's voice in his ear was absent. He'd gone out raping once or twice to see if the Lord of Pillage could be roused to take part in His favorite sport. But the god had not rustled around in his head since New Year's day; the resultant fear of harm to those who loved him by the curse that denied him love had made a solitary man withdraw even further into himself; only the Froth Daughter Jihan, hardly human, though woman in form, kept him company now.

And that, as much as anything, irked the Stepsons. Theirs was a closed fraternity, open only to the paired lovers of the Sacred Band and distinguished single mercenaries culled from a score of nations and diverted, by Tempus's service and Kittycat's gold, from the northern insurrection they'd drifted through Sanctuary en route to join.

He, too, ached to war, to fight a declared enemy, to lead his cohort north. But there was his word to a Rankan faction to do his best for a petty prince, and there was this thrice-cursed fleet of merchant warriors come to harbor talking "peaceful trade" while their vessels rode too low in the water to be filled with grain or cloth or spices—if not barter, his instinct told him, the Burek faction of Beysib would settle for conquest.

He was past caring; things in Sanctuary were too confuted for one man, even one near-immortal, god-ridden avatar of a man, to set aright. He would take Jihan and go north, with or without the Stepsons—his accursed presence among them and the love they bore him would kill them if he let it continue: if the god was truly gone, then he must follow. Beyond Sanctuary's borders, other Storm Gods held sway, other names were hallowed. The primal Lord Storm (Enlil), whom Niko venerated, had heard a petition from Tempus for a clearing of his path and his heart: he wanted to know what status his life, his curse, and his god-bond had, these days. He awaited only a sign.

Once, long ago, when he went abroad as a philosopher and sought a calmer life in a calmer world, he had said that to gods all things are beautiful and good and just, but men have supposed some things to be unjust, others just. If the god had died, or been banished, though it didn't seem that this could be so, then it was meet that this occurred. But those who thought it so did not realize that one could not escape the intelligible light: the notice of that which never sets: the apprehension of the elder gods. So he had asked, and so he waited.

He had no doubt that the answer would be forthcoming, as he had no doubt that he would not mistake it when it came.

On his way to the Maze he brooded over his curse, which kept him unloved by the living and spurned by

any he favored if they be mortal. In heaven he had a
brace of lovers, ghosts like the original Stepson, Abarsis. But to heaven he could not repair: his flesh regener-
ated itself immemorially; to make sure this was still the
case, last night he had gone to the river and slit both
wrists. By the time he'd counted to fifty the blood had
ceased to flow and healing had begun. That gift of healing—if gift it was—still remained his, and since it was
god-given, some power more than mortal "loved" him
still.

It was whim that made him stop by the weapons shop
the mercenaries favored. Three horses tethered out
front were known to him; one was Niko's stallion, a big
black with points like rust and a jughead on thickening
neck perpetually sweatbanded with sheepskin to keep its
jowls modest. The horse, as mean as it was ugly, snorted
a challenge to Tempus's Trôs—the black resented that
the Trôs had climbed Niko's mare.

He tethered it at the far end of the line and went inside, among the crossbows, the flying wings, the steel
and wooden quarrels and the swords.

Only a woman sat behind the counter, pulchritudin-
ous and vain, her neck hung with a wealth of baubles,
her flesh perfumed. She knew him, and in seconds his
nose detected acrid, nervous sweat and the defensive
musk a woman can exude.

"Marc's out with the boys in back, sighting-in the
high-torque bows. Shall I get him, Lord Marshal? Or
may I help you? What's here's yours, my lord, on trial
or as our gift—" Her arm spread wide, bangles tinkling,
indicating the racked weapons.

"I'll take a look out back, madam; don't disturb
yourself."

She settled back, not calm, but bidden to remain and
obedient.

In the ochre-walled yard ten men were gathered
behind the log fence that marked the range; a hundred

yards away three oxhides had been fastened to the encircling wall, targets painted red upon them; between the hides, three cuirasses of four-ply hardened leather armored with bronze plates were propped and filled with straw.

The smith was down on his knees, a crossbow fixed in a vise with its owner hovering close by. The smith hammered the sights twice more, put down his file, grunted and said, "You try it, Straton; it should shoot true. I got a hand-breadth group with it this morning; it's your eye I've got to match. . . ."

The large-headed, raw-boned smith, sporting a beard which evened a rough complexion, rose with exaggerated effort and turned to another customer, just stepping up to the firing line. "No, Stealth, not like that, or, if you must, I'll change the tension—" Marc moved in, telling Niko to throw the bow up to his shoulder and fire from there, then saw Tempus and left the group, hands spreading on his apron.

Bolts spat and thunked from five shooters when the morning's range officer hollered "Clear" and "Fire," then "Hold," so that all could go to the wall to check their aim and the depths to which the shafts had sunk.

Shaking his head, the smith confided: "Straton's got a problem I can't solve. I've had it truly sighted—perfect for me—three times, but when he shoots, it's as if he's aiming two feet low."

"For the bow, the name is life, but the work is death. In combat it will shoot true for him; here, he's worried how they judge his prowess. He's not thinking enough of his weapon, too much of his friends."

The smith's keen eyes shifted; he rubbed his smile with a greasy hand. "Aye, and that's the truth. And for you, Lord Tempus? We've the new hard-steel, though why they're all so hot to pay twice the price when men're soft as clay and even wood will pierce the boldest belly, I can't say."

"No steel, just a case of iron-tipped short-flights, when you can."

"I'll select them myself. Come and watch them, now? We'll see what their nerve's like, if you call score . . ."

"A moment or two, Marc. Go back to your work, I'll sniff around on my own."

And so he approached Niko, on pretense of admiring the Stepson's new bow, and saw the shadowed eyes, blank as ever but veiled like the beginning beard that masked his jaw: "How goes it, Niko? Has your *maat* returned to you?"

"Not likely," the young fighter, cranking the spring and lever so a bolt notched, said and triggered the quarrel which whispered straight and true to center his target. "Did Crit send you? I'm fine, commander. He worries too much. We can handle her, no matter how it seems. It's just time we need . . . she's suspicious, wants us to prove our faith. Shall I, by whatever means?"

"Another week on this is all I can give you. Use discretion, your judgment's fine with me. What you think she's worth, she's worth. If Critias questions that, your orders came from me and you may tell him so."

"I will, and with pleasure. I'm not his to wetnurse; he can't keep that in his head."

"And Janni?"

"It's hard on him, pretending to be . . . what we're pretending to be. The men talk to him about coming back out to the barracks, about forgetting what's past and resuming his duties. But we'll weather it. He's man enough."

Niko's hazel eyes flicked back and forth, judging the other men: who watched; who pretended he did not, but listened hard. He loosed another bolt, a third, and said quietly that he had to collect his flights. Tempus eased away, heard the range officer call "Clear" and watched Niko go retrieve his grouped quarrels.

If this one could not breach the witch's defenses, then she was unbreachable.

Content, he left then, and found Jihan, his de facto right-side partner, waiting astride his other Trôs horse, her more than human strength and beauty brightening Smith Street's ramshackle façade as if real gold lay beside fool's gold in a dusty pan.

Though one of the matters estranging him from his Stepsons was his pairing with this foreign "woman," only Niko knew her to be the daughter of a power who spawned all contentious gods and even the concept of divinity; he felt the cool her flesh gave off, cutting the midday heat like wind from a snowcapped peak.

"Life to you, Tempus." Her voice was thick as ale, and he realized he was thirsty. Promise Park and the Alekeep, an east-side establishment considered upper class by those who could tell classes of Ilsigs, were right around the corner, a block up the Street of Gold from where they met. He proposed to take her there for lunch. She was delighted—all things mortal were new to her; the whole business of being in flesh and attending to it was yet novel. A novice at life, Jihan was hungry for the whole of it.

For him, she served a special purpose: her loveplay was rough and her constitution hardier than his Trôs horses—he could not couple gently; with her, he did not inflict permanent harm on his partner; she was born of violence inchoate and savored what would kill or cripple mortals.

At the Alekeep, they were welcome. They talked in a back and private room of the god's absence and what could be made of it and the owner served them himself, an avuncular sort still grateful that Tempus's men had kept his daughters safe when wizard weather roamed the streets. "My girl's graduating school today, Lord Marshal—my youngest. We've a fete set and you and your companion would be most welcome guests."

Jihan touched his arm as he began to decline, her stormy eyes flecked red and glowing.

". . . ah, perhaps we will drop by, then, if business permits."

But they didn't, having found pressing matters of lust to attend to, and all things that happened then might have been avoided if they hadn't been out of touch with the Stepsons, unreachable down by the creek that ran north of the barracks when sorcery met machination and all things went awry.

On their way to work, Niko and Janni stopped at the Vulgar Unicorn to wait for the moon to rise. The moon would be full this evening, a blessing since anonymous death squads roamed the town—whether they were Rankan army regulars, Jubal's scattered hawkmasks, fish-eyed Beysib spoilers, or Nisibisi assassins, none could say.

The one thing that could be said of them for certain was that they weren't Stepsons or Sacred Banders or nonaligned mercenaries from the guild hostel. But there was no convincing the terrorized populace of that.

And Niko and Janni—under the guise of disaffected mercenaries who had quit the Stepsons, been thrown out of the guild hostel for unspeakable acts, and were currently degenerating Sanctuary-style in the filthy streets of the town—thought that they were close to identifying the death squads' leader. Hopefully, this evening or the next, they would be asked to join the murderers in their squalid sport.

Not that murder was uncommon in Sanctuary, or squalor. The Maze, now that Niko knew it like his horses' needs or Janni's limits, was not the town's true nadir, only the multi-tiered slum's upper echelon. Worse than the Maze was Shambles Cross, filled with the weak and the meek; worse than the Shambles was Downwind, where nothing moved in the light of day and at night hellish sounds rode the stench on the prevailing east wind across the White Foal. A tri-level hell, then, filled with murderers, sold souls and succubi, began here in the Maze.

If the death squads had confined themselves to Maze, Shambles, and Downwind, no one would have known about them. Bodies in those streets were nothing new; neither Stepsons nor Rankan soldiers bothered counting them; near the slaughterhouses cheap crematoriums flourished; for those too poor even for that, there was the White Foal, taking ambiguous dross to the sea without complaint. But the squads ventured uptown, to the east side and the center of Sanctuary itself where the palace hierophants and the merchants lived and looked away from downtown, scented pomanders to their noses.

The Unicorn crowd no longer turned quiet when Niko and Janni entered; their scruffy faces and shabby gear and bleary eyes proclaimed them no threat to the mendicants or the whores. Competition, they were now considered, and it had been hard to float the legend, harder to live it. Or to live it down, since none of the Stepsons but their task force leader, Crit (who himself had never moved among the barracks ranks, proud and shining with oil and fine weapons and finer ideals) knew that they had not quit but only worked shrouded in subterfuge on Tempus's orders to flush the Nisibisi witch.

But the emergence of the death squads had raised the pitch, the ante, given the matter a new urgency. Some said it was because Shadowspawn, the thief, was right: the god Vashanka had died and the Rankans would suffer their due. Their due or not, traders, politicians, and moneylenders—the "oppressors"—were nightly dragged out into the streets, whole families slaughtered or burned alive in their houses, or hacked to pieces in their festooned wagons.

The agents ordered draughts from One-Thumb's new

girl and she came back, cowering but determined, saying that One-Thumb must see their money first. They had started this venture with the barman's help; he knew their provenance; they knew his secret.

"Let's kill the swillmonger, Stealth," Janni growled. They had little cash—a few soldats and some Machadi coppers—and couldn't draw their pay until their work was done.

"Steady, Janni. I'll talk to him. Girl, fetch two Rankan ales or you won't be able to close your legs for a week."

He pushed back his bench and strode to the bar, aware that he was only half joking, that Sanctuary was rubbing him raw. *Was* the god dead? *Was* Tempus in thrall to the Froth Daughter who kept his company? *Was* Sanctuary the honeypot of chaos? A hell from which no man emerged? He pushed a threesome of young puds aside and whistled piercingly when he reached the bar. The big bartender looked around elaborately, raised a scar-crossed eyebrow, and ignored him. Stealth counted to ten and then methodically began emptying other patrons' drinks onto the counter. Men were few here; approximations cursed him and backed away; one went for a beltknife but Stealth had a dirk in hand that gave him pause. Niko's gear was dirty, but better than any of these had. And he was ready to clean his soiled blade in any one of them. They sensed it; his peripheral perception read their moods, though he couldn't read their minds. Where his *maat*—his balance—once had been was a cold, sick anger. In Sanctuary he had learned despair and futility, and these had introduced him to fury. Options he once had considered last resorts, off the battlefield, came easily to mind now. Son of the armies, he was learning a different kind of war in Sanctuary, and learning to love the havoc his own right arm could wreak. It was not a substitute for the equilibrium he'd lost when his left-side leader died

down by the docks, but if his partner needed souls to
buy a better place in heaven, Niko would gladly send
him double his comfort's price.

The ploy brought One-Thumb down to stop him.
"Stealth, I've had enough of you." One-Thumb's
mouth was swollen, his upper lip crusted with sores, but
his ponderous bulk loomed large; from the corner of his
eye Niko could see the Unicorn's bouncer leave his post
and Janni intercept him.

Niko reached out and grabbed One-Thumb by the
throat, even as the man's paw reached under the bar,
where a weapon might lie. He pulled him close: "What
you've had isn't even a shadow of what you're going to
get, Tum-Tum, if you don't mind your tongue. Turn
back into the well-mannered little troll we both know
and love, or you won't *have* a bar to hide behind by
morning." Then, sotto voce: "What's up?"

"*She* wants you," the barkeep gasped, his face
purpling, "to go to her place by the White Foal at high
moon. If it's con*ven*ient, of course, my *lord*."

Niko let him go before his eyes popped out of his
head. "You'll put this on our tab?"

"Just this one more time, beggar boy. Your
Whoreson bugger-buddies won't lift a leg to help you;
your threats are as empty as your purse."

"Care to bet on it?"

They carried on a bit more, for the crowd's benefit,
Janni and the bouncer engaged in a staring match the
while. "Call your cur off, then, and we'll forget about
this—this once." Niko turned, neck aprickle, and
headed back toward his seat, hoping that it wouldn't go
any further. Not one of the four—bouncer, bar owner,
Stepsons—was entirely playing to the crowd.

When he'd reached his door-facing table, Lastel/
One-Thumb called his bruiser off and Janni backed
toward Niko, white-faced and trembling with eagerness:
"Let me geld one of them, Stealth. It'll do our reputations no end of good."

"Save it for the witch-bitch."

Janni brightened, straddling his seat, both arms on the table, digging fiercely with his dirk into the wood: "You've got a rendezvous?"

"Tonight, high moon. Don't drink too much."

It wasn't the drink that skewed them, but the krrf they snorted, little piles poured into clenched fists where thumb muscles made a well. Still, the drug would keep them alert: it was a long time until high moon, and they had to patrol for marauders while seeming to be marauding themselves. It was almost more than Niko could bear. He'd infiltrated a score of camps, lines and palaces on reconnaissance sorties with his deceased partner, but those were cleaner, quicker actions than this protracted infiltration of Sanctuary, bunghole of the known world. If this evening made an end to it and he could wash and shave and stable his horses better, he'd make a sacrifice to Enlil which the god would not soon forget.

An hour later, mounted, they set off on their tour of the Maze, Niko thinking that not since the affair with the archmage Aškelon and Tempus's sister Cime had his gut rolled up into a ball with this feeling of unmitigated dread. The Nisibisi witch might know him—she might have known him all along. He'd been interrogated by Nisibisi before, and he would fall upon his sword rather than endure it again now, when his dead teammate's ghost still haunted his mental refuge and meditation could not offer him shelter as it once had.

A boy came running up calling his name and his jughead black tossed its rust nose high and snorted, ears back, waiting for a command to kill or maim.

"By Vashanka's sulfurous balls, what now?" Janni wondered.

They sat their mounts in the narrow street; the moon was just rising over the shantytops; people slammed their shutters tight and bolted their doors. Niko could catch wisps of fear and loathing from behind the houses' façades; two mounted men in these streets meant trouble, no matter whose they were.

The youth trotted up, breathing hard. "Niko! Niko! The master's so upset. Thanks Ils I've found you. . . ." The delicate eunuch's lisp identified him: a servant of the Alekeep's owner, one of the few men Niko thought of as a friend here.

"What's wrong, then?" He leaned down in his saddle.

The boy raised a hand and the black snaked his head around fast to bite it. Niko clouted the horse between the ears as the boy scrambled back out of range. "Come on, come here. He won't try it again. Now, what's your master's message?"

"Tamzen! Tamzen's gone out without her body-guard, with—" The boy named six of the richest Sanctuary families' fast-living youngsters. "They said they'd be right back, but they didn't come. It's *her* party she's missing. The master's beside himself. He said if you can't help him, he'll call the Hell Hounds—the palace guard, or go out to the Stepsons' barracks. But there's no time, no time!" the frail eunuch wailed.

"Calm down, pud. We'll find her. Tell her father to send word to Tempus anyway, it can't hurt to alert the authorities. And say exactly this: that I'll help if I can, but he knows I'm not empowered to do more than any citizen. Say it back, now."

Once the eunuch had repeated the words and run off, Janni said: "How're you going to be in two places at once, Stealth? Why'd you tell him that? It's a job for the regulars, not for us. We can't miss this meet, not after all the bedbugs I've let chomp on me for this . . ."

"*Seh!*" The word meant offal in the Nisi tongue. "We'll round her and her friends up in short order. They're just blowing off steam—it's the heat and school's end. Come on, let's start at Promise Park."

When they got there, the moon showed round and

preternaturally large above the palace and the wind had died. Thoughts of the witch he must meet still troubled Niko, and Janni's grousing buzzed in his ears: ". . . we should check in with Crit, let the girl meet her fate —ours will be worse if we're snared by enchantment and no backup alerted to where or how."

"We'll send word or stop by the Shambles drop; stop worrying." But Janni was not about to stop, and Niko's attempts to calm himself, to find transcendent perception in his rest-place and pick up the girl's trail by the heat-track she'd left and the things she'd said and done here were made more difficult by Janni's worries, which jarred him back to concerns he must put aside, and Janni's words, which startled him, over-loud and disruptive, every time he got himself calmed enough to sense Tamzen's energy trail among so many others like red/yellow/pink yarn twined among chiaroscuro trees.

Tamzen, thirteen and beautiful, pure and full of fun, who loved him with all her heart and had made him promise to "wait" for her: He'd had her, a thing he'd never meant to do, and had her with her father's knowledge, confronted by the concerned man one night when Niko, arm around the girl's waist, had walked her through the park. "Is this how you repay a friend's kindness, Stealth?" the father'd asked. "Better me than any of this trash, my friend. I'll do it right. She's ready, and it wouldn't be long, in any case," he'd replied while the girl looked between the soldier, twelve years older, and her father, with uncomprehending eyes. He had to find her.

Janni, as if in receipt of the perceptive spirit Niko tried now to reclaim, swore and mentioned that Niko'd had no business getting involved with her, a child.

"I'm not *your* type, and as for women, I drink from no other man's tainted cup." So Niko broached an uneasy subject: Janni was no Sacred Bander; his camaraderie had limits; Niko's need for touch and love

the other man knew but could not fill; they had an at-
tenuated pairbond, not complete as Sacred Banders
knew it, and Janni was uncomfortable with the in-
nuendo and assumptions of the other singles, and
Niko's unsated needs as well.

The silence come between them then gave Stealth his
chance to find the girl's red time-shadow, a hot ghost-
trail to follow southwest through the Maze . . .

As the moon climbed high its light shone brighter,
giving Maze and then Shambles shape and teasing light;
color was almost present among the streets, so bright it
shone, a reddish cast like blood upon its face, so that
when common Sanctuary horrors lay revealed at in-
tersections, they seemed worse even than they were.
Janni saw two whores fight for a client; he saw blood
run black in gutters from thugs and just incautious folk.
Their horses' hoofbeats cleared their path, though, and
Maze was left behind, as willing to let them go as they to
leave it, although Janni muttered at every vile encounter
their presence interrupted, wishing they could intervene.

Once he thought they'd glimpsed a death squad, and
urged Stealth to come alert, but the strange young
fighter shook his head and hushed him, slouched loose
upon his horse as if entranced, following some trail that
neither Janni nor any mortal man with God's good fear
of magic should have seen. Janni's heart was troubled
by this boy who was too good at craft, who had a
charmed sword and dagger given him by the entelechy
of dreams, yet left them in the barracks, decrying
magic's price. But what was this, if not sorcery? Janni
watched Niko watch the night and take them deep into
shadowed alleys with all the confidence a mage would
flaunt. The youth had offered to teach him "controls"
of mind, to take him "up through the planes and get
your guide and your twelfth-plane name." But Janni
was no connoisseur of witchcraft; like boy-loving, he
left it to the Sacred Banders and the priests. He'd gotten

into this with Niko for worldly advantage; the youth ten years his junior was pure genius in a fight; he'd seen him work at Jubal's and marveled even in the melee of the sack. Niko's reputation for prowess in the field was matched only by Straton's, and the stories told of Niko's past. The boy had trained among Successors, the Nisibisi's bane, wild guerrillas, mountain commandos who let none through Wizardwall's defiles without gold or life in tithe, who'd sworn to reclaim their mountains from the mages and the warlocks and held out, outlaws, countering sorcery with swords. In a campaign such as the northern one coming, Niko's skills and languages and friends might prove invaluable. Janni, from Machad, had no love for Rankans, but it was said Niko served despite a blood hatred: Rankans had sacked his town nameless; his father had died fighting Rankan expansion when the boy was five. Yet he'd come south on Abarsis's venture, and stayed when Tempus inherited the band.

When they crossed the Street of Shingles and headed into Shambles Cross, the pragmatic Janni spoke a soldier's safe-conduct prayer and touched his warding charm. A confusion of turns within the ways high-grown with hovels which cut off view and sky, they heard commotion, shouting men and running feet.

They spurred their horses and careened round corners, forgetful of their pose as independent reavers, for they'd heard Stepsons calling maneuver codes. So it was that they came, sliding their horses down on haunches so hard sparks flew from iron-shod hooves, cutting off the retreat of three running on foot from Stepsons, and vaulted down to the cobbles to lend a hand.

Niko's horse, itself, took it in its mind to help, and charged past them, reins dragging, head held high, to back a fugitive against a mudbrick wall. "*Seh!* Run, Vis!" they heard, and more in a tongue Janni thought might be Nisi, for the exclamation was.

By then Niko had one by the collar and two quarrels shot by close to Janni's ear. He hollered out his identity and called to the shooters to cease their fire before he was skewered like the second fugitive, pinned by two bolts against the wall. The third quarry struggled now between the two on-duty Stepsons, one of whom called out to Janni to hold the second. It was Straton's voice, Janni realized, and Straton's quarrels pinning the indigent by cape and crotch against the wall. Lucky for the delinquent it had been: Straton's bolts had pierced no vital spot, just clothing.

It was not till then that Janni realized that Niko was talking to the first fugitive, the one his horse had pinned, in Nisi, and the other answering back, fast and low, his eyes upon the vicious horse, quivering and covered with phosphorescent froth, who stood watchful by his master, hoping still that Niko would let him pound the quarry into gory mud.

Straton and his partner, dragging the first unfortunate between them, came up, full of thanks and victory: "... finally got one, alive. Janni, how's yours?"

The one he held at crossbow-point was quiet, submissive, a Sanctuarite, he thought, until Straton lit a torch. Then they saw a slave's face, dark and arch like Nisibisi's were, and Straton's partner spoke for the first time: "That's Haught, the slave-bait." Critias moved forward, torch in hand. "Hello, pretty. We'd thought you'd run or died. We've lots to ask you, puppy, and nothing we'd rather do tonight. . . ." As Crit moved in and Janni stepped back, Janni was conscious that Niko and his prisoner had fallen silent.

Then the slave, amazingly, straightened up and raised its head, reaching within its jerkin. Janni levered his bow, but the hand came out with a crumpled paper in it, and this he held forth, saying: "She freed me. She said this says so. Please . . . I know nothing, but that she's freed me. . . ."

Crit snatched the feathered parchment from him, held it squinting in the torch's light. "That's right, that's what it says here." He rubbed his jaw; then stepped forward. The slave flinched, his handsome face turned away. Crit pulled out the bolts that held him pinned, grunting; no blood followed; Straton's quarrels penetrated clothing only; the slave crouched down, unscathed but incapacitated by his fear. "Come as a free man, then, and talk to us. We won't hurt you, boy. Talk and you can go."

Niko, then, intruded, his prisoner beside him, his horse following close behind. "Let them go, Crit."

"*What?* Niko, forget the game, tonight. They'll not live to tell you helped us. We've been needing this advantage too long—"

"Let them go, Crit." Beside him his prisoner cursed or hissed or intoned a spell, but did not break to run. Niko stepped close to his task force leader, whispering: "This one's an ex-commando, a fighter from Wizard-wall come upon hard times. Do him a service, as I must, for services done."

"Nisibisi? More's the reason, then, to take them and break them—"

"No. He's on the other side from warlocks; he'll do us more good free in the streets. Won't you, Vis?"

The foreign-looking ruffian agreed, his voice thick with an accent detectable even in his three clipped syllables.

Niko nodded. "See, Crit? This is Vis. Vis, this is Crit. I'll be the contact for his reports. Go on, now. You, too, freedman, go. Run!"

And the two, taking Niko at his word, dashed away before Crit could object.

The third, in Straton's grasp, writhed wildly. This was a failed hawkmask, very likely, in Straton's estimation the prize of the three and one no word from Niko could make the mercenary loose.

Niko agreed that he'd not try to save any of Jubal's
minions, and that was that . . . almost. They had to keep
their meeting brief; any could be peeking out from win-
dowsill or shadowed door; but as they mounted up to
ride away, Janni saw a cowled figure rising from a pool
of darkness occluding the intersection. It stood, full up,
momentarily, and moonrays struck its face. Janni shuddered; it was a face with hellish eyes, too far to be so big
or so frightening, yet their met glance shocked him like
icy water and made his limbs to shake.

"Stealth! Did you see that?"

"What?" Niko snapped, defensive over interfering in
Crit's operation. "See what?"

"That—thing . . ." Nothing was there, where he had
seen it. "Nothing. . . . I'm seeing things." Crit and
Straton had reached their horses; they heard hoofbeats
receding in the night.

"Show me where, and tell me what."

Janni swung up on his mount and led the way; when
they got there they found a crumpled body, a youth with
bloated tongue outstuck and rolled up eyes as if a fit
had taken him, dead as Abarsis in the street. "Oh,
no. . . ." Niko, dismounted, rolled the corpse. "It's one
of Tamzen's friends." The silk-and-linened body came
clearer as Janni's eyes accustomed themselves to moonlight after the glare of the torch. They heaved the corpse
up upon Janni's horse who snorted to bear a dead thing
but forbore to refuse outright. "Let's take it somewhere, Stealth. We can't carry it about all night." Only
then did Janni remember they'd failed to report to Crit
their evening's plan.

At his insistence, Niko agreed to ride by the Shambles
Cross safe haven, caulked and shuttered in iron, where
Stepsons and street men and Ilsig/Rankan garrison per-
sonnel, engaged in chasing hawkmasks and other covert
enterprises, made their slum reports *in situ*.

They managed to leave the body there, but not to

alert the task force leader; Crit had taken the hawkmask wherever he thought the catch would serve them best; nothing was in the room but the interrogation wheel and bags of lime to tie on unlucky noses and truncheons of sailcloth filled with gravel and iron filings to change the most steadfast heart. They left a note, carefully coded, and hurried back onto the street. Niko's brow was furrowed, and Janni, too, was in a hurry to see if they might find Tamzen and her friends as a living group, not one by one, cold corpses in the gutter.

The witch Roxane had house snakes, a pair brought down from Nisibis, green and six feet long, each one. She brought them into her study and set their baskets by the hearth. Then, bowl of water by her side, she spoke the words that turned them into men. The facsimiles aped a pair of Stepsons; she got them clothes and sent them off. Then she took the water bowl and stirred it with her finger until a whirlpool sucked and writhed. This she spoke over, and out to sea beyond the harbor a like disturbance began to rage. She took from her table six carven ships with Beysib sails, small and filled with wax miniatures of men. These she launched into the basin with its whirlpool and spun and spun her finger round until the flagships of the fleet foundered, then were sunk and sucked to lie, at last, upon the bottom of the bowl. Even after she withdrew her finger the water raged awhile. The witch looked calmly into her maelstrom and nodded once, content. The diversion would be timely; the moon, outside her window, was nearly high, scant hours from its zenith.

Then it was time to take Jagat's report and send the death squads—or dead squads, for none of those who served in them had life of their own to lead—into town.

Tamzen's heart was pounding, her mouth dry and her lungs burning. They had run a long way. They were lost

and all six knew it; Phryne was weeping and her sister
was shaking and crying she couldn't run, her knees
wouldn't hold her; the three boys left were talking loud
and telling all how they'd get home if they just stayed in
a group—the girls had no need to fear. More krrf was
shared, though it made things worse, not better, so that
a toothless crone who tapped her stick and smacked her
gums sent them flying through the streets.

No one talked about Mehta's fate; they'd seen him
with the dark-clad whore, seen him mesmerized, seen
him take her hand. They'd hid until the pair walked on,
then followed—the group had sworn to stay together,
wicked adventure on their minds; all were officially
adults now; none could keep them from the forbidden
pleasures of men and women—to see if Mehta would
really lay the whore, thinking they'd regroup right after,
and find out what fun he'd had.

They'd seen him fall, and gag, and die once he'd
raised her skirts and had her, his buttocks thrusting
hard as he pinned her to the alley wall. They'd seen her
bend down over him and raise her head and the glowing
twin hells there had sent them pell-mell, fleeing what
they knew was no human whore.

Now they'd calmed, but they were deep in the Shambles, near its end where Caravan Square began. There
was light there, from midnight merchants engaged in
double-dealing; it was not safe there, one of the boys
said: slaves were made this way: children taken, sold
north and never seen again.

"It's safe *here*, then?" Tamzen blurted, her teeth
chattering but the krrf making her bold and angry. She
strode ahead, not waiting to see them follow; they
would; she knew this bunch better than their mothers.
The thing to do, she was sure, was to stride bravely on
until they came upon the Square and found the streets
home, or came upon some Hell Hounds, palace soldiers, or Stepsons. Niko's friends would ride them home
on horseback if they found some; Tamzen's acquain-

tance among the men of steel was her fondest prize.

Niko. . . . If *he* were here, she'd have no fear, nor
need to pretend to valor. . . . Her eyes filled with tears,
thinking what he'd say when he heard. She was never
going to convince him she was grown if all her attempts
to do so made her seem the more a child. A *child's*
error, this, for sure . . . and one dead on her account.
Her father would beat her rump to blue and he'd keep
her in her room for a month. She began to fret—the
krrf's doing, though she was too far gone in the drug's
sway to tell—and saw an alley from which torchlight
shone. She took it; the others followed, she heard them
close behind. They had money aplenty; they would hire
an escort, perhaps with a wagon, to take them home.
All taverns had men looking for hire in them; if they
chanced Caravan Square, and fell afoul of slavers, she'd
never see her poppa or Niko or her room filled with
stuffed toys and ruffles again.

The inn was called the Sow's Ear, and it was foul. In
its doorway, one of the boys, panting, caught her arm
and jerked her back. "Show money in that place, and
you'll get all our throats slit quick."

He was right. They huddled in the street and sniffed
more krrf and shook and argued. Phryne began to wail
aloud and her sister stopped her mouth with a clapped
hand. Just as the two girls, terrified and defeated,
crouched down in the street and one of the boys, his
bladder loosed by fear, sought a corner wall, a woman
appeared before them, her hood thrown back, her face
hidden by a trick of light. But the voice was a gen-
tlewoman's voice and the words were compassionate.
"Lost, children? There, there, it's all right now, just
come with me. We'll have mulled wine and pastries and
I'll have my man form an escort to see you home.
You're the Alekeep owner's daughter, if I'm right? Ah,
good, then; your father's a friend of my husband . . .
surely you remember me?"

She gave a name and Tamzen, her sense swimming in

drugs and her heart filled with relief and the sweet taste
of salvation, lied and said she did. All six went along
with the woman, skirting the square until they came to a
curious house behind a high gate, well lit and gardened
and full of chaotic splendor. At its rear, the rush of the
White Foal could be heard.

"Now sit, sit, little ones. Who needs to wash off the
street grime? Who needs a pot?" The rooms were shadowed, no longer well lit; the woman's eyes were comforting, calming like sedative draughts for sleepless
nights. They sat among the silks and the carven chairs
and they drank what she offered and began to giggle.
Phryne went and washed, and her sister and Tamzen
followed. When they came back, the boys were nowhere
in sight. Tamzen was just going to ask about that when
the woman offered fruit, and somehow she forgot the
words on her tongue-tip, and even that the boys had
been there at all, so fine was the krrf the woman smoked
with them. She knew she'd remember in a bit, though,
whatever it was she'd forgot. . . .

When Crit and Straton arrived with the hawkmask
they'd captured at the Foalside home of Ischade, the
vampire woman, all its lights were on, it seemed, yet
little of that radiance cut the gloom.

"By the god's four mouths, Crit, I still don't understand why you let those others go. And for Niko.
What—?"

"Don't ask me, Straton, what his reasons are; I don't
know. Something about the one being of that Successors band, revolutionaries who want Wizardwall back
from the Nisibisi mages—there's more to Nisibis than
the warlocks. If that Vis *was* one, then he's an outlaw as
far as Nisibisi law goes, and maybe a fighter. So we let
him go, do him a favor, see if maybe he'll come to us,
do us a service in his turn. But as for the other—you saw
Ischade's writ of freedom—we gave him to her and she

let him go. If we want to use her . . . if she'll *ever* help us
find Jubal—and she *does* know where he is; this freeing
of the slave was a message: she's telling us we've got to
up the ante—we've got to honor her wishes as far as this
slave-bait goes.''

"But this . . . coming here *ourselves?* You know what
she can do to a man . . .''

"Maybe we'll like it; maybe it's time to die. I don't
know. I *do* know we can't leave it to the garrison—every
time they find us a hawkmask he's too damaged to tell
us anything. We'll never recruit what's left of them if
the army keeps killing them slowly and we take the
blame. And also,'' Crit paused, dismounted his horse,
pulled the trussed and gagged hawkmask he had slung
over his saddle like a haunch of meat down after him, so
that the prisoner fell heavily to the ground, "we've been
told by the garrison's intelligence liaison that the army
thinks Stepsons fear this woman.''

"Anybody with a dram of common sense would.''
Straton, rubbing his eyes, dismounted also, notched
crossbow held at the ready as soon as his feet touched
the ground.

"They don't mean that. You know what they mean;
they can't tell a Sacred Bander from a straight mercenary. They think we're all sodomizers and sneer at us
for that.''

"Let 'em. I'd rather be alive and misunderstood than
dead and respected.'' Straton blinked, trying to clear his
blurred vision. It was remarkable that Critias would
undertake this action on his own; he wasn't supposed to
take part in field actions, but command them. Tempus
had been to see him, though, and since then the task
force leader had been more taciturn and even more impatient than usual. Straton knew there was no use in
arguing with Critias, but he was one of the few who
could claim the privilege of voicing his opinion to the
leader, even when they disagreed.

They'd interrogated the hawkmask briefly; it didn't take long; Straton was a specialist in exactly that. He was a pretty one, and substantively undamaged. The vampire was discerning, loved beauty; she'd take to this one, the few bruises on him might well make him more attractive to a creature such as she: not only would she have him in her power but it would be in her power to save him from a much worse death than that she'd give. By the look of the tall, lithe hawkmask, by his clothes and his pinched face in which sensitive, liquid eyes roamed furtively, a pleasant death would be welcome. His ilk were hunted by more factions in Sanctuary than any but Nisibisi spies.

Crit said, "Ready, Strat?"

"I own I'm not, but I'll pretend if you do. If you get through this and I don't, my horses are yours."

"And mine, yours." Crit bared his teeth. "But I don't expect that to happen. She's reasonable, I'm wagering. She couldn't have turned that slave loose that way if she wasn't in control of her lust. And she's smart—smarter than Kadakithis's so-called 'intelligence staff,' or Hell Hounds, we've seen that for a fact."

So, despite sane cautions, they unlatched the gate, their horses drop-tied behind them, cut the hawkmask's ankle bonds and walked him to the door. His eyes went wide above his gag, pupils gigantic in the torchlight on her threshold, then squeezed shut as Ischade herself came to greet them when, after knocking thrice and waiting long, they were about to turn away, convinced she wasn't home after all.

She looked them up and down, her eyes half-lidded. Straton, for once, was grateful for the shimmer in his vision, the blur he couldn't blink away. The hawkmask shivered and lurched backward in their grasp as Crit spoke first:

"Good evening, madam. We thought the time had come to meet, face to face. We've brought you this gift, a token of our good will." He spoke blandly, matter-of-factly, letting her know they knew all about her and didn't really care what she did to the unwary or the unfortunate. Straton's mouth dried and his tongue stuck to the roof of it. None was colder than Crit, or more tenacious when work was under way.

The woman, Ischade, dusky-skinned but not the ruddy tone of Nisibis, an olive cast that made the whites of her teeth and eyes very bright, bade them enter. "Bring him in, then, and we'll see what can be seen."

"No, no. We'll leave him—an article of faith. We'd like to know what you hear of Jubal, or his band—whereabouts, that sort of thing. If you come to think of any such information, you can find me at the mercenaries' hostel."

"Or in your hidey-hole in Shambles Cross?"

"Sometimes." Crit stood firm. Straton, his relief a flood, now that he knew they weren't going *in* there, gave the hawkmask a shove. "Go on, boy, go to your mistress."

"A slave, then, is this one?" she asked Strat and that glance chilled his soul when it fixed on him. He'd seen butchers look at sheep like that. He half expected her to reach out and tweak his biceps.

He said: "What you wish, he is."

She said: "And you?"

Crit said: "Forbearance has its limits."

She replied: "Yours, perhaps, not mine. Take him with you; I want him not. What you Stepsons think of me, I shall not even ask. But cheap, I shall never come."

Crit loosed his hold on the youth, who wriggled then, but Straton held him, thinking that Ischade was without doubt the most beautiful woman he'd ever seen, and the hawkmask was luckier than most. If death was the gateway to heaven, she was the sort of gatekeep he'd like to admit him, when his time came.

She remarked, though he had not spoken aloud, that

such could easily be arranged.

Crit, at that, looked between them, then shook his head. "Go wait with the horses, Straton. I thought I heard them, just now."

So Straton never did find out exactly what was—or was not—arranged between his task force leader and the vampire woman, but when he reached the horses, he had his hands full calming them, as if his own had scented Niko's black, whom his gray detested above all other studs. When they'd both been stabled in the same barn, the din had been terrible, and stallboards shattered as regularly as stalls were mucked, from those two trying to get at each other. Horses, like men, love and hate, and those two stallions wanted a piece of each other the way Strat wanted a chance at the garrison commander or Vashanka at the Wrigglies' Ils.

Soon after, Crit came sauntering down the walk, unscathed, alone, and silent.

Straton wanted to ask, but did not, what had been arranged: his leader's sour expression warned him off. And an hour later, at the Shambles Cross safe haven, when one of the street men came running in saying there was a disturbance and Tempus could not be found, so Crit would have to come, it was too late.

What they could do about waterspouts and whirlpools in the harbor was unclear.

When Straton and Crit had ridden away, Niko eased his black out from hiding. The spirit-track he'd followed had led them here; Tamzen and the others were inside. The spoor met up with the pale blue traces of the house's owner near the Sow's Ear and did not separate thereafter. Blue was no human's color, unless that human was an enchanter, a witch, accursed or charmed. Both Niko and Janni knew whose house this was, but what Crit and Straton were doing here, neither wanted to guess or say.

"We can't rush the place, Stealth. You know what she is."

"I know."

"Why didn't you let me hail them? Four would be better than two, for this problem's solving."

"Whatever they're doing here, I don't want to know about. And we've broken cover as it is tonight." Niko crooked a leg over his horse's neck, cavalry style. Janni rolled a smoke and offered him one; he took it and lit it with a flint from his belt pouch just as two men with a wagon came driving up from Downwind, wheels and hooves thundering across the White Foal's bridge.

"Too much traffic," Janni muttered, as they pulled their horses back into shadows and watched the men stop their team before the odd home's door; the wagon was screened and curtained; if someone was within, it was impossible to tell.

The men went in and when they came out they had three smallish people with them swathed in robes and hooded. These were put into the carriage and it then drove away, turning onto the cart-track leading south from the bridge—there was nothing down there but swamp, and wasteland, and at the end of it, Fisherman's Row and the sea . . . nothing, that is, but the witch Roxane's fortified estate.

"Do you think—Stealth, was that them?"

"Quiet, curse you; I'm trying to tell." It might have been; his heart was far from quiet, and the passengers he sensed were drugged and nearly somnambulent.

But from the house, he could no longer sense the girlish trails which had been there, among the blue/archmagical/anguished ones of its owner and those of men. Boys' auras still remained there, he thought, but quiet, weaker, perhaps dying, maybe dead. It could be the fellow Crit had left there, and not the young scions of east-side homes.

The moon, above Niko's head, was near at zenith.

Seeing him look up, Janni anticipated what he was
going to say: "Well, Stealth, we've got to go down there
anyway; let's follow the wagon. Mayhap we'll catch it.
Perchance we'll find out whom they've got there, if we
do. And we've little time to lose—girls or no, we've a
witch to attend to."

"Aye." Niko reined his horse around and set it at a
lope after the wagon, not fast enough to catch it too
soon, but fast enough to keep it in earshot. When
Janni's horse came up beside his, the other mercenary
called: "Convenience of this magnitude makes me
nervous; you'd think the witch sent that wagon, even
snared those children, to be sure we'd have to come."

Janni was right; Niko said nothing; they were com-
mitted; there was nothing to do but follow; whatever
was going to happen was well upon them, now.

A dozen riders materialized out of the wasteland near
the swamp and surrounded the two Stepsons; none had
faces; all had glowing pure-white eyes. They fought as
best they could with mortal weapons, but ropes of spit-
ting power came round them and blue sparks bit them
and their flesh sizzled through their linen chitons and,
unhorsed, they were dragged along behind the riders until they no longer knew where they were or what was
happening to them or even felt the pain. The last thing
Niko remembered, before he awoke bound to a tree in
some featureless grove, was the wagon ahead, stopping,
and his horse, on its own trying to win the day. The big
black had climbed the mount of the rider who dragged
Niko on a tether, and he'd seen the valiant beast's thick
jowls pierced through by arrows glowing blue with
magic, seen his horse falter, jaws gaping, then fall as he
was dragged away.

Now he struggled, helpless in his bonds, trying to
clear his vision and will his pain away.

Before him he saw figures, a bonfire limning silhouettes. Among them, as consciousness came full upon him and he began to wish he'd never waked, was Tamzen, struggling in grisly embraces and wailing out his name, and the other girls, and Janni, spreadeagled, staked out on the ground, his mouth open, screaming at the sky.

"Ah," he heard, "Nikodemos. So kind of you to join us."

Then a woman's face swam before him, beautiful, though that just made it worse. It was the Nisibisi witch and she was smiling, itself an awful sign. A score of minions ringed her, creatures roused from graves, and two with ophidian eyes and lipless mouths whose skins had a greenish cast.

She began to tell him softly the things she wished to know. For a time he only shook his head and closed his ears and tried to flee his flesh. If he could retire his mind to his rest-place, he could ignore it all; the pain, the screams which split the night; he would know none of what occurred here, and die without the shame of capitulation: she'd kill him anyway, when she was done. So he counted determinedly backward, eyes squeezed shut, envisioning the runes which would save him. But Tamzen's screams, her sobs to him for help, and Janni's animal anguish, kept interfering, and he could not reach the quiet place and stay: he kept being dragged back by the sounds.

Still, when she asked him questions he only stared back at her in silence: Tempus's plans and state of mind were things he knew little of; he couldn't have stopped this if he'd wanted to; he didn't know enough. But when at length, knowing it, he closed his eyes again, she came up close and pried them open, impaling his lids with wooden splinters so that he would see what made Janni cry.

They had staked the Stepson over a wild creature's burrow—a badger, he later saw, when it had gnawed and clawed its way to freedom—and were smoking the rodent out by setting fire to its tunnel. When Janni's stomach began to show the outline of the animal within, Niko, capitulating, told all he knew and made up more besides.

By then the girls had long since been silenced.

All he heard was the witch's voice; all he remembered was the horror of her eyes and the message she bade him give to Tempus, and when he had repeated it, she pulled the splinters from his lids. . . . The darkness she allowed him became complete, and he found a danker rest-place than meditation's quiet cave.

In Roxane's "manor house" commotion raged; slaves went running and men cried orders, and in the court the caravan was being readied to make away.

She herself sat petulant and wroth, among the brocades of her study and the implements of her craft: water and fire and earth and air, and minerals and plants, and a globe sculpted from high peaks clay with precious stones inset.

A wave of hand would serve to load these in her wagon. The house spells' undoing would take much less than that—a finger's wave, a word unsaid, and all would be no more than it appeared: rickety and threadbare. But the evening's errors and all the work she'd done to amend them had drained her strength.

She sat, and Niko, in a corner, propped up but not awake, breathed raspingly: another error—those damn snakes took everything too literally, as well as being incapable of following simple orders to their completion.

The snakes she'd sent out, charmed to look like Stepsons, should have found the children in the streets; as Niko and Janni, their disguises were complete. But a vampire bitch, a cursed and accursed third-rater possessed of meager spells, had chanced upon the quarry and taken it home. Then she'd had to change all plans and make the wagon and send the snakes to retrieve the bait—the girls alone, the boys were expendable—and snakes were not up to fooling women grown and knowledgeable of spells. Ischade had given up her female prizes, rather than confront Nisibisi magic, pretending for her own sake that she believed the "Stepsons" who came to claim Tamzen and her friends.

Had Roxane not been leaving town this evening, she'd have had to wipe the vampire's soul—or at least her memory—away.

So she took the snakes out once more from their baskets and held their heads up to her face. Tongues darted out and reptilian eyes pled mercy, but Roxane had forgotten mercy long ago. And strength was what she needed, which in part these had helped to drain away. Holding them high she picked herself up and, speaking words of power, took them both and cast them in the blazing hearth. The flames roared up and snakes writhed in agony and roasted. When they were done she fetched them out with silver tongs and ate their tails and heads.

Thus fortified, she turned to Niko, still hiding mind and soul in his precious mental refuge, a version of it she'd altered when her magic saw it. This place of peace and perfect relaxation, a cave behind the meadow of his mind, had a ghost in it, a friend who loved him. In its guise she'd spoken long to him and gained his spirit's trust. He was hers, now, as her lover-lord had promised; all things he learned she'd know as soon as he. None of it he'd remember, just go about his business of war and death. Through him she'd herd Tempus whither she willed and through him she'd know the Riddler's every plan.

For Nikodemos, the Nisibisi bondservant, had never shed his brand or slipped his chains: though her lover had freed his body, deep within his soul a string was tied. Any time, her lord could pull it; and she, too, now, had it twined around her pinky.

He remembered none of what occurred after his interrogation in the grove; he recalled just what she pleased
and nothing more. Oh, he'd think he'd dreamed deliri-
ous nightmares, as he sweated now to feel her touch.

She woke him with a tap upon his eyes and told him
what he was: her pawn, her tool, even that he would not
recall their little talk or coming here. And she warned
him of undeads, and shriveled his soul when she showed
him, in her mirror-eyes, what Tamzen and her friends
could be, should he even remember what passed between them here.

Then she put her pleasure by and touched the bruised
and battered face: one more thing she took from him, to
show his spirit who was slave and who was master. She
had him service her and took strength from his swollen
mouth and then, with a laugh, made him forget it all.

Then she sent her servant forth, unwitting, the extra
satisfaction—gleaned from knowing that his spirit
knew, and deep within him cried and struggled—giving
the whole endeavor spice.

Jagat's men would see him to the road out near the
Stepsons' barracks; they took his sagging weight in
brawny arms.

And Roxane, for a time, was free to quit this scrofu-
lous town and wend her way northward: she might be
back, but for the nonce the journey to her lord's embrace was all she craved. They'd leave a trail well
marked in place and plane for Tempus; she'd lie in high-
peak splendor, with her lover-lord well pleased by what
she'd brought him: some Stepsons, and a Froth
Daughter, and a man the gods immortalized.

It took until nearly dawn to calm the fish-faces who'd
lost their five best ships; "lucky" for everyone that the
Burek faction's nobility had been enjoying Kadakithis's
hospitality, ensconced in the summer palace on the

lighthouse spit and not aboard when the ships snapped anchor and headed like creatures with wills of their own toward the maelstrom that had opened at the harbor's mouth.

Crit, through all, was taciturn; he was not supposed to surface; Tempus, when found, would not be pleased. But Kadakithis needed counsel badly; the young prince would give away his imperial curls for "harmonious relations with our fellows from across the sea."

Nobody could prove that this was other than a natural disaster; an "act of gods" was the unfortunate turn of phrase.

When at last Crit and Strat had done with the dicey process of standing around looking inconsequential while in fact, by handsign and courier, they mitigated Kadakithis's bent to compromise (for which there was no need except in the Beysib matriarch's mind) they retired from the dockside.

Crit wanted to get drunk, as drunk as humanly possible: helping the Mageguild defend its innocence, when like as not some mage or other had called the storm, was more than distasteful; it was counterproductive. As far as Critias was concerned, the newly elected First Hazard ought to step forward and take responsibility for his guild's malevolent mischief. When frogs fell from the sky, Straton prognosticated, such would be the case.

They'd done some good there: they'd conscripted Wrigglies and deputized fishermen and bullied the garrison duty officer into sending some of his men out with the long boats and Beysib dinghies and slave-powered tenders which searched shoals and coastline for survivors. But with the confusion of healers and thrill-seeking civilians and boat owners and Beysibs on the docks, they'd had to call in all the Stepsons and troops from road patrols and country posts in case the Beysibs took their loss too much to heart and turned upon the townsfolk.

On every corner, now, a mounted pair stood watch; beyond, the roads were desolate, unguarded. Crit worried that if diversion was some culprit's purpose, it had worked all too well: an army headed south would be upon them with no warning. If he'd not known that yesterday there'd been no sign of southward troop movement, he confided to Straton, he'd be sure some such evil was afoot.

To make things worse, when they found an open bar it was the Alekeep, and its owner was wringing his hands in a corner with five other upscale fathers. Their sons and daughters had been out all night; word to Tempus at the Stepsons' barracks had brought no answer; the skeleton crew at the garrison had more urgent things to do than attend to demands for search parties when manpower was suddenly at a premium; the fathers sat awaiting their own men's return and thus had kept the Alekeep's graveyard shift from closing.

They got out of there as soon as politic, weary as their horses and squinting in the lightening dark.

The only place where peace and quiet could be had now that the town was waking, Crit said sourly, was the Shambles drop. They rode there and fastened the iron shutters down against the dawn, thinking to get an hour or so of sleep, and found Niko's coded note.

"Why wouldn't the old barkeep have told us that he'd set them on his daughter's trail?" Strat sighed, rubbing his eyes with his palms.

"Niko's legend says he's defected to the slums, remember?" Crit was shrugging into his chiton, which he'd just tugged off and thrown upon the floor.

"We're not going back out."

"I am."

"To look for *Niko? Where?*"

"Niko and *Janni.* And I don't *know* where. But if that pair hasn't turned up those youngsters yet, it's no simple adolescent prank or graduation romp. Let's hope it's just that their meet with Roxane took precedence and it's inopportune for them to leave her." Crit stood.

Straton didn't.

"Coming?" Crit asked.

"Somebody should be where authority is expected to be found. You should be here or at the hostel, not chasing after someone who might be chasing after you."

So in the end, Straton won that battle and they went up to the hostel, stopping, since the sun had risen, at Marc's to pick up Straton's case of flights along the way.

The shop's door was ajar, though the opening hour painted on it hadn't come yet. Inside, the smith was hunched over a mug of tea, a crossbow's trigger mechanism dismantled before him on a split of suede, scowling at the crossbow's guts spread upon his counter as if at a recalcitrant child.

He looked up when they entered, wished them a better morning than he'd had so far this day, and went to get Straton's case of flights.

Behind the counter an assortment of high-torque bows was hung.

When Marc returned with the wooden case, Straton pointed: "That's Niko's, isn't it—or are my eyes that bad?"

"I'm holding it for him, until he pays," explained the smith with the unflinching gaze.

"We'll pay for it now and he can pick it up from me," Crit said.

"I don't know if he'd . . ." Marc, half into someone else's business, stepped back out of it with a nod of head: "All right, then, if you want. I'll tell him you've got it. That's four soldats, three . . . I've done a lot of work on it for him. Shall I tell him to seek you at the guild hostel?"

"Thereabouts."

Taking it down from the wall, the smith wound and

levered, then dry-fired the crossbow, its mechanism to his ear. A smile came over his face at what he heard. "Good enough, then," he declared and wrapped it in its case of padded hide.

This way, Straton realized, Niko would come direct to Crit and report when Marc told him what they'd done.

By the time dawn had cracked the world's egg, Tempus as well as Jihan was sated, even tired. For a man who chased sleep like other men chased power or women, it was wondrous that this was so. For a being only recently become woman, it was a triumph. They walked back toward the Stepsons' barracks, following the creekbed, all pink and gold in sunrise, content and even playful, his chuckle and her occasional laugh startling sleepy squirrels and flushing birds from their nests.

He'd been morose, but she'd cured it, convincing him that life might take a better turn, if he'd just let it. They'd spoken of her father, called Stormbringer in lieu of name, and arcane matters of their joint preoccupation: whether humanity had inherent value, whether gods could die or merely lie, whether Vashanka was hiding out somewhere, petulant in godhead, only waiting for generous sacrifices and heartfelt prayers to coax him back among his Rankan people—or, twelfth plane powers forfend, really "dead."

He'd spoken openly to her of his affliction, reminding her that those who loved him died by violence and those he loved were bound to spurn him, and what that could mean in the case of his Stepsons, and herself, if Vashanka's power did not return to mitigate his curse. He'd told her of his plea to Enlil, an ancient deity of universal scope, and that he awaited godsign.

She'd been relieved at that, afraid, she admitted, that the lord of dreams might tempt him from her side. For when Askelon the dream lord had come to take Tempus's sister off to his metaphysical kingdom of delights, he'd offered the brother the boon of mortality. Now that she'd just found him, Jihan had added throatily, she could not bear it if he chose to die.

And she'd spent that evening proving to Tempus that it might be well to stay alive with her, who loved life the more for having only just begun it, and yet could not succumb to mortal death or be placed in mortal danger by his curse, his strength, or whatever he might do.

The high moon had laved them and her legs had embraced him and her red-glowing eyes like her father's had transfixed him while her cool flesh enflamed him. Yes, with Jihan beside him, he'd swallow his pride and his pique and give even Sanctuary's Kadakithis the benefit of the doubt—he'd stay though his heart tugged him northward, although he'd thought, when he took her to their creekbed bower, to chase her away.

When they'd slipped into his barracks quarters from the back, he was no longer so certain. He heard from a lieutenant all about the waterspouts and whirlpools, thinking while the man talked that this was his godsign, however obscure its meaning, and then he regretted having made an accommodation with the Froth Daughter: all his angst came back upon him, and he wished he'd hugged his resolve firmly to his breast and driven Jihan hence.

But when the disturbance at the outer gates penetrated to the slaver's old apartments which he had made his own, rousting them out to seek its cause, he was glad enough she'd remained.

The two of them had to shoulder their way through the gathered crowd of Stepsons, astir with bitter mutters; no one made way for them; none had come to their commander's billet with news of what had been brought up to the gatehouse in the dawn.

He heard a harsh whisper from a Stepson too angry to be careful, wondering if Tempus had sent Janni's team

deliberately to destruction because Stealth had rejected
the Riddler's offered pairbond.

One who knew better answered sagely that this was a
Mygdonian message, a Nisibisi warning of some an-
tiquity, and *he* had heard it straight from Stealth's
broken lips.

"What *did* that?" Jihan moaned, bending low over
Janni's remains. Tempus did not answer her but said
generally: "And Niko?" and followed a man who
headed off toward the whitewashed barracks, hearing as
he went a voice choked with grief explaining to Jihan
what happens when you tie a man spreadeagled over an
animal's burrow and smoke the creature out.

The Stepson, guiding him to where Niko lay, said that
the man who'd brought them wished to speak to Tempus. "Let him wait for his reward," Tempus snapped,
and questioned the mercenary about the samaritan
who'd delivered the two Stepsons home. But the Sacred
Bander had gotten nothing from the stranger who'd
rapped upon the gates and braved the angry sentries
who almost killed him when they saw what burden he'd
brought in. The stranger would say only that he must
wait for Tempus.

The Stepson's commander stood around helplessly
with three others, friends of Niko's, until the barber-
surgeon had finished with needle and gut, then chased
them all away, shuttering windows, barring doors. Cup
in hand, then, he gave the battered, beaten youth his
painkilling draught in silence, only sitting and letting
Niko sip while he assessed the Stepson's injuries and
made black guesses as to how the boy had come by
green and purple blood-filled bruises, rope burns at
wrist and neck, and a face like doom.

Quite soon he heard from Nikodemos, concisely but
through a slur that comes when teeth have been loosed
or broken in a dislocated jaw, what had transpired: they
had gone seeking the Alekeep owner's daughter, deep

into Shambles where drug dens and cheap whores promise dreamless nights, found them at Ischade's, seen them hustled into a wagon and driven away toward Roxane's. Following, for they were due to see the witch at high moon in her lair in any case, they'd been accosted, surprised by a death squad armed with magic and visaged like the dead, roped and dragged from their horses. The next lucid interval Niko recalled was one of being propped against dense trees, tied to one while the Nisibisi witch used children's plights and spells and finally Janni's tortured, drawn-out death to extract from him what little he knew of Tempus's intentions and Rankan strategies of defense for the lower land. "Was I wrong to try not to tell them?" Niko asked, eyes swollen half-shut but filled with hurt. "I thought they'd kill us all, whatever. Then I thought I could hold out . . . Tamzen and the other girls were past help . . . but Janni—" He shook his head. "Then they . . . thought I was lying, when I couldn't answer . . . questions they should have asked of *you*—Then I did lie, to please them, but she . . . the witch knew. . . ."

"Never mind. Was One-Thumb a party to this?"

A twitch of lips meant "no" or "I don't know."

Then Niko found the strength to add: "If I hadn't tried to keep my silence—I've been interrogated before by Nisibisi. . . . I hid in my rest-place . . . until Janni —They killed him to get to me."

Tempus saw bright tears threatening to spill and changed the subject: "Your rest-place? So your *maat* returned to you?"

He whispered, "After a fashion. . . . I don't care about that now. Going to need all my anger . . . no time for balance anymore."

Tempus blew out a breath and set down Niko's cup and looked between his legs at the packed clay floor. "I'm going north, tomorrow. I'll leave sortie assignments and schedules with Critias—he'll be in command

here—and a rendezvous for those who want to join in
the settling up. Did you recognize any Ilsigs in her company? A servant, a menial, anyone at all?''

''No, they all look alike. . . . Someone found us, got
us to the gates. Some trainees of ours, maybe—they
knew my name. The witch said come ahead and die up-
country. Each reprisal of ours, they'll match fourfold.''

''Are you telling me not to go?''

Niko struggled to sit up, cursed, fell back with blood
oozing from between his teeth. Tempus made no move
to help him. They stared at each other until Niko said,
''It will seem that you've been driven from Sanctuary,
that you've failed here. . . .''

''Let it seem so; it may well be true.''

''Wait, then, until I can accompany—''

''You know better. I will leave instructions for you.''
He got up and left quickly, before his temper got the
best of him where the boy could see.

The samaritan who had brought their wounded and
their dead was waiting outside Tempus's quarters. His
name was Vis and though he looked Nisibisi he claimed
he had a message from Jubal. Because of his skin and
his accent Tempus almost took him prisoner, thinking
to give him to Straton, for whom all manner of men
bared their souls, but he marshaled his anger and sent
the young man away with a pocket full of soldats and
instructions to convey Jubal's message to Critias. Crit
would be in charge of the Stepsons henceforth; what
Jubal and Crit might arrange was up to them. The
reward was for bringing home the casualties, dead and
living, a favor cheap at the price.

Then Tempus went to find Jihan. When he did, he
asked her to put him in touch with Askelon, dream lord,
if she could.

''So that you can punish yourself with mortality?
This is not your fault.''

''A kind, if unsound, opinion. Mortality will break
the curse. Can you help me?''

"I will not, not now, when you are like this," she replied, concern knitting her brows in the harsh morning light. "But I will accompany you north. Perhaps another day, when you are calmer. . . ."

He cursed her for acting like a woman and set about scheduling sorties and sketching maps, so that each of his men would have worked out his debt to Kadakithis and be in good standing with the mercenaries' guild when and if they joined him in Tyse, at the very foot of Wizardwall.

It took no longer to draft his resignation and Critias's appointment in his stead and send them off to Kadakithis than it took to clear his actions with the Rankan representatives of the mercenaries' guild: his task here (assessing Kadakithis for a Rankan faction desirous of a change in emperors) was accomplished; he could honestly say that neither town nor townspeople nor effete prince was worth struggling to ennoble. For good measure he was willing to throw into the stewpot of disgust boiling in him both Vashanka and the child he had co-fathered with the god, by means of whom certain interests thought to hold him here: he disliked children, as a class, and even Vashanka had turned his back on this one.

Still, there were things he had to do. He went and found Crit in the guild hostel's common room and told him all that had transpired. If Crit had refused the appointment outright, Tempus would have had to tarry, but Critias only smiled cynically, saying that he'd be along with his best fighters as soon as matters here allowed. He left One-Thumb's case in Critias's hands; they both knew that Straton could determine the degree of the barkeep's complicity quickly enough.

Crit asked, as Tempus was leaving the dark and comforting common room for the last time, whether any children's bodies had been found—three girls and boys still were missing; one young corpse had turned up cold in Shambles Cross.

"No," Tempus said, and thought no more about it. "Life to you, Critias."

"And to you, Riddler. And everlasting glory."

Outside, Jihan was waiting on one Trôs horse, the other's reins in her hand.

They went first southwest to see if perhaps the witch or her agents might be found at home, but the manor house and its surrounds were deserted, the yard criss-crossed with cart-tracks from heavily laden wagons' wheels.

The caravan's track was easy to follow.

Riding north without a backward glance on his Trôs horse, Jihan swaying in her saddle on his right, he had one last impulse: he ripped the problematical Storm God's amulet from around his throat, dropped it into a quaggy marsh. Where he was going, Vashanka's name was meaningless. Other names were hallowed, and other attributes given to the weather gods.

When he was sure he had successfully cast it aside, and the god's voice had not come ringing with awful laughter in his ear (for all gods are tricksters, and war gods worst of any), he relaxed in his saddle. The omens for this venture were good: they'd completed their preparations in half the time he'd anticipated, so that he could start it while the day was young.

Crit sat long at his customary table in the common room after Tempus had gone. By rights it should have been Straton or some Sacred Band pair who succeeded Tempus, someone . . . anyone but him. After a time he pulled out his pouch and emptied its contents onto the plank table: three tiny metal figures, a fishhook made from an eagle's claw and abalone shell, a single die, an old field decoration won in Azehur while the Slaughter Priest still led the original Sacred Band.

He scooped them up and threw them as a man might throw in wager: the little gold Storm God fell beneath

the lead figurine of a fighter, propping the man upright;
the fishhook embraced the die, which came to rest with
one dot facing up—Strat's war name was Ace. The third
figure, a silver rider mounted, sat square atop the field
star—Abarsis had slipped it over his head so long ago
the ribbon had crumbled away.

Content with the omens his private prognosticators
gave, he collected them and put them away. He'd
wanted Tempus to ask him to join him, not hand him
fifty men's lives to yea or nay. He took such work too
much to heart; it lay heavy on him, worse than the task
force's weight had been, and he'd only just begun. But
that was why Tempus picked him—he was conscientious
to a fault.

He sighed and rose and quit the hostel, riding aim-
lessly through the fetid streets. Damned town was a pit,
a buboe, a sore that wouldn't heal. He couldn't trust his
task force to some subordinate, though how he was going to run them while stomping around vainly trying to
fill Tempus's sandals, he couldn't say.

His horse, picking his route, took him by the Vulgar
Unicorn where Straton would soon be "discussing sensitive matters" with One-Thumb.

By rights he should go up to the palace, pay a call on
Kadakithis, "make nice" (as Straton said) to Vash-
anka's priest-of-record Molin, visit the Mageguild. . . .
He shook his head and spat over his horse's shoulder.
He hated politics.

And what Tempus had told him about Niko's misfor-
tune and Janni's death still rankled. He remembered the
foreign fighter Niko had made him turn loose—Vis.
Vis, who'd come to Tempus, bearing hurt and slain,
with a message from Jubal. That, and what Straton had
gotten from the hawkmask they'd given Ischade, plus
the vampire woman's own hints, allowed him to triang-
ulate Jubal's position like a sailor navigating by the
stars. Vis was supposed to come to him, though. He'd

wait. If his hunch was right, he could put Jubal and his
hawkmasks to work for Kadakithis without either
knowing—or at least having to admit—that was the
case.

If so, he'd be free to take the band north—what they
wanted, expected, and would now fret to do with Tempus gone. Only Tempus's mystique had kept them this
long; Crit would have a mutiny, or empty barracks, if
he couldn't meet their expectation of war to come. They
weren't babysitters, slum police, or palace praetorians;
they collected exploits, not soldats. He began to form a
plan, shape up a scenario, answer questions sure to be
asked him later, rehearsing replies in his mind.

Unguided, his horse led him slumward—a barn-rat, it
was taking the quickest, straightest way home. When he
looked up and out, rather than down and in, he was
almost through the Shambles, near White Foal Bridge
and the vampire's house, quiet now, unprepossessing in
the light of day. Did she sleep in the day? He didn't
think she was that kind of vampire; there had been no
bloodloss, no punctures on the boy stiff against the
drop's back door when one of the street men found it.
But what did she do, then, to her victims? He thought of
Straton, the way he'd looked at the vampire, the exchange between the two he'd overheard and partly understood. He'd have to keep those two quite separate,
even if Ischade was putatively willing to work with,
rather than against, them. He spurred his horse on by.

Across the bridge, he rode southwest, skirting the
thick of Downwind. When he sighted the Stepsons'
barracks, he still didn't know if he could succeed in
leading Stepsons. He rehearsed it wryly in his mind:
"Life to all. Most of you don't know me but by
reputation, but I'm here to ask you to bet your lives on
me, not once, but as a matter of course over the next
months. . . ."

Still, someone had to do it. And he'd have no trouble

with the Sacred Band teams, who knew him in the old days, when he'd had a right-side partner, before that vulnerability was made painfully clear, and he gave up loving the death-seekers—or anything else which could disappoint him.

It mattered not a whit, he decided, if he won or if he lost, if they let him advise them or deserted post and duty to follow Tempus north, as he would have done if the sly old soldier hadn't bound him here with promise and responsibility.

He'd brought Niko's bow. The first thing he did— after leaving the stables, where he saw to his horse and checked on Niko's pregnant mare—was seek the wounded fighter.

The young officer peered at him through swollen, blackened eyes, saw the bow and nodded, unlaced its case and stroked the wood recurve when Critias laid it on the bed. Half a dozen men were there when he'd knocked and entered—three teams who'd come with Niko and his partner down to Ranke on Sacred Band business. They left, warning softly that Crit mustn't tire him—they'd just got him back.

"He's left me the command," Crit said, though he'd thought to talk of hawkmasks and death squads and Nisibisi—a witch and one named Vis.

"Gilgamesh sat by Enkidu seven days, until a maggot fell from his nose." It was the oldest legend the fighters shared, one from Enlil's time when the Lord Storm and Enki (Lord Earth) ruled the world, and a fighter and his friend roamed far.

Crit shrugged and ran a spread hand through feathery hair. "Enkidu was dead; you're not. Tempus has just gone ahead to prepare our way."

Niko rolled his head, propped against the white-washed wall, until he could see Crit clearly: "He followed godsign; I know that look."

"Or witchsign." Crit squinted, though the light was

good, three windows wide and afternoon sun raying the room. "Are you all right—beyond the obvious, I mean?"

"I lost two partners, too close in time. I'll mend."

Let's hope, Crit thought but didn't say, watching Niko's expressionless eyes. "I saw to your mare."

"My thanks. And for the bow. Janni's bier is set for morning. Will you help me with it? Say the words?"

Crit rose; the operator in him still couldn't bear to officiate in public, yet if he didn't, he'd never hold these men. "With pleasure. Life to you, Stepson."

"And to you, Commander."

And that was that. His first test, passed; Niko and Tempus had shared a special bond.

That night, he called them out behind the barracks, ordering a feast to be served on the training field, a wooden amphitheatre of sorts. By then Straton had come out to join him, and Strat wasn't bashful with the mess staff or the hired help.

Maybe it would work out; maybe together they could make half a Tempus, which was the least this endeavor needed, though Crit would never pair again. . . .

He put it to them when all were well disposed from wine and roasted pig and lamb, standing and flatly telling them Tempus had left, putting them in his charge. There fell a silence and in it he could hear his heart pound. He'd been calmer ringed with Tyse hillmen, or alone, his partner slain, against a Rankan squadron.

"Now, we've got each other, and for good and fair, I say to you, the quicker we quit this cesspool for the clean air of high peaks war, the happier I'll be."

He could hardly see their faces in the dark with the torches snapping right before his face. But it didn't matter; they had to see him, not he them. Crit heard a raucous growl from fifty throats become assent, and then a cheer, and laughter, and Strat, beside and off a bit, gave him a soldier's sign: all's well.

He raised a hand, and they fell quiet; it was a power he'd never tried before: "But the only way to leave with honor is to work your tours out." They grumbled. He continued: "The Riddler's left busy-work sorties enough—hazardous duty actions, by guild book rules; I'll post a list—that we can work off our debt to Kittycat in a month or so."

Someone nay'd that. Someone else called: "Let him finish, then we'll have our say."

"It means naught to me, who deserts to follow. But to *us*, to cadre honor, it's a slur. So I've thought about it, since I'm hot to leave myself, and here's what I propose. All stay, or go. You take your vote. I'll wait. But Tempus wants no man on his right at Wizardwall who hasn't left in good standing with the guild."

When they'd voted, with Straton overseeing the count, to abide by the rules they'd lived to enforce, he said honestly that he was glad about the choice they'd made. "Now I'm going to split you into units, and each unit has a choice: find a person, a mercenary not among us now, a warm body trained enough to hold a sword and fill your bed, and call him 'brother'—long enough to induct him in your stead. Then we'll leave the town yet guarded by 'Stepsons' and that name's enough, with what we've done here, to keep the peace. The guild has provisions for man-steading; we'll collect from each to fill a pot to hire them; they'll billet here, and we'll ride north a unit at a time and meet up in Tyse, next high moon, and surprise the Riddler."

So he put it to them, and so they agreed.

NECROMANT

C. J. Cherryh

The wind came from the north tonight, out of chilly distances, sending an unaccustomed rain-washed freshness through the streets of Downwind, along the White Foal where traffic came and went across the only bridge. The Stepsons had finally done the obvious and set up a guard post here; in these fractious times, things were bad indeed. Previous holders of power in Sanctuary had been content to watch and gather information. Now (when subtlety is lacking, one tries the clenched fist) they meant to control every move between Downwind and the Maze.

Tonight another guard was dead, pinned to the post beside the guardhouse; the second one—no one knew where. The word spread in all those quarters where folk were interested to know, so that traffic on the bridge increased despite the rumbles of oncoming thunder, and those who for a day or two had been caught on one side of the White Foal or the other heard and went skit-

tering, wind-blown, across the White Foal bridge, some
shuddering at the erstwhile guard whose eyes still stared;
some mocking the dead, how whimsical he looked, thus
open-mouthed as if about to speak.

For those who knew, the stationing of that corpse was
a signature: the Downwind knew and did not gossip, not
even in the security of Mama Becho's, which sat, a
scruffy, doors-open building, a tolerable walk from the
White Foal bridge. Only the fact was reported there,
that for the third time that week the bridge guard had
come to grief; there was general grim laughter.

The news found its way to the Maze on the other side
and drew thoughtful stares and considerably less mirth.
Certain folk left the Vulgar Unicorn with news to carry;
certain ones called for another drink; and if there was
gossip of what this chain of murders might mean, it was
done in the quietest places and with worried looks.
Those who had left did so with that skill of Maze-born
skulkers, pretending indirection. They shivered at the
sight of beggars in the streets, at urchins and old men,
who were back again at posts deserted while the bridge
guard had (briefly) stood.

The news had not yet reached the strange ships rocking to the wind in Sanctuary's harbor, or the glittering
luxury of Kadakithis, who amused himself in his palace
this night and who would not, without understanding
more things than he did, have known that the underpinnings of his safety trembled. The report did, and soon,
reach the Stepsons' Sanctuary-side headquarters, after
which a certain man sat alone with uncertainties. Dolon
was his name. Critias had left him in charge, when the
senior Stepsons had gone, quietly, band by band, to the
northern war. "You've got all you need," Critias had
said. Now Dolon, in charge of all there was, sat listening
to the first patter of rain against the wall and wondering
whether he dared, tonight, the morale of his command
being what it was, send a band to the bridge to gather up

the one available body before the dawn.

Of even more concern to him was the missing one, what might have become of Stilcho; whether he had gone into the river, or run away, or whether he might have been carried off alive, to some worse and slower fate, spilling secrets while he died. The house by the bridge was a burned-out shell; but burning the beggars' headquarters and creating a few Downwinder corpses had not solved the matter, only scattered it.

He heard steps outside the building, splashing through the rain. Someone knocked at the outside door; he heard that door groan open, heard the burr of quiet voices as his own guards passed someone through. The matter reached his door then, a second, louder rap.

"Mor-am, sir." The door opened, and his guard let in the one he had sent for, this wreckage of a man. Handsome once . . . at least they said that he had been. The youth's eyes remained untouched by the burn-scars, dark-lashed and dark-browed eyes. Haunted, yes; long habituated to terrors.

The commander indicated a chair and the one-time hawkmask limped to it and sat down, staring at him from those dark eyes. The nose was broken, scarred across the bridge; the fine mouth remained intact, but twitched at times with an uncontrollable tic that might be fear—not enviable was Mor-am's state, nowadays, among latter-day Stepsons.

"There's a man," Dolon said at once, in a low, soft voice, "pinned to the White Foal bridge tonight. How would this go on happening? Shall I guess?"

The tic grew more pronounced, spread to the left, scar-edged eye. The hands jerked as well, until they found each other and clasped for stability. "Stepson?" Mor-am asked needlessly, a hoarse thin voice: that too the fire had ruined.

Dolon nodded and waited, demanding far more than that.

"They would," Mor-am said, lifting his shoulder, seeming to give apologies for those that had ruined him for life and made him what he was. "The bridge, you know—they—h-have to come and go—"

"So now we and the hawkmasks have a thing in common."

"It's the same t-thing. Hawkmasks and Stepsons. To t-them."

Dolon thought on that a moment, without affront, but he assumed a scowl. "Certainly," he said, "it's the same thing where you're concerned. Isn't it?"

"I d-don't t-take Jubal's pay."

"You take your life," Dolon whispered, elbows on the desk, "from us. Every day you live."

"Y-you're not the same S-Stepsons."

Now the scowl was real, and the moment's sneer cleared itself from the man's ruined face.

"I don't like losing men," Dolon said. "And it comes to me—hawkmask, that we *might* find a use for you." He let that lie a moment, enjoying the anxiety that caused, letting the hawkmask sweat. "You know," he said further, "we're talking about your life. Now there's this woman, hawkmask, there's this woman—we know. Maybe you do. You will. Jubal's hired her, just to keep her out of play. Maybe for more just now. But a hawkmask like yourself—maybe you could tell her just what you just told me. . . . Common cause. That's what it is. You know how long you'd live if we put you on the streets. You know who's looking for you? I'm sure you know. I'm sure you know what those enemies can do. What we might do; who knows?"

The tic became steady, like a pulse. Sweat glistened on Mor-am's brow.

"So, well," Dolon said, "I want you to go to a certain place and take a message. There's those will watch you—just so you get there safe and sound. You can trust that. And you talk to this woman and you tell her how Stepsons happen to send her a hawkmask for a messenger, how you're hunted—oh, tell her anything you like. Or lie. It's all the same. Just give the paper to her.''

"What's it s-say?"

"Curiosity, hawkmask? It's an offer of employ. *Trust* us, hawkmask. Her name's Ischade. Tell her this: we want this beggar-king. More, we've got one man missing on that bridge tonight. Alive, maybe. And we want him back. You're another matter . . . but I'd *advise* you come back to us. I'd advise you don't look her in the eye if you can avoid it. Friendly advice, hawkmask. And it's all the truth.''

Mor-am had gone very pale. So perhaps he had heard the rumors of the woman. Sweat ran, in that portion of his face unglazed by scars. The tic had stopped, for whatever reason.

The wind caught Haught's cloak as he ran, rain spattered his face and he let it go, splashing through the puddles as he approached the under-stair door within the Maze.

He rapped a pattern, heard the stirring within and the bar thrust up. The door swung inward, on light and warmth and a woman, on Moria, who whisked him inside and snatched his dripping wrap. He put chilled arms about her, hugged her tight, still shivering, still out of breath.

"They got a Stepson," he said. "By the bridge. Like before. Mradhon's coming—another way."

"Who?" Moria gripped his arms in violence. "Who did they get?"

"Not him. Not your brother. I know that." His teeth wanted to chatter, not from the chill. He remembered the scurrying in the alley, the footsteps behind him for a way. He had lost them. He believed he had. He left Moria's grasp and went to the fireside, to stand by the tiny hearthside, the twisted, mislaid bricks. He looked back at Moria standing by the door, feeling aches in all his scars. "They almost got us."

"They."

"Beggars."

She wrapped her arms about herself, rolled a glance toward the door as someone came racing up at speed, splashing through the rain. A knock followed, the right one, and she whisked the door open a second time, for Mradhon Vis, who came in drenched and spattered with mud on the left side.

Moria stared half a heartbeat and slammed shut the door, dropping the bar down. Mradhon stamped a muddy puddle on the aged boards and stripped his cloak off, showing a drowned, dark-bearded face, eyes still wild with the chase.

"Slid," he said, taking his breath. "There's a patrol out. There's watchers—You get it?"

Haught reached inside his doublet, pulled out a small leather purse. He tossed it at Mradhon Vis with a touch of confidence recovered. At least this they had done right.

Then Moria's eyes lightened. The hope came back to them, as Mradhon shook the bright spill of coins into her palm, three, four, five of them, good silver; a handful of coppers.

But the darkness came back again when she looked up at them, one and the other. "Where did you get it, for what?"

"Lifted it," Haught said.

"Who from?" Moria's eyes blazed. "You by-Shalpa double fools, you lifted it from where?"

Haught shrugged. "A greater fool."

She hefted coin and purse, down-browed. "At this hour, a merchant abroad in the Maze? No, not likely, not at all. *What did I teach you?* Where did you get this haul? From what thief?" They neither one answered, and she cast the prize onto the table. Four silver coins among the copper.

"Light-fingers," Mradhon said. "Share and share alike."

"Oh, and share the trouble too?" She held up the missing coin and dropped it down her bodice, dark eyes flashing. "Share it when someone marks you out? I don't doubt I will." She walked away, took a cup of wine from the table, and sipped at it. She drank too much lately, did Moria. Far too much.

"Someone has to do it," Haught said.

"Fool," Moria said again. "I'm telling you, there's those about don't take kindly to amateurs cutting in on their territory. Still less to being robbed themselves. Did you kill him?"

"No," Mradhon said. "We did it just the way you said."

"What's this about beggars? You get spotted?"

"There was one near," Haught said. "Then—there were three of them. All at once."

"Fine," said Moria in steely patience. "That's fine. You're not half good. My brother and I—"

But that was not a thing Moria spoke of often. She took another drink, sat down at the table in the only chair.

"We got the money," Haught protested, trying to cheer her.

"And we're counting," said Mradhon. "You go ahead and keep that silver, bitch. I'm not going after it. But that's all you get, 'til you're worth something again."

"Don't you tell me who's worth something. You'll get our throats cut, rolling the wrong man."

"Then you by-the-gods do something. You want to lose this place? You want us on the street? Is that what you want?"

"Who's dead over by the bridge?"

"Don't know."

"But beggars sent you running. Didn't they?"

Mradhon shrugged.

"What more do we need?" she asked. "Stepsons. Now Becho's vermin. Thieves. Beggars, for Shipri's sake, *beggars* sniffing round here."

"Jubal," Mradhon said. "Jubal's what we need. Until you come through with Jubal's money—"

"He's going to send for us again." Her lip set hard. "Sooner or later. We just go on checking the drops. It's slow, that's all: it's a new kind of business, this setting up again. But he won't touch us if you get the heat on us; if you go off making your own deals. You stay out of trouble. Hear me? You're not cut out for thieves. It's not in you. You want to go through life left-handed?"

"Stay sober enough to do it yourself, why don't you?" Mradhon said.

The cup came down on the tabletop. Moria stood up; the wine spilled over the scarred surface, dripping off the edge.

But Haught thrust himself into Mradhon's way in his own temper. Something seized up in him when he did; his gut knotted. Ex-slave that he was, his nerves did not forget. Old reflexes. "Don't talk to her that way."

Mradhon stared at him, northron like himself, broad-shouldered, sullen. Friend, sometimes. A moment ago, if not now. More, he suspected Mradhon Vis of pity, the way Mradhon stared at him, and that was harder than the blow.

Mradhon Vis turned his shoulder and walked away across the room, leaving him nothing.

He put his hand on Moria's then, but she snatched it away, out of humor. So he stood there.

"Don't be scattering that mud about," Moria said to Mradhon's back. "You do it, you clean it up."

Mradhon sat down on the single bed, on the blankets, began pulling off his boots, heedless of puddles forming, of their bed soaking and blanket muddied.

"Get up from there," Haught said, pushing it further.

But Mradhon only fixed him with a stare. *Come and do something,* it said, and Haught stood still.

"You listen to me," Mradhon said. "It takes money keeping her in wine. And until *she* comes across with some cash out of Jubal, what better have we got? Or maybe—" A second boot joined the other on the floor. "Maybe we ought to go looking for Jubal on our own. Or the Stepsons. They're running short of men."

"*No!*" Moria yelled.

"They pay. *Jubal* dealt with them, for the gods' sake."

"Well, he's not dealing now. You don't make deals on your own. *No.*"

"So when are you going out again? When are you going to make that contact, eh? Or maybe Jubal's dead. Or not interested in you. Maybe he's broke as we are, hey?"

"I'll find him."

"You know what I begin to think? Jubal's done. The beggars seem to think so. They don't think it's enough to take on hawkmasks. Now they take on Stepsons. Nothing they can't handle. They're loose. You understand that? This Jubal—I'll believe he's something if he can take them on. The day he nails a beggar to that bridge, I'll believe Jubal's worth something. Meanwhile—meanwhile, there's a roof over our heads. A bar on the door. And we've got money. We're out of Becho's territory. And keeping out takes money."

"We're never out," Haught said, remembering the beggars, the ragged shapes rising out of the shadows like spiders from their webs, small moving humps in the lightning-flash that might have showed their faces to these beggar-witnesses.

The chill had seeped inward from Haught's wet

clothes. He felt cold, beyond shivering. He sneezed, wiped his nose on his sleeve, went over to the fire to sit disconsolate. Quietly he tried a small scrying, to see something. Once he had had the means, but it had left him, with his luck; with his freedom.

"I'll go out tomorrow," Moria said, walking over near the fire.

"Don't," said Haught. There was a small premonition on him. It might be the scrying. It might be nothing, but he felt a deep unease, the same panic that he had felt seeing the beggars moving through the dark. "Don't let him talk you into it. It's not safe. We've got enough for a little while. Let him find us, this Jubal."

"I'll find him," she said. "I'll get money." But she said that often. She went and picked up the cup again, wiped the spilled wine with a rag. Sniffed loudly. Haught turned his back to her, staring at the fire, the leaping shapes. The heat burned, almost to the point of pain, but it took that, to reach the cold inside his bones, in his marrow; easier to watch the future than to dwell on the past, to remember Wizardwall, or Carronne, or slavery.

This Jubal the slaver who was their hope had sold him once. But he chose to forget that too. He had nerved himself to walk the streets, at least by dark, to look free men in the eye, to do a hundred things any free man took for granted. Mradhon Vis gave him that; Moria did. If they looked to Jubal, so must he. But in the fire he saw things, twisted shapes in the coals. A face stared back at him, and its eyes—

Mradhon came over and dumped the boots by him, spread his clothes on the stones, himself wrapped in a blanket.

"What do you learn?" Mradhon asked.

He shrugged. "I'm blind to the future. You know that."

A hand came down on his shoulder, pressed it, in the way of an apology.

"You shouldn't talk to her that way," Haught said again.

The hand pressed his shoulder a second time. He shivered, despite the heat.

"Scared?" Mradhon said. Haught took it for challenge, and the cold stayed in his heart. Scared he was. He had not had a friend, but Mradhon Vis. Distrust gnawed at him, not bitter, but only the habit of weighing his value—to anyone. He had learned that he was for using and when he stopped being useful he could not see what there was in him that anyone would want. Moria needed him; no woman ever had, not really. This man did, sometimes; for a while; but a shout from him —a harsh word—made him flinch, and reminded him what he was even when he had a paper that said otherwise. Challenged, he might fight from fear. Nothing else. And never Mradhon Vis.

"I talk to her like that," Mradhon said, not whispering, "when it does her good. Brooding over that brother of hers—"

"Shut up," Moria said from behind them.

"*Mor-am's dead,*" Mradhon said. "Or good as dead. Forget your brother, hear? It's your good I'm thinking of."

"My good." Came a soft, hateful laugh. "So I can steal again, that's the thing. Because Jubal knows me, not you." A chair scraped. Haught looked round as two slim-booted feet came beside them, as Moria squatted down and put a hand on Mradhon's arm. "You hate me. Hate me, don't you? Hate women. Who did that, Vis? You born that way?"

"Don't," Haught said, to both of them. He gripped Mradhon's arm, which had gone to iron. "Moria, let him be."

"No," Mradhon said. And for some reason Moria drew back her hand and had a sobered look.

"Go to bed," said Haught. "Now." He sensed the violence beside him, sensed it worse than other times.

He could calm this violence, draw it to himself, if there was nothing else to do. He was not afraid of that, viewed it with fatalistic patience. But Moria was so small, and Mradhon's hate so much.

She lingered, looking at them both. "You come," she said, in a quiet, fearful voice, "too."

Mradhon said nothing, but stared into the fire. *Go*, Haught shaped with his lips, nodded toward the bed, and so Moria went, paused by the table, and finished off the wine all at a draught.

"Sot," Mradhon said under his breath.

"She just gets started at it sometimes," Haught said. "Alone—the storm. . . ."

The rain spatted against the door. The wind knocked something over that went skittering along the alley outside. The door rattled. Twice. And ceased.

Mradhon Vis looked that way, long and keenly. Sweat ran on his brow.

"It's just the wind," Haught said.

Thunder cracked, distantly, outside, and the shingles of the small riverhouse fluttered like living things. The gate creaked, not the wind, and disturbed a warding-spell that quivered like a strand of spider web, while the spider within that lair stirred in a silken bed, opened eyes, stretched languorous limbs.

The visitor took time getting to the door: she read his hesitancy, his fear, in the sound of uneven steps her hearing registered. No natural hearing could have pierced the rain sound. She slipped on a robe, an inkiness in the dark. She wished for light, and there was, in the fireplace, atop the logs that were nothing but focus and never were consumed; atop candles that smelled musty and strange and perfumed with something sweet and dreadful.

Her pulse quickened as the visitor tried the latch. She relaxed the ward that sealed the door, and it swung inward, a gust that guttered the candles, amid that gust a cloaked, hunched man who smelled of fear. She tightened the ward again and the door closed, against the wind, with a thump that made the visitor turn, startled, in his tracks.

He did not try it. He looked back again, cast the hood back from a face fire had touched. His eyes were dilated, wild.

"Why do you come?" she asked, intrigued, despite a life that had long since lacked variety. In the casual matter of the door she had dropped pretenses that she wore like robes; he knew, must know, that he was in deadly jeopardy. "Who sent you?" He seemed the sort not to plan, but to do what others planned.

"I'm one of the h-hawkm-masks. M-mor-am." The face jerked, twisting the mouth; the whole head nodded with the effort of speech. "M-message." He fumbled out a paper and offered it to her in a shaking hand.

"So." He was not so unhandsome, viewed from the right side. She walked around him, to that view, but he followed her with his eyes, and that was error, to meet her stare for stare. She smiled at him, being in that mood. *Mor-am.* The name nudged memory, and wakened interest. *Mor-am.* The underground pricked up its ears in interest at that name—could this man be running Jubal's errands again? Likely as summer frost. She tilted her head and considered him, this wreckage. "*Whose* message?" she asked.

"T-take it." The paper fluttered in his hand.

She took it, felt of it. "What does it say?" she asked, never taking her eyes from his.

"The Stepsons—t-there's another d-dead. They s-sent me."

"Did they?"

"C-common problem. M-Moruth. The beggars. They're k-killing us both."

"Stepsons," she said. "Do you know my name, Mor-

am? It's Ischade.'' She kept walking, saw the panic
grow. ''Have you heard that name before?''

A violent shake of the head, a clamping of the jaw.

''But you are more notorious than I—in certain quarters. Jubal misses you. And you carry Stepson messages
—what do they say to tell me?''

''Anyt-thing you a-asked m-me.''

''Mor-am.'' She stopped before him, held him with
her eyes. Her hand that had rested on his shoulder
touched the side of his jaw, stilled the tic, the jerking of
muscles, his rapid breathing. Slowly the contorted body
straightened to stand tall; the drawn muscles of his face
relaxed. She began to move again, and he followed her,
turning as she wove spells of compulsion, until she
stood before the great bronze mirror in its shroud of
carelessly thrown silks. At times in this mirror she cast
spells. Now she cast another, and showed him himself,
smiled at him the while. ''So you will tell me,'' she said,
''anything.''

''What did you do?'' he asked. Even the voice was
changed. Tears leapt to eyes, to voice. ''What did you
do?''

''I took the pain. A small spell. Not difficult for me.''
She moved again, so that he must turn to follow her,
with dreamlike slowness. ''Tell me—what you know.
Tell me who you are. Everything. Jubal will want to
know.''

''They caught me, the Stepsons caught me, they made
me—''

She felt the lie and sent the pain back, watched the
body twist back to its former shape.

''I—t-turned—traitor,'' the traitor said, wept,
sobbed. ''I s-s-sold them, sold other hawkmasks—to the
Stepsons. My sister and I—we had to live, after Jubal
lost it all. I mean, how were we going to live?—We
didn't know. We had to. I had to. My sister—didn't
know.'' She had let go the pain and the words kept com-

ing, with the tears. His eyes strayed from her to the mirror. "O gods—"

"Go on," she said, ever so softly, for this was truth, she knew. "What do the Stepsons want? What do you want? What are you prepared to pay?"

"*Get Moruth*. That's what they want. The beggar-lord. And this man—this man of theirs, they think the beggars have got, get him back—safe."

"These are not trifles."

"They'll pay—I'm sure—they'll pay."

She unfolded the note, perused it carefully, holding it before the light. It said much of that. It offered gold. It promised—immunities—at which she smiled, not humorously. "Why, it mentions you," she said. "It says I might lend you back to Jubal. Do you think he would be amused?"

"No," he said. There was fear, multiplying fear: she could smell it. It prickled at her nerves.

"But when you carry messages for rogues," she said, "you should expect such small jokes." She folded the note carefully, folded it several times until it was quite small, until she opened her hand, being whimsical, and the paper note was gone.

He watched this, this magician's trick, this cheap comedy of bazaars. It amused her to confound him, to suddenly brighten all the fires 'til the candles gleamed like suns, 'til he flinched and looked as if he would go fleeing for the door.

It would not have yielded. And he did not. He stood still, with his little shred of dignity, his body clenched, the tic working at his face as she let the spell fade.

So this was a man. At least the remnant of one. The remnant of what had almost been one. He was still young. She began to pace round him, back of him, to the scarred left side. He turned the other way to look at her. The tic grew more and more pronounced.

"And what if I could not do what they wish? I have

turned their betters down before. You come carrying their messages. Is there nothing—more personal you would want?"

"The p-pain."

"Oh. That. Yes, I can ease it for a time. If you come back to me. If you keep your bargains." She stepped closer still, took the marred face between her hands. "Jubal, on the other hand, would like you the way the beggars left you. He would flay you inch by inch. Your sister—" She brushed her lips across his own, gazed close into his eyes. "She has been under a certain shadow for your sake. For what you did."

"Where is she? Ils blast you, *where?*"

"A place I know. Look at me, go on looking, that's right. That's very good. No pain, none at all. Do you understand—Mor-am, what you have to do?"

"The Stepsons—"

"I know. There's someone watching the house." She kissed him long and lingeringly, her arms twined behind his neck, smiled into his eyes. "My friend, a hawk-mask's a candle in the wind these days; a hawkmask other hawkmasks hunt—hasn't a chance in the world. The contagion's even gotten to your sister. *Her* life, you understand. It's very fragile. The Stepsons might take her. Hawkmasks use her only to talk to Stepsons. Right now they're not talking at all. Not to these. Not to stupid men who've thrown away every alliance better men had made. Moruth, too—Moruth the beggar knows your name. And hers. He remembers the fire, and you, and her, and it's a guess where he casts the blame—as if he needed an excuse at any time. What will you pay for my help? What coin do you have, Mor-am?"

"What do you want?"

"Whatever. Whenever. That does change. As you can. Never forget that, hear? They name me vampire. Not quite the case—but very close. And they will tell you so. Does that put you off, Mor-am? Or is there worse?"

He grew brave then and kissed her on the lips.

"O be very careful," she said. "*Very* careful. There will be times—when I tell you go, you do not question me. Not for your life, Mor-am, not for your soul, such as it is." Another kiss, lighter than all the rest. "We shall go do the Stepsons a favor, you and I. We shall go walking—oh, here and there tonight. I need amusement."

"They'll kill me on the street."

She smiled, letting him go. "Not with me, my friend. Not while you're with me." She turned away, gathering up her cloak, looked back again. "It's widely said I'm mad. A beast, they call me. Lacking self-control. This is not so. Do you believe me?"

And she laughed when he said nothing. "That man of theirs—go outside. Tell Dolon's spy to keep to his own affairs tonight. Tell him—tell him *maybe*." She dimmed the lights, unwarded the door, a howl of wind and rain. Mor-am's face contorted in fright. He ran out to do as he was told, limping still, but not so much as before. She took back the spell: he would be limping in truth when he reached the watcher, would be the old Mor-am, in pain, to convince the Stepsons. And that also amused her.

She shut the door, walked through the small strange house, which at one time seemed to have one room and disclosed others behind clutter—oddments, books, books, hangings, cloaks, discarded garments, bits of silk or brocade which had taken her fancy and lost it again, for she never wore ornament, only kept it for the pleasure of having it; and the cloaks, the men's cloaks —that was another sort of amusement. Her bare feet trod costly silk strewn on time-smoothed boards, and thick carpet of miniscule silk threads, hand knotted, dyed in rarest opalescent dyes—collected for a fee, pro-

venance forgotten. Had someone plundered the hoard,
she might not have cared or missed the theft—or might
have cared greatly, depending on her mood. Material
comfort meant little to her. Only satiation—when the
need was on her.

And lately—lately that need had quickened in a different way.

One had affronted her. She had, in the beginning,
dismissed the matter, clinging to her indolence, but it
gnawed at her. She had thought upon this thing, as one
will think on an affront long after the moment, turning
it from one side to the other to discover the motive of it,
and she had discovered not malice, not anger, but insouciance, even humor on the part of the perpetrator,
this witch, this northron demigoddess, be she what she
was. The affront lay there a good long while, gnawing at
the laissez-faire on which her peace was founded—for,
without that habit of laziness, she hungered more often;
and that hunger led to tragedies.

Such a thing had happened because she was lazy,
because there were costs of power she had never wished
to pay. This witch slaughtered children, plucking them
from her hands; and dropped the matter at her door.
This witch went her way, indifferent, having fouled her
nest, her eyes set on further ambitions, in professional
disregard. This was worth, after thought, a certain
anger; and anger eroded itself a place and grew. She
ought, Ischade thought, to *thank* the Nisi witch for this
discovery, that there were other appetites, and one great
one which could assuage that moon-driven hunger that
had held her, so, so long.

She understood—oh, very much of what passed in the
streets, having been on the bridge, having been everywhere in Sanctuary, black-robed, wrapped in more than
robes when she chose to be. The world tottered. The
sea-folk intruded, assuming power; Wizardwall and
Stepsons fought, with ambitions all their own; Jubal

planned—whatever Jubal planned; young hotheads
dealt in swords on either side; death squads invaded
uptown; while across the White Foal the beggar-king
Moruth made his own bid. All the while the prince sat in
his palace and intrigued with thieves, invaders, all, a
wiser fool than some; priests connived, gods perished in
this and other planes—and Ranke, the heart of empire,
was in no less disarray, with every lord conniving and
every priest conspiring. She heard the rain upon the
roof, heard the thunder rattling the walls of the world
and heard her own catspaw returning up the path. She
shod herself, flung her cloak about her, opened the door
on Mor-am's rain-washed presence.

"Take a dry cloak," she said, catching up a fine one,
dark as hers. "Man, you'll catch your death."

He was not amused; but she unwound the pain from
him, cast one cloak aside, and adjusted the finer one
about his newly straightened shoulders, tenderly as a
mother her son, looking him closely in the eyes.

"Gone?" she asked.

"They'll try to trick you."

"Of course they will." She closed the front door,
opened the back, never glancing at either. "Come
along," she said, flinging up her hood, the wide wings
of her cape flying in the wind that swirled the random,
garish draperies of the house like multicolored fire. The
gust struggled with the candles and the fireplace and
failed to extinguish them, while mad shadows ran the
walls, 'til she winked the lights out, having no more
need of them.

Something rattled. Mradhon Vis opened an eye, in dark
lit by the dying fire in its crooked hearth. Beside him
Haught and Moria lay inert, lost in sleep, curled
together in the threadbare quilt. But this sound came,
and with it a chill, as if someone had opened a door on
winter in the room, while his heart beat in that blind

terror only dreams can give, or those things that have the unreality of dreams. He had no idea whether that rattle had been the door—the wind, he thought, the wind blowing something; but why this night-terror, this sickly sweat, this conviction it boded something?

Then he saw the man standing in the room. Not—standing—but existing there, as if he were part of the shadows, and light from somewhere (not the fire) falling on golden curling hair, and on a bewildered expression. He was young, this man, his shirt open, a charm hung on a cord about his neck, his skin glistening with wine-heat and summer warmth as it had been one night; while sweat like ice poured down Mradhon's sides beneath the thin blanket.

Sjekso. But the man was dead, in an alley not so far from here. In some unmarked grave he was food for worms.

Mradhon watched the while this apparition wavered like a reflection in wind-blown water, all in dark, and while its mouth moved, saying something that had no sound—as, suddenly, treacherously swift, it came drifting toward the bed, closer, closer, and the air grew numb with cold. Mradhon yelled in revulsion, waved his arm at it, felt it pass through icy air, and his bedmates woke, stirred in the nest—

"Mradhon!" Haught caught his arm, held him.

"*The door,*" Moria said, thrusting up from beside them, "O gods, the door—"

Mradhon rolled, saw the lifting of the bar with no hands upon it, saw it totter—it fell and crashed, and he was scrambling for the side of the bed, the bedpost where his sword hung even while he felt the blast of rain-soaked air, while Haught and Moria likewise scrambled for weapons. He whirled about, his shoulders to the wall, and there was no one there at all, but the lightning-flashes casting a lurid glow on the flooded cobbles outside, and the door banging with the wind.

Terror loosened his bones, set him shivering; instinct sent his hand groping after a cloak, his feet moving toward the door, his sword in hand the while he whipped the cloak about himself, towellike. He leapt out suddenly into the rain-swimming alley, barefoot, trusting the corners of his eyes, and swung at once to that side that had anomaly in it, a tall shape, a cloaked figure standing in the rain.

And then he was easy prey for anything, for that cloaked form, its height, its manner, waked memories. He heard a presence near, Haught or Moria at his back, or both, but he could not have moved, not from the beginning. That figure well belonged with ghosts, with witchery, with nightmares that waked him cold with sweat. Lightning flashed and showed him a pale face within the hood.

"For Ils' sake get in!" Moria's voice. A hand tugging at his naked shoulder. But it was a potential trap, that room, lacking any other door; while somewhere, somehow in his most secret nightmares he knew, had known, that Ischade had always known how to find him when she wished.

"What do you want?" he asked.

"Come to the bridge," the witch said. "Meet me there."

He had gazed once into those eyes. He could not forget. He stood there with the rain pelting him, with his feet numb in icewater, his shoulders numb under the force of it off the eaves. "Why?" he asked. "Witch, why?"

The figure was blank again, lacking illumination. "You have employ again, Mradhon Vis. Bring the others. Haught—he knows me, oh, quite, quite well. 'Twas I freed him, after all; and he will be grateful, will he not? For Moria—indeed, this must be Moria—I have a gift: something she has misplaced. Meet me beneath the bridge."

"Gods blast you!"

"Don't trade curses with *me*, Mradhon Vis. You would not profit in the exchange."

And with that the witch turned her back and walked away, merged with the night. Mradhon stood there, chilled and numb, the sword sinking in his hand. He felt distantly the touch against him, a hand taking his arm—"For Ils' sweet sake," Moria said, "get inside. Come *on*."

He yielded, came inside, chilled through, and Moria flung shut the door, barred it, went to the fire and threw a stick on it, so that the yellow light leapt up and cast fleeting shadows about the walls. They led him to the fire, set him down, tucked the blanket about him, and finally he could shiver, when he had gotten back the strength.

"Get my clothes," he said.

"We don't have to go," Moria said, crouching there by him. She turned her head toward Haught, who came bringing the clothes he had asked for. "*We don't have to go.*"

But Haught knew. Mradhon took the offered clothes, cast off the sodden blanket, and began to dress, while Haught started pulling on his own.

"Ils save us," Moria said, clutching her wrap to her. Her eyes looked bruised, her hair streaming wet about her face. "What's the matter with you? Are you both out of your minds?"

Mradhon fastened his belt and gathered up his boots, having no answer that made sense. In some part of him panic existed, and hate, but it was a further and cooler hate, and held a certain peace. He did not ask Haught his own reasons, or whether Haught even knew what he was doing or why; he did not want to know. He went in the way he would draw his hand from fire: it hurt too much not to.

And with scalding curses at them both, Moria began

getting dressed, calling on them to wait, swearing impotence on them both in Downwind patois, in terms even the garrison had lacked.

"Stay here," he said, "little fool; you want to save your neck? Stay out of this."

He said it because somewhere deep inside he understood a difference between this woman and the other, which he had never fully seen, that Moria with her thin sharp knife was on his side and Haught's because they were fools themselves, and three fools seemed better odds.

"Rot you," Moria said, and when he took his muddy cloak and headed for the door, when Haught overtook him in the alley, Mradhon heard her panting after, still cursing.

He gave her no help, no sign that he heard. The rain had abated, sunk to a steady drizzle, a dripping off the eaves, a river down the cobbled alley, which sluiced filth along toward the sewers and so toward the bay where the foreign ships rode, insanity to heap upon the other insanities that life was here, where the likes of Ischade prowled.

If he could have loved, he thought, if he could have loved anything, Moria, Haught, known a friend outside himself, he might have made that a charm against what drew him now. But that had gone from him. There was only Ischade's cold face, cold purposes, cold needs: he could not even regret that Moria and Haught were with him: he felt safe now only because she had summoned them together, and not called him alone, not alone into that house. And he was ashamed.

Moria came up on his left hand, Haught on his right, and so they took that street under the eaves of the Unicorn and passed on by its light, by its shuttered, furtive safety that did not ask what prowled the streets outside.

•   •   •

"*Where?*" Dolon asked, at his desk, the sodden watcher standing dripping on the floor before him. "Where has he gotten to?"

"I don't know," the would-be Stepson said: Erato; his partner was still out. He stood with his hands behind him, head bowed. "He—just said he had a message to take, to carry for her. He said her answer was *maybe*. I take it she wasn't sure she could do anything."

"You take it. *You* take it. And where did they go, then? Where's your left-hand man? Where's Stilcho? Where's our informer?"

"I—" The Stepson stared off somewhere vague, his face contracted as if at something that just escaped his wits.

"Why didn't you do something?"

"I don't know," the Stepson said in the faintest, most puzzled of voices. "I don't know."

Dolon stared at the man and felt the flesh crawling on his nape. "We're being used," he said. "Something's out of joint. Wake up, man. Hear me? Get yourself a dozen men and get out there on the streets. Now. I want a watch on that bridge—not a guard, a watch. I want that woman found. I want Mor-am watched. Finesse, hear me? It's not a random thing we're dealing with. *I want Stilcho back. I don't care what it takes.*"

The Stepson left in all due haste. Dolon leaned head on hands, staring at the map that showed the Maze, the streets leading to the bridge. It was not the only thing on his desk. Death squads. A murder uptown. Factions were armed. The beggars were on the streets. And somehow every contact had dried up, frozen solid.

He saw things slipping. He called in others, gave them orders, sent them to apply force where it might loosen tongues.

"Make examples," he said.

The streets gave way to one naked rim along the White

Foal shore, an openness that faced the rare lights of Downwind, across the White Foal's rain-swollen flood. The black water had risen far up on the pilings of the bridge and gnawed away at the rock-faced banks, trying at this winding to break its confinement and take the buildings down, this ordinarily sluggish stream. Tonight it was another, noisier river, a shape-changer, full of violence; and Mradhon Vis moved carefully along its edge, in this soundless darkness of deafening sound, in the lead because of the three of them, he was most reckless and perhaps the most afraid.

So they came up in the place he had aimed for, in the underpinnings of the bridge on the Mazeward side; in this deepest dark. But a star glimmered here like swampfire, and above it was a pale, hooded face.

He felt one of his two companions set a warning hand on his arm. He kept walking all the same, watching his footing on this treacherous ground. He could look away from that face, or look back again, and a strange peace came on him, facing this creature who was the center of all his fears. No more running. No more evasion. There was a certain security in loss. He stopped, took an easy stance, there above the flood.

"What's the job?" he asked, as if there had never been an interlude.

The light brightened fitfully, in the witch's outheld hand. "Mor-am," she said. A shadow moved from among the pilings to stand by her. Light fell on a ruined, still-familiar face.

"O gods," Mradhon heard beside him, Moria lunged and he caught her arm. Hers was hard and tense; she twisted like a cat, but he held on.

"Moria," her twin said, no longer twin, "for Ils' sake listen—"

She stopped fighting then. Perhaps it was the face, which was vastly, horribly changed. Perhaps it was Haught, who moved in the way of her knifehand,

making himself the barrier, too careless of his life.
Haught was a madman. And he could win what no one
else could. Moria stood still, still heaving for breath,
while Mor-am stood still at Ischade's side.

"See what love is worth," Ischade said, smiling
without love at all. "And loyalty, of course." She
walked a pace nearer, on the slanted stones. "Mor-am's
loyalty, now—it's to himself, his own interests; he
knows."

"Don't," Mor-am said, with more earnestness than
ever Mradhon had heard from the hardnosed, streetwise
seller of his friends; for a moment the face seemed
twisted, the body diminished, then straightened again
—a trick of the light, perhaps, but in the same moment
Moria's arm went limp and listless in his hand.

"You'd live well," Ischade said in her quiet voice, an
intimate tone which yet rose above the river-sound. "I
reward—loyalty."

"With *what*?" Mradhon asked.

She favored Mradhon with a long, slow stare,
ophidian and, at this moment, amused.

"Gold. Fine wines. Your life and comfort. Follow
me—across the bridge. I need four brave souls."

"What for? To do what for you?"

"Why, to save a life," she said, "maybe. The burned
house. I'm sure you know it. Meet me there."

The light went, the shadow rippled, and in the half-
dark between the pilings and the flagstone bank, one
shadow deserted them. The second started then to
follow. "*The patrols*—" he said to the dark, but she
was gone then. Mor-am stopped, abandoned, his voice
swallowed by the river-sound. He turned hastily, facing
them.

"Moria—I had a reason."

"Where have you been?" The knife was still in
Moria's hand. Mradhon remembered and took her by
the sleeve.

"Don't," Mradhon said, not for love of Mor-am, the gods knew; rather, a deep unease, in which he wished to disturb nothing, do nothing.

"What's this about?" Moria asked. "Answer me, Mor-am."

"Stepsons—They—they hired her. They sent— Moria, for Ils' sake, they had me locked up, they used me to bargain with—with her."

"What are you worth?" Moria asked.

"She works for Jubal."

That hung there on the air, dying of unbelief.

"She does," Mor-am said.

"And you work for her."

"I have to." Mor-am turned, amorphous in his cloak, began to vanish among the pilings.

"Mor-am—" Moria started forward, brought up short in Mradhon's grip.

"Let him go," Mradhon said, and in his mind was a faint far dream of doing something rash, breaking with sanity and heading for somewhere safe. To the Stepsons, might be. But that was, lately, no way to a long life.

Haught was on his way—why, he had no idea, whether it was despair or ensorcelment. "Wait," he called to Haught, losing control of things, but he had lost that when he had come out here, blind-sotted as Moria at her worst. He let her draw him up the stone facing, among the pilings, chasing after Haught at the first, but then joining him in the open, where anyone might spy them.

There was the empty guard station, the pole standing vacant.

"They got him down," Haught said.

"Someone did," Mradhon muttered, looking about. He felt naked, exposed to view. The rain spattered away at the board surface of the bridge, a shadowed span leading through the dark to Downwind, to Ischade. A distant, solitary figure flitted like illusion at its other end, lost itself into Downwind, among its shuttered buildings. Here they stood, neither one place nor the other, neither in the Maze of Sanctuary nor in the Downwind, belonging now to no one.

And there was no hiding now.

Haught started across the bridge. Mradhon followed, with Moria beside him, and all he could think of now was how long it took to get across, to get out of this nakedness. Someone was coming their way, a shambling, raggedy figure. He clutched his cloak about him, gripped his sword as this beggar passed; he dared not look when the apparition had gone by, but Moria swung on his arm, feigning drunkenness like some doxy.

" 'S just a beggar," she said in full voice, hanging on him, terrifying him with the noise. Haught spun half-about, turned again, and kept walking like some honest man with disreputable followers—but no honest man crossed the bridge.

"Beggar," Moria whined, leaning on Mradhon's arm. He jerked at her and cursed, knowing this mentality, this bloody-minded humor that he had had beside him in the field, soldiers who got this affliction. Heroes all. Dead ones. Soon. "Straighten up," he said, knowing her, knowing her brother, knowing that this was a game both played. He twisted at her arm. "You see your brother? You see what games won *him*?"

She grew quiet then. Subdued. She walked beside him at Haught's back, past the tall end-pilings that themselves bore nail-holes from the time that hawkmasks, not Stepsons, were the prey.

To the right, a huddle of blackened timbers, of tumbled brick, was the burned shell of a house. Haught went that way, entering the shadow of Downwind, and they came after, out of choices now.

Erato slipped back into shadow, his pulse beating

double-time, for a shadow had passed that disturbed him. He felt a presence at his shoulder, where it belonged, but he trusted nothing now. He scanned the figure at near range, his heart still thumping away until he had (pretending calm) resolved his left-hand man still beside him, and not some further threat, some shape-changer, nightwalker. He had no taste for this witch-stalking. "They're across," the partner said.

"They're across. We're not the only ones moving. Get back along the bank. Get the squad in place. Get a message back to base." Erato moved back along the alley, headed toward the river house.

It smelled of double-cross, the whole business. His partner jogged off, holding his cloak tight to him, muffling his armor. They kept well away from the grounds, wary of traps.

This was the place to watch. Here. He was sure of that.

He settled in then, watching the storm clouds lose themselves on the seaward horizon in the dark, down that split that divided Downwind from Sanctuary, poor from rich, that division no bridge could span. He had been smug once, had Erato, well-paid, well-armed as he was, convinced of his own skill, of the reputation that would keep challenges off his neck. And somewhere in Downwind that bluff was called, and they dared not go in, dared not pass the streets except by day—had effectively lost nighttime access to their own base beyond the Downwind, the slaver's old estate, and relied more and more on the city command. And their enemies knew it.

It would be a long, cold wait. It eroded morale, that view of the bridge, the river, the Downwind. The realization came to him that he was sitting now in the same kind of position the bridge guard had been in, alone out here. Sounds came and went in the streets, rustled in the thin line of brush that rimmed the rivershore. Wild fears dawned on him, to wonder whether the others were there, whether those sounds masked murder, creepings through cover, throats cut, or worse, his comrades snatched away as Stilcho had gone.

He wanted to call out, to ask the others were they safe; but that was craziness. He heard the rustling again near himself.

Some vermin creeping about; they grew rats large here on riverside. So he told himself. Something feeding on the garbage that swept down the sewers, the gutters, some choice tidbit brought down from the dwellings of the rich, to tempt the rats and snakes. And the fear grew and grew, so that he eased his sword from its sheath and crouched there with his back pressed to the stones and his eyes constantly scanning the dark that he had view of.

There was nothing anywhere but the splash of rain, the steady drip off eaves of buildings that still had eaves. Beside them, the shell, the timbers, the loose piles of brick.

One moved with a dull chink. Mradhon whirled about, saw a figure close against the wall, at the corner.

"Come," Ischade said.

"Where's my brother?" Moria asked.

But the witch was gone around the corner.

Mradhon cursed beneath his breath, adding things as he went, as Haught did, as Moria stayed with them. There was no way of retreat, now, against the flow of things. The beggar on the bridge—someone was watching. The body was gone. There were likely Stepsons on the loose. He came round the corner, down the alley where once he had waited in ambush, where the three of them had, before the Stepsons had chosen to make a bonfire of the place, to use the clenched fist.

He knew this place. Knew it because he had lived here. They had. He knew the law here, how it worked apart from Kadakithis' law, from Molin Torchholder's, from any governance of Ranke. Law this side flowed from a place called Becho's. It flourished on the trade of vice, on things that went dear Across the Bridge, that most men never thought to sell, or never planned to. He remembered the smell of it, the reek that clung to clothes; the smell of Mama Becho's brew.

Haught stopped, for the witch had, waiting in their way, a tall shadow-shape; and a second had joined her.

"Now you earn your pay," Ischade said, when they had come close. The dark surrounded them, buildings leaned close overhead where listeners could have heard, perhaps did hear, but Ischade seemed not to care. "I have a matter to discuss. A man who certain folk want back, in whatever case. Mor-am knows. The second Stepson. Stilcho is his name."

"Moruth," Mradhon said.

"Oh, yes, Moruth has him. I do think this is the case. But Moruth will be reasonable, with me."

"Wait," Mradhon said, for she had moved to drift away again. This time she did wait, looked at him, faceless in the dark; and this time the question died stillborn. *Why?*

"Is there something?" she asked.

"What are we supposed to do—that you can't?"

"Why, to have mercy," Ischade said. "This man wants rescuing. That's your business."

And she was off again, a shadow along the way.

"Becho's," Mor-am said, all hoarse, keeping a safe distance from them. "Follow me."

But they knew the streets, every route that led to that place, that center of this hell.

"No luck," the man said, in the commander's doorway. "Everything's gone underground. This time of night—"

There was disturbance beyond; the outer doorway

opened, creating a draft that blew papers out of order.
Dolon slammed his hand onto them to stop the fall.
"Get someone," he said. "I don't care—"

One of his aides appeared behind the man, signaling
with a nod of his head. "What?" Dolon said.

"Erato sends word," the aide said, "the woman's
gone to the Downwind. Taken the informer with her."

Dolon stood up. "Who says? Get him in here."

"By your leave," the other said, trying graceful exit.

"You stay." Dolon walked round the desk and met
the man that came in. Erato's partner. "Where's Erato
now?"

"Set up to watch the shore. Figuring she'll come
home—sooner or later, whatever she comes up with."

Dolon drew a breath, the first easy one in hours.
Something worked. Someone was where he ought to be,
taking advantage of the situation. "All right," he said.
"You get back there right now—Tassi."

"Sir," the other said.

"Get ten more men. I want them down there on that
rivershore. I want every access under watch, from both
directions. I want no surprises out of this. You get down
there. You get those streets blocked. When the witch
shows up, I want an account from her. I want names,
places, bodies—I don't care how you get them. If she
cooperates, fine. If not—stop her. Dead. Understood?"

There was hesitance.

"Sir," Erato's partner said.

"*Understood?*"

"Yes, sir."

"They say fire works on her sort. You get what you
can."

"She's—"

Heat rose to his face. Breath grew short. "—gone un-
dependable. If she ever was. You cure it. Hear? You get
what you can, then you settle her. I want Stilcho *quiet*,
you understand: back here safe, number one; but if he's

become expendable, expend him. You know the rule. Now move!''

There was flight from the doorway, a clatter in the outer room, one injudicious unhappy oath. Dolon stood gathering his breath. Critias's list of reliables was itself the problem; unstable informants; men on double payrolls. A witch, for the gods' sake, an ex-slaver, a judge on the take.

There was, he began to reckon, a need to purify that list. His discretion, Critias had said. Critias had delayed too long in passing power, that was what it was. Uncertainty set in. The opportunists wanted convincing again.

Then the rest would fall in line.

It was near Becho's. Mradhon Vis knew that much, and it set off nerves, this approach. Tygoth would be in his alley, patroling up and down, banging at the wall with his stick to let all Downwind know that Mama's property was secure. The surviving crowd of drunks would have collapsed in the streets. Gods knew who might have inherited that room in the alley now. He did not want to know. He wanted out of this place, with all his soul he wanted out of it, and he was where he had never looked to be again, following Mor-am through the labyrinth of alleys, with Haught at his back—and Moria between them. He glanced back from time to time, when there was too much silence; but they still followed.

And now Mor-am stopped. Waited, signaled silence, outside a street that had gotten overbuilt with lean-tos.

Beggar-kingdom, this. Mradhon grabbed a handful of Mor-am's cloak, pulled, meaning retreat.

No, Mor-am insisted. He pointed just ahead, where suddenly a figure darker than the night was treading amid the ragged, lumpish shelters. Ischade paused and beckoned to them.

Mor-am followed, and Mradhon did, taking it on himself whatever the others did, wishing now they would keep their feckless help out of this. He gripped his sword, meaning to kill a few if it came to that, but Ischade kept her pace slow, down that street of furtive eyes, of watchers within collections of board, canvas, anything that might fend away rain and wind. The stench rose up about them, of human waste, of something dead and rotting. He heard steps at his back and dared not turn his head, praying to Ilsigi gods that he knew who it was. His eyes were all for Mor-am, for the wand-slender darkness of Ischade, who walked before them through this aisle of misery.

And none offered to touch, none offered violence. A building made this lane a cul de sac, a dilapidated, boarded-up building, but light showed from the cracks about the door.

Sound got out. Mor-am wavered at that whimpering, that human, wretched sound. At voices. At laughter. He stopped altogether, and Mradhon shoved him, put him into motion, not because he wanted to go, but because it was not a good moment to stop, not here, not now, without any path of retreat. There was a moment in battles, the downhill moment past which there was no way to stop, and they had reached it now. Things seemed to slow, just as they began to move in earnest, when the door flew open outward with no one touching it at all, when light flung out into the dark and there were dark figures leaping to their feet inside that building, but none darker than Ischade's, who occupied that doorway.

And silence then, after momentary outcry. Dire silence, as if everyone inside had stopped, just stopped. Mor-am stood stock still. But Mradhon stepped up the single step to stand behind Ischade.

"Give him to me," Ischade said very quietly, as if everything was sleeping and voices ought to be hushed. "Mradhon Vis—" She had never looked around, and knew him, somehow, by means that set his teeth on edge. So did calling his name—here. "This man they have. Get him up. Whatever you can do for him. Mor-am knows the way."

He looked past her, to the wretch on the floor, to what this ragged, awful crowd had left of a man. He had seen corpses, of various kinds. This one looked worse than most and might still be alive, which daunted him more than death. But it was a question of downhill. He walked in, among the beggar-horde, among ragged men and women. Gods! there was a child, feral, with a rat's sharp, frozen grin. He bent above this seeming corpse and picked it up, not even thinking of broken bones, only struggling with limp weight; the head lolled. It only had one eye. Blood was everywhere.

Haught met him, passing Ischade, got the other arm of this perhaps-living thing, and they took it to the door. Moria was there. Mor-am stood against the wall.

"*Mor-am,*" Ischade said, never turning her head. "Remember." And more quietly: "Get him away now. I have further dealings with these here."

The nightmare lasted. The silence held, that chill quiet lying over all the alley with its sea of tents. Not the look of her eyes that had wrought this quiet, no, Mradhon reckoned, but some subtler spell. Or fear. Perhaps they knew her. Perhaps here in Downwind she was better understood than across the river, for what she was, and what her visitations meant.

"Come on," Mradhon said. He heaved the limp arm further across his shoulder. "Gods blast you," he said to Moria, "get going—" for Mor-am began to run, limping, down the lane between the tents and shelters, off into the dark.

It would hold, he thought, only so long as Ischade was in the way, only so long as Ischade dealt with Moruth, who was somewhere in that room. What estate would distinguish a beggar king, he wondered in a mad distraction, panting through the tents, managing with

Haught to drag the bleeding half-corpse past obstacles, boxes, litter and heaped-up offal of the beggar-king's court. He wished he had known the face, had gotten the image clear, but he had focused clearly on none of them, not one, the way he had not focused on the man he was carrying. He had nightmares enough to last him; he bore this one with him, past the end of the street, around the corner. He twisted his neck to look to his side.

"Moria. Little fool," he panted, "get up ahead, get in front of us, don't straggle."

"Where's my brother?" she asked, her voice verging on panic. She had her knife; he saw the dull gleam. "Where has he gotten to?"

"Back to the street," Haught guessed, between breaths, and they labored along, dragging the dead weight, back the way they had come. No sign of Mor-am. Nothing.

"Bridge," Mradhon gasped, working with Haught to run with their burden as best they could. "Stepsons want this bastard, they get themselves out there and hold that Ils-forsaken bridge."

It was a long way through the streets, a long, long course, the noise of their footsteps, of their ragged breathing like the movement of an army. Moria ran ahead of them, checked corners.

Then one moment she failed to bob into sight again. Haught began to pull forward, doubling his pace. Mradhon resisted.

Then Moria reappeared, dodging round the corner, flat shadow, her hand up as if the knife was in it, and another shadow came shambling round wide of her, standing in the way—Mor-am was back.

"B-b-boat," he said. His breath came raw and hoarse. "Sh-she says—this p-place. O g-g-gods, c-come on."

"The river's up," Mradhon hissed, the limp weight

sagging against his shoulder, the feel of chase behind.
"The river's up to the bridge bottom, hear? No boat can
handle that current."

"Sh-she says. C-come."

Mor-am lurched off, dragging one foot. Moria stood
where she was, plastered to the wall. *Wrong,* a small
faint voice was saying inside Mradhon Vis, a prickling
of his nerves where Moria's twin was concerned. And
another voice said *she. The river.* Ischade.

"Come on," he said, deciding, and Haught shoul-
dered up his side as they headed after Mor-am.

Moria cursed as they passed and came too, jogging
along with them in the dark, under the dripping eaves.
She took the lead again, serving as their eyes in this
winding gut of a street.

Now there were sounds, many of them.

"Behind us," Haught gasped; and where they were
Mradhon could not have sworn, but it sounded like
behind. He threw all he had into running, pulled a stitch
in his side as Haught stumbled and recovered, and now
Moria was gone again, in the turning of the streets.

They staggered the last alley and onto the downslope
to the river, splashing through the outpourings of
Downwind's streets, past a low wall and down again.
"This way," Moria said, materializing again out of the
brushy dark, in the sound of the river, which lay like a
black gulf downslope. Mradhon went, steadied his
footing for Haught's sake. There was the reek of blood
from their unconscious burden, and now the taste of it
was in Mradhon's mouth, coppery; his lungs ached; he
was blind except that Moria was at his right telling him
come on, come on, down to the river, to the flooded
dark, the curling waters that could snatch any misstep
and make it fatal. He flung his head up, sweat running
in his eyes, sucked air, staggered on the uneven stony
shore and nearly went to his knees on the rain-slick
rock.

There was a boat. He saw Mor-am struggling with it,
and Moria running to it, a black shell amid the brush,
not distinguishable as a boat if he had not known what
it was. There was a muddy slide: boats *were* launched
here, from Downwind, in sane weather, when the river
was tamer. But this one hit the water and rode calm,
stayed close as if there were no currents tearing at it, as
if it and the river obeyed two madly different laws.

"G-get him in," Mor-am said, and coming to the
edge, Mradhon took the limp weight all to his side,
going into water to the knee to reach the boat, stagger-
ing as he flung the body down. The boat hardly rocked.
He gripped the side of it, stood there, uselessly, to
steady it. Haught crouched on the muddy shore, head
down, breathing in great gulps.

"Sh-she said *w-wait*," Mor-am said.

Mradhon stood, still leaning on the side, his feet
going numb and the sweat pouring down his face into
his eyes. Go out in this against orders—no. He saw
Moria collapsed, head and arms between her knees, in
the clearing of the sky that afforded them some star-
light; saw Mor-am's hooded shape standing further up,
holding to the rope. When he glanced across the river,
he could see Sanctuary's lights, few at this hour, could
see the bridge, sane and reasonable crossing.

And from the man they had carried all this way, there
was no sound, no movement—dead, Mradhon thought.
They had just carried a corpse away from Moruth; and
everyone was robbed.

Stones rattled, high among the brush. Heads lifted,
all round; and *she* was there, coming down, gliding
down the rocks like a fall of living dark, making only
occasional sound. "So," she said, reaching them. She
put out a hand and brushed Mor-am. "You've re-
deemed yourself."

He said nothing, but limped down to the water's
edge, and Haught and Moria were on their feet.

"Get in," said Ischade. "It will take us all."

Mradhon climbed aboard, stepping over the corpse, which moved, which moaned, and his nerves prickled at that unexpected life. Greater mercy, he thought, with this stirring between his feet, to use the sword: he had seen deaths such as this Stepson faced when the wounds went bad, the gaping socket of the missing eye thus close to the brain—it would be bad, he thought, while the boat rocked with the others getting in. He reached over the side, dipped up water with his hand, passed it over the Stepson's lips, felt movement in response.

Ischade's robe brushed him as she took her place. She knelt there all too close for any comfort; she bent her head, bowed over, her hands on the wounded face. There was suddenly outcry, a struggling of limbs beneath them. . . . "For the gods' sake!" Mradhon exclaimed, his gorge rising; he thrust at Ischade, shoved her back, froze at the lifting of her face, the direction of that basilisk stare at him.

"Pain is life," she said.

And the boat began to move, slowly, like a dream, the while the wind swirled about them and the river roared beneath. His companions—they were hazy shapes in the night about Ischade. The wounded man stirred and moaned, threatening instability in the boat should his thrashing become severe. Mradhon reached down and held him, gently. The witch touched him too, and the struggles took harder and harder restraint. The moans were pitiful.

"He will live," she said. "*Stilcho*. I am calling you. Come back."

The Stepson cried out, once, sharply, back arching, but the river took the sound.

It was a boat, running on the flood. Erato saw it, his first thought that some riverfisher's skiff had come untied in the White Foal's violence.

But the boat came skimming, running slowly like a cloud before the wind *across* the current, in a straight line no boat could achieve in any river. Erato stirred in his concealment, hair rising at his nape. He scrambled higher amongst the brush, disturbed one of his men.

"Pass the word," he said. "Something's coming."

"Where?"

"River."

That got a stare, a silence in the dark.

"*Get the rest,*" Erato hissed, shoving at the man. "They're going to come ashore. Hear me? Tell them pass it on. The back of the house: that's where they'll come."

The man went. Erato slipped along the bank at the same level, toward the brambles, which served as effective barrier. The house they watched—they did not venture liberties with it, did not try the low iron gate, the hedges. Try reason, he thought. He was in command. It was on him to try reason with the witch; and it had to be the witch out there: there was nothing in all sanity that ought to be doing what that boat did. He moved quietly, gathered up men here and there while the boat came on.

The bow grated onto rock and kept grating, pushing itself ashore, and the Stepson moaned anew, leaning against the gunwales of the boat.

"Bring him," Ischade said, and Mradhon looked up as the witch stepped ashore, on the landing which rose in steps up to the brambles. He flung an arm about the Stepson, accepted Haught's help as he stood up, as now the Stepson fought to get his own feet under him, more than dead weight. The boat rocked as Mor-am went past and stepped out, close to Ischade. They went next, stepping over the bow to solid if water-washed stone footing, and Moria came up by Haught's side, while Ischade stood gazing into the dark beside them.

Men were there, armed and armored. A half a dozen visible. Stepsons.

The foremost came out a few steps. "You surprise us," that one said. "You did it."

"Yes," Ischade said. "Now go away. Be wise."

"Our man—"

"Not yours," she said.

"There's more of them," Mradhon muttered to her; there was the light of torches up on the height of the bank, just the merest wink of red through the brush. "Give him over, woman." He was holding the Stepson still, and the man was standing much on his own between himself and Haught, standing, having no strength, perhaps, to speak for himself. Or no will to do so—as there seemed a curious lack of initiative on the part of the Stepsons who faced them in the dark.

"Go away," Ischade said, and walked past, walked up to the iron gate that closed the bramble hedge at the back of her house. She turned there and looked back at them, lifted her hand.

Come. Mradhon felt it, a shiver in his nerves. The man they were carrying took a step on his own, faltering, and they went on carrying him, up the steps, to the gate Ischade held open for them, into a garden overgrown with weeds and brush. The back door of the house swung open abruptly, gaping dark; and they went toward this, up the backdoor steps—heard hasty footfalls behind them, Moria's swift pace, Mor-am's dragging foot. The iron gate creaked shut.

"Get him in," Ischade hissed at their backs; and there was not, at the moment, any choice.

Light flickered, the beginnings of fire in the fireplace, candles beginning to light all at once. Mradhon looked about in panic, at too many windows, a house too open to defend. The Stepson dragged at him. He sought a place and with Haught's help bestowed the man on the orange silk-strewn bed, the gruesomeness of it all niggling at his mind—that and the windows. He looked about, saw Moria close to the shelf-cluttered wall, by the window—saw the gleam of fire through the shutter-slats.

"Come out!" a thin voice cried, "or burn inside."

"The hedges," Haught said, and Ischade's face was set and cold. She lifted her hand, waved it as at inconsequence. The lights all brightened, all about the room, white as day.

"The hedges," said Mor-am. "They'll burn."

"They're close." Moria had sneaked a look, got back to the safe solidity of the wall. "They're moving up."

Ischade ignored them all. She brought a bowl, dipped a rag, laid a wet cloth on the Stepson's ravaged face, so, so tenderly. Straightened his hair. "Stilcho," she addressed the man. "Lie easy now. They'll not come inside."

"They won't need to," Mradhon said between his teeth. "Woman, they don't care if he fries along with us. If you've got a trick, use it. *Now*."

"This is your warning," the voice came from outside the walls. "Come out or burn!"

Ischade straightened.

Beyond the window slats a fire arced, flared. Kept flaring, sunbright. There were screams, a rush of wind. Mradhon whirled, saw the blaze of light at every window and Ischade standing black and still in the midst of them, her eyes—

He averted his, gazed at Haught's pale face. And the screams went on outside. Fire roared like a furnace about the house, went from white to red to white again outside, and the screams died.

There was silence then. The fire-glow vanished. Even the light of the candles, the fire in the fireplace sank lower. He turned toward Ischade, saw her let go a breath. Her face—he had never seen it angry; and saw it now.

But she walked to a table, quietly poured wine, a rich, rich red. She turned up other cups, two, four, the sixth. She filled only the one. "Make yourselves at home," she said. "Food, if you wish it. Drink. It will be safe for you. I say that it is."

None of them moved. Not one. Ischade drained her cup and drew a quiet breath.

"There is night left," she said. "An hour or more to dawn. Sit down. Sit down where you choose."

And she set the cup aside. She took off her cloak, draped it over a chair, bent and pulled off one boot and the other, then rose to stand barefoot on the litter that carpeted this place; she drew off her rings and cast them on the table, looked up again, for still no one had moved.

"Please yourselves," she said, and her eyes masked in insouciance something very dark.

Mradhon edged back.

"I would not," she said, "try the door. Not now."

She walked out to the middle of the silk-strewn floor. "Stilcho," she said; and a man who had been near dead moved, tried to sit.

"Don't," Moria said, a strangled, small voice—not love of Stepsons, it was sure; Mradhon felt the same, a knot of sickness in his throat.

Ischade held out her hands. The Stepson rose, swayed, walked to her. She took his hands, drew him to sit, with her, on the floor; he knelt, carefully.

"No," Haught said, quietly, a small, lost voice. "*No. Don't.*"

But Ischade had no glance for him. She began to speak, whispering, as if she shared secrets with the man. His lips began to move, mouthing words she spoke.

Mradhon seized Haught's arm, for Haught stood closest, drew him back, and Haught got back against the wall. Moria came close. Mor-am sought their corner, the furthest that there was.

"What's she doing?" Mradhon asked, tried to ask, but the room drank up sound and nothing at all came out.

She dreamed, deeply dreamed. The man who touched her—*Stilcho*. He had been deep within that territory of dreams, as deep as it was possible to go and still come back. He wanted it now: his mind wanted to go fleeting away down those dark corridors and bright—*Sjekso,* she chanted, over and over: that was the easiest to call of all her many ghosts. *Sjekso.* She had his attention now. *Sjekso. This is Stilcho. Follow him. Come up to me.*

The young rowdy was there, just verging the light. He attempted his old nonchalance, but he was shivering in the cold of a remembered alleyway, in the violence of her wrath.

She named other names and called them; she sent them deep, deep into the depths, remembering them— all her men, most ruffians, a few gentle, a few obsessed with hate. One had been a robber, dumped his victims in the harbor after carving up their faces. One had been a Hell Hound: Rynner was his name; he used to play games with prostitutes—his commander never knew. They were hate, raw hate: there were some souls that responded best to them. There was a boy, come with tears on his face; one of Moruth's beggars; one of Kadakithis' court, silver-tongued, with honey hair and the blackest, vilest heart. Up and up they came, swirled near, a veritable cloud.

She spoke, through Stilcho's lips, words in a language Stilcho would not have known, that few living did. "Til dawn, til dawn, til dawn—"

The dream stretched wide, passed beyond her control in a moment of panic. She tried to call them back, but that would have been dangerous.

Til dawn, she had said.

• • •

There were so many pressing at the gates, so very many—*Sanctuary*, the whisper went, *Sanctuary's open*—and some went in simple longing for home, for wives, husbands, children; some in anger, many, many in anger—the town inspired that, in those it trapped.

A wealthy widow turned in bed from the slave she kept and stared into a dead husband's reproachful eyes: a yell rang out through marble halls, high on the hill.

A judge waked, feeling something cold, and stared round at all the ghosts who had cause to remember him. He did not scream; he joined them, for his heart failed him on the spot.

In the Maze there was the sound of children's voices, running frenzied through the streets—*O Mama, Papa! Here I am!* One such wandered alone, among the merchants' fine houses, and rapped on a door. *I'm home —o Mama, let me in!*

A thief stirred in his sleep, rubbed his eyes and rubbed them twice. "Cudget," he said, knowing that he was dreaming, and yet he felt the cold drifting from the old man. "Cudget?" The old man swore at him just as he used to do, and Hanse Shadowspawn sat up in bed, petrified as his old mentor gazed on him, sitting on his foot.

Outside, the streets rustled with the gathering of the dead. One hammered at a door with thin rattling result: *Where's my money?* it wailed. *One-Thumb, where's my money?*

The booths at the Vulgar Unicorn grew crowded, buzzed with whispers, and the few diehard patrons went fleeing out the door.

Brother, a ghost said to the fat man in an uptown bed, and to the woman beside him—*is he worth it, Thea?*

Screams rose, long ones, echoing above the streets, a thin clamoring that the wind took and carried through the air.

A Beysib woman felt the stirring of the snake that

shared her bed, opened dark strange eyes and stared in wonder at the pale nightgowned figure that stood within the room: *Usurper*, it said. *Get out of my bed. Get out of my house. You have no right.*

No one had ever told her that. She blinked, confused, hearing the screams, as if the town were being sacked.

Across the river Moruth hurried along, hastening in the night for a newer, more secure place, in the madness of the hour, in streets insane with screams.

He stopped, seeing the way closed off. They were hawkmasks, four of them, who began to come toward him; he turned, and there were Stepsons, armed with swords.

In the guardroom a Hell Hound wakened, bleary-eyed from drink, looked up with the interest of one who hears the step of a friend returning, a singular pattern, so familiar and loved among a thousand others; and then with a sinking of the heart remembered it impossible. But Zalbar looked all the same, and stood up, overturning the chair with a crash.

Raskuli was standing there, unmarred, his head firmly on his shoulders. *I can't stay long,* he said.

And higher in the palace, Kadakithis screamed and yelled for guards, waking to find strangers in his room, a horde of ghosts, some with ropes about their necks; and soldiers all dusty in tattered armor; and his grandfather, who did not belong in Sanctuary, wearing a shadow-crown.

Shame, his grandfather said.

Walegrin sat up in bed, in the barracks below the wall—heard the clash of bracelets, ominous and clear. He reached for his knife, beneath the pillow. But as the sound ceased, faint as it was, he heard screams from beyond the walls, and leapt up, knife in hand, to fling the window wide.

Jubal the ex-slaver waked, hearing the murmur of a sea—and not a sea, but a horde of slaves about his bed, lacking limbs, with scars, some clutching their entrails to them. He spat at them, and felt the cold at the same time.

It's your fault, Kurd said, and from that ghost the others fled, deserting the place, leaving only the pale old man, the visitor with hollow eyes. *We should sit and talk,* Kurd said.

Sir? asked a wan, lost ghost, accosting a drunk who staggered by the Unicorn, stopping up his ears. *Sir? What street is this? I got to get home, me wife'll kill me, sure.*

On the street of gods a priestess screamed, waking to find a tiny ghost lying at her breast, all wet and dripping with riverweed, an infant of dark and accusing eyes.

A clatter of hooves rang through the Stepson barracks courtyard, a rattle of armor, a breath of cold wind.

And in the headquarters in the town, Dolon gave orders, dispatched men here and there—stopped cold as, alone, he realized other men had come, with their blackened skin and flesh hanging from their limbs.

We've lost, Erato said.

Fool! A different presence burst among them, whose armor shone, whose look was bronze and gold; he came striding in from out of the wall itself and the others fled. The air smelled suddenly of dust and heat. *O fool, what have you done?*

And Dolon backed away, knowing legend when he saw it.

The presence faded and left cold in its stead.

Ischade stirred, feeling the pain of long-rigid limbs. A heavy weight poured against her, Stilcho in collapse. And one last thing she did, without thinking of it, holding the Stepson in her arms: "Come back," she said, knowing it was dawn.

No, the almost-ghost said, weeping, but she compelled it. The body grew warm again. Moaned with pain.

"Help me," she said, looking up at the others who sat huddled in the corner.

It was Haught who came. Even Mor-am was too afraid; but Haught—who touched her, with his hands and in a different way, like the flickering of a fire. He took Stilcho up; Mor-am helped, and Vis, and Moria last of all.

Ischade drew herself to her feet, walked over to the window and unshuttered it by hand, considerate of her guests. There were some things they might bear with in the dark of night; but by day—that seemed unkind, and she felt washed clean this morning. A bird was perched on the untouched hedge. It was a carrion crow; it hopped down out of sight, in a fluttering of unseen wings.

Mradhon Vis strode along the street in the silence of the morning—free, inhaling air that had, even with its stench, a more wholesome quality than that within the riverhouse.

Haught, Moria, Mor-am—they were afraid. The Stepson slept, unharmed, in Ischade's silken bed, while the witch herself—gods knew where she was.

"Come *on*," he had pleaded, with Haught—with Moria, even. Mor-am he had not asked. Even the Stepson: him he would have gotten out of there if he could. But maybe it would be a corpse he was carrying before he had gotten to the street.

"No," Moria had said, seeming shamed. Haught had said nothing, but a hell was in his eyes, so he had it bad. "Don't—touch her," Mradhon had said then, shaking him by the shoulders. But Haught turned away, head bowed, passed his hand over one of the dead candles. A bit of smoke curled up on its own. Died. So Mradhon knew what hold Ischade had on Haught. And he went away, went out the door with no one to stop him.

She would find him if she wished. He was sure of that. There was a long list of those who might be interested to find him—but he walked the street past the bridge by daylight in the town. Traffic had begun, if late. There were walkers on the street, folk with unhappy, hunted looks.

"Vis," someone said. He heard rapid steps. His heart turned in him as he looked back and saw a man of the garrison. "Vis, is it?"

He thought of his sword, but daytime, on the streets —even in Sanctuary—was no time or place for that kind of craziness. He struck an easy stance, impatient attention, nodded to the man.

"Got a message," the soldier said. "Captain wants to see you. Mind?"

THE ART OF ALLIANCE

Robert Lynn Asprin

A large blackbird perched on the awning of the small jeweler's shop, its head cocked to fix the approaching trio with an unblinking eye, as if it knew of the drama about to unfold.

"There it is, Bantu, just like I told you. I'm sure it wasn't there last week."

The leader of the group nodded curtly, never taking his eyes from the small symbol scratched on one of the awning posts. It was a simple design: a horizontal line curved downward at the left, with a small circle at its lower right end. No rune or letter of any known alphabet matched it, yet it spoke volumes to those in the know.

"Not last week," Bantu said, his jaw muscles tightening, "and not next week. Come on."

The three were so intent on their mission within that they failed to note the loiterer across the street, who regarded them with much the same careful scrutiny that they had given the symbol. As they vanished into the shop, the watcher closed his eyes to evaluate the details of what he'd seen.

Three youths . . . well monied from the cut and newness of their clothes . . . swords and daggers only . . . no armor . . . none of the habitual wariness of warriors about them . . .

Satisfied that the facts were clear in his mind, the watcher opened his eyes, turned, and made his way quickly down the street, suddenly aware of the pressures of time in the performance of his duties.

There was a middle-aged couple in the shop, but the youths ignored them as completely as they did the displays. Instead they moved to confront the shopkeeper.

"Can . . . may I show you gentlemen something?" that notable inquired hesitantly.

"We'd like to know more about the sign scratched on the post outside," Bantu proclaimed bluntly.

"Sign?" the shopkeeper frowned. "There's no sign on my posts. Perhaps the children . . ."

"Spare us your feigned innocence, old fool," the youth snapped, swaggering forward. "Next you'll be telling us you don't even recognize Jubal's mark."

The shopkeeper paled at the mention of the ex-crimelord's name, and shot a quick glance at his other customers. The couple had drawn away from the disturbance and were attempting to appear unaware that anything was amiss.

"Tell us what that mark means," Bantu said. "Are you one of his killers or just a spy? Are these goods you're selling stolen or merely smuggled? How much blood was paid for your stock?"

The other customers exchanged a few mumbled words and began edging toward the door.

"Please," the storekeeper begged, "I . . ."

"That black bastard's power has been smashed once," the youth raged. "Do you think honest citizens will just stand by while he spreads his web again? That sign . . ."

The shop door flew open with a crash, cutting off the customers' escape. Half a dozen figures crowded into the limited space, swords drawn and ready.

Before Bantu had finished turning, the newcomers had shoved his comrades roughly against the walls of the shop, pinning them there with bared blades against their throats. The youth started to reach for his own weapon, then thought better of it and let his hand fall away from his sword hilt.

These men had the cold, easy confidence of those who make their living by the sword. There was near-military precision to their movements, though no soldier ever worked with such silent efficiency. As confident as he was at terrorizing storekeepers, Bantu knew he was now outclassed; there was no doubt in his mind what the outcome would be if he or his comrades offered any resistance.

A short, swarthy man came forward with a step that was more a glide. He leaned casually in front of the storekeeper, yet never took his eyes from Bantu. "Are these boys bothering you, citizen?"

"No, these . . . men were just asking about the sign on my post outside. They . . . seemed to think it was Jubal's mark."

"Jubal?" the swarthy man repeated, raising his eyebrows in mock surprise. "Haven't you heard, lad? The Black Devil of Sanctuary's dead now, or so everybody says. Lucky for you, too."

A knife glinted suddenly in the man's hand as he advanced on Bantu, a glint that was echoed in his narrowed eyes.

". . . because *if* he were alive, and *if* this shop were under his protection, and *if* he or his men caught you coming between him and a paying customer, then he'd have to make an example of you and your friends!"

The man was close now, and Bantu's throat tightened
as the knife moved up and down in the air between
them, gracefully serving as a pointer during the speech.

"Maybe your ears should be cut off to save you from
hearing troublesome rumors . . . or your tongue cut out
to keep you from repeating them. . . . Better still the
nose . . . yes, chop off the nose to keep it out of other
people's business . . ."

Bantu felt faint now. This couldn't be happening.
Not in broad daylight on the east side of town. These
things might happen in the Maze, but not here! Not to
him!

"Please, sir," the shopkeeper interrupted. "If anything happens in my shop . . ."

"Of course," the swarthy man continued, as if he
hadn't heard, "all this is pure conjecture. Jubal is dead,
so nothing need be done . . . or *said*. Correct?"

He turned away abruptly, summoning his men back
to the door with a jerk of his head.

"Yes, Jubal is dead," he repeated, "along with his
hawkmasks. As such, no one need concern themselves
with silly symbols scratched on shopfronts. I trust we
did not interrupt your business, citizens, for I'm sure
you are all here to purchase some of this man's excellent
stock . . . and you *will* each buy something before you
leave."

Jubal, the not-so-dead ex-crimelord of Sanctuary,
paced the confines of the small room like a caged animal. The process that had healed his terrible wounds
after the raid on his estate had aged him physically.
Mentally, however, he was still agile, and that agility
rebelled at these new restrictions on his movement. Still,
it was a small price to pay for rebuilding his lost power.

"So the alliance is finalized?" he asked. "We will
warn and guard the Stepsons whenever possible in return for their abandoning the hunt for the remaining
hawkmasks?"

"As you ordered," his aide acknowledged.

Jubal caught the tone of voice and hesitated in his pacing.

"You still don't approve of this treaty, do you Saliman?"

"Tempus and his Whoresons raided our holdings, wounded you nearly unto death, scattered our power, and have since been occupying their time killing our old comrades. Why should I object to allying with them . . . any more than I'd object to bedding a mad dog that's bitten me not once, but several times."

"But you yourself counseled not seeking vengeance on him!"

"Avoiding confrontation is one thing. Pledging to help an enemy is yet another. Forming an alliance was your idea, Jubal, not mine."

Jubal smiled slowly, and for a moment Saliman saw a flash of the old crimelord, the one who had once all but ruled Sanctuary.

"The alliance is at best temporary, old friend," the ex-gladiator murmured. "Eventually there will be a reckoning. In the meantime, where better to study an enemy than from within his own camp?"

"Tempus is smarter than that," his aide argued. "Do you really think he'll be trusting enough to relax his guard?"

"Of course not," said Jubal. "But Tempus has moved north to fight at Wizardwall. I have less respect for those he's left behind. However, their efforts to locate old hawkmasks are an annoyance we can ill afford at this time."

"The rebuilding goes well. Resistance is minimal, and . . ."

"I'm not talking about the rebuilding, and you know it!" Jubal interrupted viciously. "It's those Beysib that have me worried."

"But everyone else in town is unconcerned."

"They're fools! Not a one of them can see beyond

their own immediate gains. Merchants don't understand
power. Power understands power. I know those fish-
folk better than most, because I know myself. They
didn't come to Sanctuary to help the town. Oh, they'll
make a big show of the benefits of their arrival to the
citizens, but eventually there'll come a parting of the
ways. A situation will arise when they'll have to choose
between what's good for their new neighbors and what's
good for the Beysib, and there's no doubt in my mind as
to how they'll choose. If we let them get strong enough,
Sanctuary will be lost when their choice goes against the
city."

"They are not exactly weak now," Saliman observed,
thoughtfully chewing his lip.

"That's right," Jubal growled, "and that's why they
concern me. What we must do . . . what the town must
do, is to gain strength through our association with the
fish-folk, while at the same time blocking their growth,
actually sapping their strength whenever possible. Fortunately, this is a role Sanctuary is well suited to."

"There are those who would confuse your zeal for
self-interest rather than a defense of the town," Saliman
said carefully. "The Beysib *do* constitute a threat to
your effort to rebuild your power base."

"Of course," the hawkmaster smiled. "Like the
invaders, I work for my own benefit. . . . Everyone
does, though most don't admit it. The difference is that
my success is linked to the continuance of Sanctuary as
we have known it. Theirs isn't."

"Of course, your success will not happen by itself,"
his aide reminded him.

"Yes, yes. I know. Affairs of business. Forgive my
ramblings, Saliman, but you know I find details tedious
now that I've attained old age."

"You found them tedious well before your aging,"
came the dry response.

". . . which is why you are so valuable to me. Enough
of your nagging. Now, what pressing matter do you

have that simply *must* be dealt with?''

"Do you recall the shop that was displaying our protection symbol without having paid for the services?''

"The artifact shop? Yes, I remember. Synab never struck me as the sort who had that kind of courage.''

For all his grumbling and protests about detail, Jubal had an infallible memory for money and people.

"Well?'' the slaver continued, "What of it? Has the investigation been completed, or does his shop still stand?''

"Both,'' Saliman smiled. "Synab claims to be innocent of offense. He says that he *did* pay us for protection.''

"And you believed him? It's not like you to be so easily bluffed.''

"I believed him, but only because we located the one who has been dealing in our name.''

"A poacher?'' Jubal scowled. "As if we didn't have enough problems. All we need is to have every cheap crook in Sanctuary borrowing our reputation for his own extortions. I want the offender caught and brought to me as soon as possible.''

"He's waiting outside,'' the aide smiled. "I thought you would want to see him.''

"Excellent, Saliman. Your efficiency improves daily. Give me a moment to get into this wretched mask and bring him in.''

To maintain appearances, Jubal always wore one of the outlawed blue hawkmasks, as well as a hooded cloak when interviewing underlings and outsiders. It would not do to have the word spread that his youth had fled him, nor did it hurt to capitalize on the terror inspired by a featureless leader. In an effort to maximize the latter effect, the ex-crimelord doused all candles but one and laid his sword on the table in front of himself before signaling that the captive's blindfold should be removed.

Their prisoner was an unwashed urchin barely into his

teens. His type were as numerous as rats in Sanctuary, harassing store owners and annoying shoppers with their arrogant stares and daring sorties. There was no defiance in this one, though. Cowed and humble, he stood blinking, trying to clear his eyes while standing with the trembling stillness of a tethered goat trying to escape the notice of a predator.

"Do you know who I am, boy?"

"J . . . Jubal, sir."

"Louder! The name came readily enough to you when you represented yourself to Synab as my agent."

"I . . . everyone said you were dead, sir. I thought the symbols were a new extortion racket and didn't see any harm in trying to cash in on it myself."

"Even if I *were* dead, it's a dangerous name to be using. Weren't you afraid of the guardsmen? Or the Stepsons? They're hunting hawkmasks, you know."

"The Stepsons," the boy sneered. "They aren't so much. One of them had me cold with my hand in his purse yesterday. I knocked him down and got away before he could untangle himself enough to draw his sword."

"Anyone can be surprised, boy. Remember that. Those men are hardened veterans who've earned their reputation as well as their pay."

"They don't scare me," the boy argued, more defiantly.

"Do I?"

"Y . . . Yes, sir," came the reply, as the youth remembered his predicament.

". . . but not enough to keep you from posing as one of my agents," Jubal finished for him. "How much did you get from Synab, anyway?"

"I don't know, sir."

The ex-crimelord raised his eyebrows in mock surprise.

"Really!" the urchin insisted. "Instead of a flat fee, I demanded a portion of his weekly sales. I told him that we . . . that you would be watching his shop and would know if he tried to cheat on the figure.''

"Interesting," Jubal murmured. "How did you arrive at that system?"

"Well, once I knew that he was scared enough to pay, I suddenly realized that I didn't know how much to ask for. If I asked for too little, he'd get suspicious, but if I named a figure too high, he'd either ruin his shop, trying to pay it, or simply refuse . . . and then I'd have to try to make good my threats.''

"So what portion did you ask for?''

"One in five. But, you see, linking his payment to his sales, the fee would grow with his business, or adjust itself if times grew lean.''

The hawkmaster pondered this for a time.

"What is your name, boy?''

"Cidin, sir.''

"Well, Cidin, if you were in my place, if you caught someone using your name without permission, what would you do to him?''

"I . . . I'd kill him, sir," the boy admitted. "You know, as an example, so other people wouldn't do the same thing.''

"Quite right," Jubal nodded, rising to his feet. "I'm glad you understand what would have to be done.''

Cidin braced himself as the ex-crimelord reached for the sword on the table, then blinked in astonishment as the weapon was returned to its scabbard, instead of being wielded with deadly intent.

". . . fortunately for both of us, that isn't the case here. You have my permission to use my name and work as my agent. Of course, two-thirds of what you collect will be paid to me for the use of that name. Agreed?''

"Yes, sir.''

"You might also think of recruiting some of your friends to help you . . . if they're as quick of wit as they are of foot.''

"I'll try, sir.''

"Now wait here for a moment while I fetch my aide. I want you to tell him what you told me about portions instead of flat fees. It's an idea worth investigating."

He started for the door, then paused, studying the boy with a thoughtful eye.

"You don't *look* like a hawkmask . . . but then again, maybe that's what our rebuilding needs. I think the days of swaggering swordsmen are numbered in Sanctuary."

"Have you reached a decision yet on Mor-am and Moria?"

Jubal shook his head. "There's no rush," he said. "Mor-am is ours anytime we want him. I don't want to eliminate him until I've made my mind up on Moria. Those two were close once, and I'm still unconvinced she has totally quelched her feelings for her brother."

"It's said she has developed a taste for wine. If we wait too long, she may not be worth the recruiting."

"All the more reason to wait. Either she is strong enough to stand alone, without brother or wine, or she isn't. We've no room for employees who need tending."

"They were good people," Saliman said softly.

"Yes, they *were*. But we can ill afford generosity at this time. What about the other? Is there any danger our spies in Walegrin's force will be discovered?"

"None that we know of. Of course, they have an advantage over the rest of us."

"What's that supposed to mean?"

"Only that they're exempt from the order to assist the Stepsons, whenever trouble arises. I've told you before, it's a dead giveaway to come to the aid of those mercenaries every time they get into a scrape. No one else in town likes them, except the whores, and it breeds suspicion when one of ours takes their side in a quarrel."

"Have they honored their pledge not to hunt the old hawkmasks?"

"Yes," Saliman admitted grudgingly. "In a way, they still go through the motions, but they have been notably ineffective since the alliance.''

"Then we'll honor our side of the bargain. If our forces are drawing unwanted attention, instruct them to be more subtle with their assistance. There are ways of helping without openly taking sides in a brawl.''

"We tried that, and the Stepsons proved inept in battle. You were the one who said we must do whatever necessary to keep them alive.''

"Then keep doing it!'' Jubal was suddenly tired of the argument. "Saliman, I fear your dislike of this alliance has slanted your reports. Those 'inept' Stepsons drove our entire force out of our mansion. I find it hard to believe that they are suddenly unable to survive a simple street skirmish.''

The small snake raised its head to study its captors, then went back to exploring the confines of its jar with the singleminded intent characteristic of reptiles.

"So this is one of the dread beynit,'' Jubal mused, resting his chin on his hands to study the specimen. "The secret weapon of the Beysib.''

"Not all that secret,'' his aide retorted. "I've told you of the bodies that have appeared marked with snake-bite. The fish-folk are not always discreet in their use of their secret weapons.''

"Let's not fall victim to our own tricks, Saliman. We were never above scattering a few extra corpses around to confuse the issue. I don't think it's safe to assume that every snakebit body is the work of the Beysib. You're sure this snake won't be missed?''

"It cost the life of one of their women, but that's unimportant. Hers isn't the only life they've lost lately. They seem remarkably stubborn about not adapting to Sanctuary's nightlife. Wherever they come from, they're used to being able to travel the streets alone.''

"Their carelessness may give us the advantage we need,'' Jubal said, tapping the side of the jar to make the snake raise its head again. "If we can unlock the secret of this venom, we'll be that much ahead if we ever have to confront the fish-folk.''

He straightened and pushed the jar across the table to his aide.

"Pass this to someone well-versed in toxins and include enough money for test-slaves. I want an antidote for this poison within the month. Too bad Tempus revenged himself on Kurd. We could use the vivisectionist's services.''

"Tempus has a knack for making our life difficult,'' Saliman agreed, dryly.

"That reminds me. How are things going with the Stepsons? You haven't said anything lately, so I assume the situation has stabilized.''

"No, it hasn't. However, you told me in no uncertain terms that you didn't want to hear any more complaining about the Alliance.''

"No more complaints, but that didn't mean I would reject *all* reports.''

"Yes, it did. All I get is complaints about the Whoresons and their inability to save themselves from the simplest of conflicts.''

"All right, Saliman,'' Jubal sighed. "Perhaps I have discounted the reports too much. Now, can you give me an impartial briefing as to what has been happening?''

The aide paused to collect his thoughts before reporting. "The Stepsons, as we knew them when they first arrived in town, were hardened warriors, able to not only survive but triumph in most situations involving armed conflict. They were feared but respected by the people of Sanctuary. This has changed radically since our alliance with them. They have grown more quarrelsome, and their ability to defend themselves seems to have diminished nearly to the point of nonexistence. A major portion of our agents' time and energies is being diverted into keeping the Stepsons out of trouble, or saving them when our preventive measures fail.''

The ex-crimelord digested this. "We both know that field soldiers left in town too long become troublesome as their fighting trim and discipline deteriorate. Is this what's happened to the Stepsons?"

Saliman shook his head. "Such deterioration would not be so rapid or complete. These warriors could not be more ineffectual if they were *trying* to lose."

"You may have the answer there. We know the Stepsons to be fearless, willing to follow Tempus's orders even unto death. They could be testing us, deliberately exposing themselves to danger to measure our intent or ability to honor our alliances. Either that, or there may be more to Tempus's leadership than meets the eye. It has been established that he derives support from at least one god. Perhaps he has found a way to transmit that power to his troops . . . a way that has grown tenuous operating at such a distance."

"Either way, we're still investing too much of our time maintaining a bad alliance."

"But until we know for sure, we can't tell if it's more to our advantage to keep or dissolve the agreement. Find me the answers and I'll reconsider. Until then, we'll maintain our current position."

"As you will."

Jubal smiled as Hakiem was led blindfolded into the room. It was not necessary to wear the hawkmask for *this* interview, and he was glad, for he wanted an unobstructed view of his guest. Had he not been forewarned, he never would have recognized the old storyteller. He waited until the blindfold had been removed before making his examination, walking slowly around the tale-spinner, while Hakiem stood blinking in the light. New clothes, hair and beard trimmed, the gauntness gone from his rib cage, and . . . Yes! The fragrant odor of perfume! Hakiem had bathed!

"I have a job," the storyteller broke the silence,

almost embarrassed by his newfound wealth.

"I know," Jubal said. "In the new court, as advisor to the Beysa."

"If you already knew that, why'd you drag me here all blindfolded," Hakiem snapped, returning momentarily to his old gutter temper.

"Because I also know you're thinking of quitting."

There were several heartbeats of silence; then the storyteller heaved a sigh. "So instead of my asking why I'm here, I guess the question is 'Why am I quitting?' Is that it?"

"You've put it a bit more bluntly than I would have, but you've captured the essence of the matter."

Jubal sank into a chair and waved Hakiem to take the seat across from him. ". . . and help yourself to the wine. We've known each other too long for you to stand on ceremony."

"Ceremony!" the old tale-spinner snorted, accepting both chair and wine. "Perhaps that's what bothers me. Like you, I come from the streets and gutters. All the pomp and bother of court life bores me and, if nothing else, my time in Sanctuary has taught me to be impatient with boredom."

"Money pays for much patience, Hakiem," Jubal observed. "That *I've* learned from this town. Besides, I've had call to discover your beginnings are not as humble as you would have others believe. Come now, the real reason for your discontent."

"And what business is it of yours? Since when did you concern yourself with my thoughts or livelihood?"

"Information is my business," the ex-gladiator shot back. "Especially when it concerns the power structure of this town. You know that. You've sold me rumors often enough. And besides . . ." Jubal's voice dropped suddenly, losing its edge of anger and authority. ". . . Not long ago I considered changing careers. Two men, an old friend and a penniless storyteller, ignored my temper and convinced me to examine my own motives. I haven't paid all my debts in life, but I don't forget them either. Will you let me try to return the favor you paid me? Of being both gadfly and confessor at a time you feel most alone?''

Hakiem stared into his wine for several moments. ''I love this town,'' he said finally, ''as you do, though we love it differently and for different reasons. When the foreigners ask me my opinions of the townfolk, to appraise their trustworthiness or weakness, I feel I'm somehow betraying my friends. The gold is nice, but it leaves a slime on me that all the perfumed baths in the world cannot remove.''

''They ask no more than I did when you served as my eyes and ears,'' Jubal suggested.

''It's not the same,'' Hakiem insisted. ''You are a part of this town, like the Bazaar or the Maze. Now I deal with strangers, and I'll not spy against my home for mere gold.''

The ex-crimelord weighed this carefully, then poured them each another round of wine.

''Listen to me, Hakiem.'' he said at last. ''And think well on what I say. Your old life is gone. You know you could no more return to being an innocent storyteller than I could go back to being a slave. Life moves forward, not backward. Just as I've had to adapt to my sudden advance in age, you must learn to live with your new station in life. No. Hear me out.

''What you tell the invaders, they would learn whether you supplied it or not. As a fellow gatherer of information, I swear to you this is true. There is always more than one way to learn any fact. If, however, you were not there, if they chose someone else to advise them, there would be a difference. Another would be too swelled with his own importance, too in love with the sound of his own words to hear and see what was actually going on around him. That, storyteller, is a weakness you have never had.

''What goes on in that court, and the logic that the

newcomers use to arrive at their decisions, can be of utmost importance to the future of our town. It worries me, but not so much as it would if anyone but yourself were monitoring their activities. Trading information we know for that which we do not is a fair enough bargain, especially when what we gain is so valuable."

"All this talk comes very smoothly, slaver," the talesmith scowled. "Perhaps I've underestimated you again. You didn't bring me here to ask my reasons for quitting. It seems my thoughts were already known to you. What you really wanted was to recruit me as your spy."

"I suspected your reasons," Jubal admitted. "But *spy* is an ugly word. Still, the life of a spy is dangerous and would command a high wage . . . say, fifty in gold each week? With bonuses for particularly valuable reports?"

"To betray the other powers of Sanctuary while feeding your strength." Hakiem laughed. "And what if the Beysib ask about you? They'll grow suspicious if there is a blind spot in my reporting."

"Answer them as truthfully as you would when questioned about anyone else." The ex-gladiator shrugged. "I'm hiring you to gather information, not to protect me at your own expense. Admit everything, including that you have ways of contacting me, should the need arise. Tell the truth as often as you can. It will increase the odds of them believing you when you do find it necessary to lie."

"I'll consider it," the storyteller said. "But I'll tell you the only reason I'd even think about such a pact is that you and your ghosts are one of the last effective forces in Sanctuary, now that the Stepsons have left."

Something flickered across Jubal's face, then was gone.

"The Stepsons?" he asked. "When last I heard, they still ruled the streets. What makes you think they're gone?"

"Don't toy with me, Hawkmaster," Hakiem scolded, reaching for more wine, only to find the bottle empty. "You, who knows even what's going on in my own head, must know that those clowns in armor who parade the streets these days are no more Stepsons than I'm a Hell Hound. Oh, they have the height and the hair of those they replaced, but they're poor substitutes for the mercenaries who long ago followed Tempus off to the Northern Wars."

"Of course." Jubal smiled vaguely.

A small purse found its way from his tunic to his hand, and he pushed it across the table to the storyteller.

"Here," he instructed, "use this to buy yourself a charm, a good one, against poison. Violence in the courts is quieter, but no less rough than that you know from the Maze, and tasters are not always reliable."

"What I really need is a guard against their snakes," Hakiem grimaced, making the purse vanish with a wave of his hand. "I'll never get used to having so many reptiles about."

"Check with me next week," Jubal answered absently. "I have people working on an antidote for that particular poison. That is, of course, assuming you decide to retain your position. A street storyteller has no need of such protection."

"You have one of the beynit?" the talesmith asked, impressed in spite of himself.

"They aren't that hard to come by," the ex-crimelord responded casually, "which reminds me. If you need a tidbit to keep your patroness happy with your services, tell her that not all the snakebite victims appearing lately are her people's work. There are those who would discredit her court by duplicating their methods."

Hakiem raised his eyebrow in silent question, but Jubal shook his head.

"None of mine," he declared, "though the idea bears further study in the future. If you'll excuse me now, I have other matters to attend to . . . and tell your escort I said to see that you reach your next destination safely.''

The sound of Jubal's laughter brought Saliman hurrying into the room.

"What is it?'' he asked, half-puzzled, half-concerned by the first outburst of gaiety he'd witnessed from Jubal for many months. "Did the old storyteller have an amusing tale? Tell me, I could use a good laugh these days.''

"It's very simple,'' the Hawkmaster explained, regaining partial control of himself. "We've been betrayed. Double-crossed.''

"And you're laughing about it?''

"It's not the intent, but the method that amuses me. Though I have no love of being tricked, even I must admit this latest effort displays a certain style.''

With a few brief sentences, he sketched out what he had learned from Hakiem.

"Substitutes?'' Saliman frowned.

"Think about it,'' Jubal argued. "You know at least *some* of the Stepsons on sight. Have you seen any familiar faces in those uniforms lately? Perhaps the one who made the alliance with us? It explains so much, like why the so-called Stepsons suddenly don't know which end of a sword to grasp. And to think I expected to take advantage of a naive second-in-command.''

"So what are we going to do now?''

"*That* I decided as soon as I learned of the deception.''

All signs of laughter faded from Jubal's eyes, to be replaced by a dangerous glitter.

"I make alliances with men, not uniforms. Now it just so happens that the *men*, the Stepsons, whom our alliance is with are now somewhere to the north, putting their lives and reputations on the line for the dear old Empire. In their efforts to be in two places at once, though, they've left themselves vulnerable. They've turned their name over to a batch of total incompetents, hoping their reputation will suffice to bluff their replacements' way through any crisis.

"While we have an alliance with the Stepsons, we have no obligation at all to the fools they left behind in their stead. What's more, we know from our own difficulties in rebuilding exactly how fragile a reputation can be."

The eyes were narrow slits now.

"Therefore, here are my orders to all under my command. All support for those in town who currently call themselves Stepsons is to be withdrawn immediately. In fact, any opportunity to harass, embarrass, or destroy those individuals is to take priority over any assignment save those directly involving the Beysib. In the shortest possible time, I want to see the name of the Stepsons held in somewhat less regard by the citizens of Sanctuary than that shown to the Downwinders."

"But what will happen when word of this reaches the *real* Stepsons?" Saliman asked.

"They will be faced with a choice. They can either stay where they are and have their name slandered in the worst hell-hole in the Rankan Empire, or they can return at all speed, risking the label of deserter from the forces at Wizardwall. With any luck, both will happen. They'll desert their post *and* find they are unable to re-establish their reputation here."

He locked gazes with his aide, then winked slowly. "And *that*, Saliman old friend, is why I'm laughing."

THE CORNERS OF MEMORY

Lynn Abbey

I

A door that had been obscured by shadows opened to admit a hunched-over figure in dark, voluminous robes. The labored wheezing of the intruder filled the little room as, with quick, birdlike movements, the winding sheet was opened and the naked corpse revealed. Light entered the austere room from a single barred window high on one wall, illuminating the face of a young woman who lay on a narrow, wooden table, masking her waxen pallor so that it seemed she rested in the gentle sleep of youth, rather than the deeper sleep of eternity.

Ulcerous fingers uncurled from the depths of the shapeless robe sleeves, fingers more morbid and repellent than the corpse they probed. From within the cowl came a sound like a laugh—or a sob—and the grotesque hands brushed the young woman's hair away from her neck. His dark robes concealed her as the crippled crea-

ture sighed, sniffed, and bent to her throat. He stepped
back, examining a slim phial of blood in the faint light.

Still silent, except for his strained breathing, the
robed figure lurched back into the shadows, where he
conjured an intense blue light and, drop by drop,
emptied the blood into it. He inhaled the vapors, extin-
guished the light with a gesture, and returned his attention to the corpse. His fingers re-examined every part
of her without finding any mark other than the small
bruise on her neck from which he had removed the
blood.

Sighing, he drew the edges of the shroud together
again and carefully rearranged the folds of coarse linen.
He smoothed her ash-brown hair over the bruise on her
neck and, reluctantly, folded the cloth over her face.
There was no doubt, this time, that a sob escaped from
the shadowed depths of his cowl. There had been many
women when he had been young and handsome. They
had pursued him and he had squandered his love on
them. Now he could remember no face more clearly
than the one he had just covered with the linen.

The mage, Enas Yorl, shuffled back into the shadows, lit an ordinary candle, and sat at a rough-plank
desk, his face cradled in his unspeakable hands. She had
been a woman from the Street of Red Lanterns; from
the Aphrodisia House, where blue-starred Lythande
was a frequent guest. Yet they'd brought her to Enas for
the postmortem. And now he understood why.

Dipping the stylus in the inkwell, he began his report
in a script that had been antique in his own youth.
*"Your suspicions are confirmed. She was poisoned by
the concentrated venom of the benyit serpent."*

Lythande had most likely suspected as much, but the
Order of the Blue Star neither knew nor taught
everything. It fell to such as himself, more shunned than
feared, to research the arcane minutiae of the eon; to
recognize the poison for what it was or was not. Enas
Yorl continued:

The mark on her neck concealed two punctures—like those of the beynit serpent, though, my colleague, I am not at all certain that a serpent slithered up her arm to strike her. Our new ruler, the Beysa Shupansea, has the venom within her—as she has shown at the executions. It is said that the Blood of Bey, the envenomed blood, flows only in the veins of the true rulers of the Beysib, but you and I, who know magic and gods, know that this is most likely untrue. Perhaps not even Shupansea knows how far the gift is spread, but surely she knows she is not the only one . . .

A weeping ulcer on Yorl's hand burst with a foul odor, and a vile ichor seeped onto the parchment. The ancient, cursed magician groaned as he swept the fluid away. A ragged hole remained on the parchment; grey-green bone poked through the ruined flesh of his hand. The movement, and the pain, had loosened his cowl. It fell back to reveal thick, chestnut-colored hair, which glittered crimson and gold in the candlelight—his own hair—if the truth were known or anyone still lived who remembered him from before the curse.

He did not often feel the pain of his assorted bodies; the curse that disguised him in ever-shifting forms did not truly affect *him*. *He* still felt as he'd felt the instant before the curse had claimed him. Except—except rarely when in mocking answer to a yearning he could not quite repress, he was himself again: Enas Yorl, a man twice, three times the age of any other man. A shambling, rotted-out wreck who could not die; whose bones would never be scoured clean in the earth. He hid the radiant, unliving, and therefore uncursed, hair.

The ulcer was congealing with a faintly blue, scaly iridescence. Yorl prayed, as much as he ever prayed and to gods no mortal would dare worship, that sometime it would end for him as it had ended for the woman on his table. He no longer wished that the curse be removed.

The blueness was beginning to spread, bringing with it disorientation and nausea. He would not be able to complete his message to Lythande. With a trembling hand, he clutched the stylus and scrawled a final warning:

> Go, or send someone you trust, to the Beysib wharf
> where their ships still lie at anchor. Whisper 'Harka Bey'
> to the waters; then leave quickly, without looking back—

The transformation sped through him, blurring his vision, softening his bones. He folded the paper with a gross, awkward gesture and left it on the shroud. Paralysis had claimed his feet by the time he'd fumbled the door open and he retreated back to his private quarters, crawling on his hands and knees.

There was much more he could have told Lythande about the powerful, legendary beynit venom and the equally powerful and legendary Harka Bey. A few months ago even he had thought that the assassin's guild was only another Ilsigi myth; but then the fish-eyed folk *had* come from beyond the horizon and it now seemed some of the other myths might be true as well. Someone had gone to considerable trouble, using distilled venom and a knife point to make the wound, to make it seem as if the Harka Bey had slain the courtesan. He did not personally believe the Harka Bey would trouble themselves over a Red Lanterns woman —and he did not truly care why she had been killed or who had killed her. His thoughts surrounded the knowledge that the methods of the Harka Bey, at least, were real and might be turned toward ending his own misery.

II

Of late life had been kinder to the woman known in the town simply as Cythen. Her high leather boots were not only new but had been made to fit her. Her warm, fur-lined cloak was new as well: made by an old Down-

winds woman who had discovered that, since the arrival
of the Beysib and their gold, there were more things to
do with a stray cat than eat it. Yes, since the Beysib had
come, life was better than it had been—

Cythen hesitated, repressed a wave of remembrance
and, reminding herself that it was dangerous folly to
remember the past, continued on her way. Perhaps life
was better for the Downwinds woman; perhaps her own
life was now better than it had been a year before, but it
was not unconditionally better.

The young woman moved easily through the inky,
twilight shadows of the Maze, avoiding the unfathomed
pools of detritus that oozed up between the ancient cobblestones. Tiny pairs of eyes focused on her at the sound
of her approach and scampered noisily away. The
larger, more feral creatures of the hell-hole watched in
utter silence from the deeper shadows of doorways and
blind alleys. She strode past them all, looking neither
right nor left, but missing no flicker of motion.

She paused by an alley apparently no different from
any of the dozens she had already passed by and, after
assuring herself that no intelligent eyes marked her,
entered it. There was no light now; she guided herself
with her fingertips brushing the grimy walls, counting
the doorways: one, two, three, four. The door was
locked, as promised, but she quickly found the hand-
holds that had been chipped into the outer walls. Her
cloak fell back as she climbed and, had there been light
enough to reveal anything, it would have shown a man's
trousers under a woman's tunic and a mid-length sword
slung low on her left hip. She swung herself over the
cornice and dropped into the littered courtyard of a
long-abandoned shrine.

A single patch of moonlight, brilliant and unwelcome
here in the Maze, shone amid the rubble of what had
been an altar. Holding her cloak as if it were the source
of all bravery and courage itself, Cythen knelt among
the stones and whispered: "My life for Harka Bey!"

Then, as no one had forbidden it, she drew her sword and laid it across her thighs.

Lythande had said—or rather implied, for magicians and their ilk seldom actually said anything—that the Harka Bey would test her before they would listen to her questions. For Bekin's sake and her own need for vengeance, Cythen vowed that they would not find her wanting. The slowly shifting moonlight fed her terror, but she sat still and silent.

The darkness, which had been a comfort while she had been a part of it, now lurked at the edge of her vision, as her memories of better times always lurked at the edge of her thoughts. For a heartbeat she was the young girl she had once been and the darkness lunged at her. A yelp of pure terror nearly escaped her lips before she pushed both memory and old fears aside.

Bekin had been her elder sister. She had been betrothed when disaster had struck. She had witnessed her lover's bloody death and then had been made the victim of the bandits' lust in the aftermath of their victory. None of the brigands had noticed Cythen: slight, wiry Cythen, dressed in a youth's clothes. The younger sister had escaped from the carnage into the darkness. Waiting until the efforts of drinking, killing, and raping had overcome each outlaw and she could bundle her senseless sister away to the relative safety of the brush.

Under Cythen's protection, Bekin's bruises had healed, but her mind was lost. She lived in her own world, believing that the bulge in her belly was the legitimate child of her betrothed, oblivious to their squalor and misery. The birthing, coming on an early spring night, much like this, with only the moonlight for a midwife, had been a long and terrifying process for both of them. Though Cythen had seen midwives start a baby's life with a spanking, she held this one still, watching Bekin's exhausted sleep, until there was no chance it would live. Remembering only the half-naked outlaws

in the firelight, she laid the little corpse on the rocks for
scavengers to find.

Again Bekin recovered her strength, but not her wits.
She never learned the cruel lessons that hardened
Cythen and never lost the delusion that each strange
man was actually her betrothed returning to her. At first
Cythen fought with Bekin's desires and agonized with
guilt whenever she failed. But she could find no work to
get them food, while the men often left Bekin a trinket
or two that could be pawned or sold in the next village
—and Bekin was willing to go with any man. So, after a
time, Bekin earned their shelter while Cythen, who had
always preferred swordplay to needlework, learned the
art of the garrote and dressed herself in dead men's
clothes.

When the pair reached Sanctuary, it was only natural
that Cythen found a place with Jubal's hawkmasked
mercenaries. Bekin slept safely in the slaver's bed
whenever he desired her and Cythen knew a measure
of peace. When the hell-sent Whoresons had raided
Jubal's Downwinds estate, the younger sister again
came to the aid of the elder. This time, she took her to
the Street of Red Lanterns, to the Aphrodisia House
itself, where Myrtis promised that only a select, discrim-
inating clientele would encounter the ever-innocent
Bekin. But now, despite Myrtis' promise, Bekin was
four days dead of a serpent's venom.

The pool of moonlight shifted as the night aged and
Cythen waited. She was bathed in silvery light and blind
to the shadows beyond it: undoubtedly the Harka Bey
had chosen the rendezvous carefully. She held only her
sword hilt and endured the cramps the cold stone left in
her legs. Rising above the pain, she sought the mindlessness she had first discovered the day her world had
ended and the future closed. It was not the fantastic
mindlessness that had claimed Bekin, but rather an alert
emptiness, waiting to be filled.

Even so, she missed the first hint of movement in the

shadows. The Harka Bey were within the ruins before
she heard the faint rustle of shoes on the crumbling
masonry.

"Greetings," she whispered as one figure separated
from the rest and whipped out a short, batonlike sword
from a sheath she wore slung like a bow across her back.
Cythen was glad of the sword beneath her palms and of
the sturdy boots that let her spring to her feet while
the advancing woman drew a second sword like the
first. She remembered all Lythande had been able to tell
her about the Harka Bey: they were women, mercenaries, assassins, magicians, and utterly ruthless.

Cythen backed away, masking her apprehension as
the woman spun the pair of blades around her with a
blinding, deadly speed. By now, five months after the
landing, almost everyone had heard of the dazzling
swordwork of the Beysib aristocracy, but few had seen
even practice bouts with wooden swords and none had
seen such lethal artistry as advanced toward Cythen.

She assumed the static *en garde* of a Rankan officer
—who until the Beysib had been the best swordsmen in
the land—and fought the mesmerizing power of the
spinning steel. The almost invisible sphere the Beysib
woman constructed with the whirling blades was both
offense and defense. Cythen saw herself sliced down
like wheat before a peasant's scythe—and cut down in
the next few heartbeats.

She was going to die.

There was serenity in that realization. The nausea
dropped away, and the terror. She still couldn't see the
individual blades as they twirled, but they seemed somehow slower. And no one, unless the Harka Bey were
demons as well, could twirl the steel forever. And
wasn't her own blade demon-forged, shedding green
sparks when it met and shattered inferior metal? The
voice of her father, a voice she thought she had forgotten, came to her: "Don't watch what I do," he'd
snarled good-naturedly after batting aside her practice

sword. "Watch what I'm not doing and attack into that weakness!"

Cythen hunched down behind her sword and no longer retreated. However fast they moved, those blades could not protect the Harka Bey everywhere, all the time. Though still believing she would die in the attempt, Cythen balanced her weight and brought her sword blade in line with her opponent's neck: a neck which would be, for some invisible fraction of time, unprotected. She lunged forward, determined that she would not die unprotesting like the wheat.

Green sparks showered as Cythen absorbed the force of two blades slamming hard against her own. The Beysib steel did not shatter—but that was less important than the fact that all three blades were entrapped by each other and the tip of Cythen's blade was a finger's width from the Harka Bey's black-scarved neck. Cythen had the advantage with both hands firmly on her sword hilt, while the Harka Bey still had her two swords, and half the strength to hold each of them with. Then Cythen heard the unmistakable sound of naked steel in the shadows around her.

"Filthy, fish-eyed bitches!" Cythen exclaimed. The local patois, usually unequalled for expressing contempt or derision, had not yet taken the measure of the invaders, but there was no mistaking the murderous disgust in Cythen's face as she beat her sword free and stepped momentarily back out of range.

"Cowards!" she added.

"Had we wished to slay you, child, we could have done so without revealing ourselves. So, you see, it was simply a test; a test which you passed," her opponent said in slightly breathless, accented tones. She sheathed her swords and, unseen still in the darkness, her companions did the same.

"You're lying, bitch."

The Harka Bey ignored Cythen's remark, but began unwinding the black scarf from her face, revealing a

woman only a little older than Cythen herself. The clear
racial stamp of the Beysib unsettled Cythen as much, or
more than, the twirling swords. It wasn't just that their
eyes were a bit too round and bulging for mainland taste
but—*flick*—and those eyes went impenetrable and
glassy. To Cythen it was like being watched by the dead,
and with the corpse of her sister still foremost in her
mind, the comparison was not at all comforting.

"Do we truly seem so strange to you?" the Beysib
woman asked, reminding Cythen that she, too, was
staring.

"I had expected someone . . . older: a crone, from
what the mages said."

The Harka Bey hunched her shoulders; the glassy
membrane over her eyes flicked open, then closed
without interrupting her stare. "No old people came on
the ships with us. They would not have survived the
journey. I have been Harka Bey since my eyes first
opened on the sun and Her blood mingled with mine.
You needn't fear that I am not Harka Bey. I am called
Prism. Now, what do you wish from the Harka Bey?"

"A woman from the Street of Red Lanterns has been
murdered. She slept secure in the most guarded House
in Sanctuary and yet someone was able to kill her—
leaving the mark of serpent fangs on her neck." Cythen
spoke the words Lythande had taught her, though they
were far from the ones she would have freely chosen.

Though the Sanctuary woman believed it impossible,
Prism's eyes grew wider, rounder and the glassy membrane fluttered wildly. Finally her eyelids closed and, as
if on cue, the loose, dark clothing she wore began to
writhe from her waist to her breasts, from her breasts to
her shoulders, until the bloodred head of the woman's
familiar peeked above her collar and regarded Cythen
with round, unblinking eyes. The serpent opened its
mouth, revealing an equally crimson maw and glistening
ivory fangs. Its tongue wove before Cythen's face,

drawing a faint murmur of disgust from her.

"You needn't fear her," Prism assured Cythen with a cold smile, "unless you're my enemy."

Cythen silently shook her head.

"But you do think that I, or my sisters, killed this woman who was, in some way, dear to you?"

"No—yes. She was mad; she was my sister. She was protected there and there was no reason for anyone to want her dead. She lived in the past, in a world that doesn't exist anymore."

The cold smile flickered across Prism's face again. "Ah, then, you see it could not have been Harka Bey. We would never kill without reason."

"There were no marks besides the snake fangs' puncture anywhere on her. Myrtis even called Lythande to examine the body—and *he* arranged for Enas Yorl to study the poison. And Enas Yorl sent us to you."

Prism turned to the shadows and spoke rapidly in her own language. Cythen recognized only the names of the two magicians; the native Beysib language was very different from the mix of dialects common in Sanctuary. A second woman joined them in the moonlight. She unwound her scarf to reveal a face that shimmered orchid as it stared at Cythen. Cythen let her hand rest once again on her sword hilt while the two women conversed rapidly in their incomprehensible tongue.

"What else did your magician, Enas Yorl, tell you about us—besides how to contact us along the wharves?"

"Nothing," Cythen replied, hesitating a bit before continuing. "Enas Yorl's cursed. We left Bekin's corpse in his vestibule and returned later to find a note tucked in her shroud. Lythande said it was incomplete; that the shifting curse had claimed him again. Beyond saying that you, the Harka Bey, would know the truth, the note was indecipherable."

There was another brief exchange of foreign words

before Prism spoke again to Cythen. "The shape-changer is known to us—as we are known to him. It is a serious charge you and he bring before us. This woman, your sister, was not our victim. You, of course, do not know us well enough to know that we speak the truth in this; you will have to trust us that this is so."

Cythen opened her mouth to protest, but the woman waved her back to silence.

"I have not doubted the truth of *your* words," Prism warned. "Do not be so foolish as to doubt mine. We will study this matter closely. The dead woman will be avenged. You will be remembered. Go now, with Bey, the Mother of us all."

"If it wasn't you, then who was it?" Cythen demanded, though the women were already melting back into the shadows. "It couldn't have been one of us. None of us has the venom, or knows of the Harka Bey . . ."

They continued to vanish, as silently and mysteriously as they had arrived. Prism lingered the longest; then she, too, vanished and Cythen was left to wonder if the alien women had been there at all.

Still full of the delayed effects of her terror, Cythen clambered loudly over the wall. The Maze was still black as ink, but now it was silent, caught in the brief moment between the activities of night and those of the day. Her soft footfalls echoed and she pulled the dark cloak high around her face, until the Maze was behind her and she was in the Street of Red Lanterns, where a few patrons still lingered in the doorways, shielding their faces from her eyes. The great lamps were out above the door of the Aphrodisia House. Myrtis and her courtesans would not rise until the sun beat on the rooftops at noon. But her staff, the ones who were invisible at night, were working in the kitchens and took Cythen's hastily scribbled, disappointed message, promising that it would be delivered as soon as Madame had breakfasted. Then, weary and yawning, Cythen slipped back into the garrison barracks where Walegrin, in deference to her sex, had allotted her a private, bolted chamber.

She slept well into the day watch, entering the mess hall when it was deserted. The gelid remains of breakfast remained on the sideboard, ignored by the endemic vermin. It would taste worse than it looked, though Cythen was long past the luxury of tasting the food she ate: one ate what was available or one starved. She filled her bowl and sat alone by the hearth.

Bekin's death was still unexplained and unavenged and that weighed more heavily upon her than the greasy porridge. For more years than she cared to remember, her only pride had been that she had somehow managed to care for Bekin. Now that was gone and she stood emotionally naked to her guilts and unbidden memories. If the Harka Bey had not appeared, she might still have blamed them but, despite their barbaric coldness, or perhaps because of it, she believed what they had said. The warmth of tears rose within her as her brooding was broken by the sound of a chair scraping along the floor in the watchroom above her. Rather than succumb to the waiting tears, she went to confront Walegrin.

The straw-blond man didn't notice as she opened the door. He was absorbed in his square of parchment and the cramped rows of figures he had made upon it. With one hand on the door, Cythen hesitated. She didn't like Walegrin; no one really did, except maybe Thrusher—and he was almost as strange. The garrison's officer repelled compassion and friendship alike and hid his emotions so thoroughly that none could find them. Still, Walegrin managed to provide leadership and direction when it was needed—and he reminded Cythen of no one else in her troubled past.

"You missed curfew," he greeted her after she closed the door, not looking up from his figures. His hands were filthy with cheap ink, the only kind available in Sanctuary. But the numbers themselves, Cythen saw as she moved closer, were clear and orderly. He could read and write as well as swing a sword; in fact, he had education and experience equal to her own, and at times her feelings for him threatened to take wild leaps beyond friendship or respect. Then she would remind herself that it was only loneliness that she was feeling and the remembering of things best left forgotten.

"I left word for you," she stated without apology.

He kicked a stool toward her. "Did you find what you were looking for?"

She shook her head and sat on the stool. "No, but I found them all right. Beysib, and from the palace, by the look of them." She shook her head again, this time recalling the strange faces of the two women she had seen. "They sneaked up on me; I couldn't see how many there were. One came after me with a pair of those long-hilted swords of theirs. She spun them so fast I couldn't see them any more. Fighting with them's like walking into the mouth of a dragon."

"But you fought and survived?" A faint trace of a smile creased Walegrin's face. He set his quill aside.

"She said they were testing me—but that's because she couldn't kill me like she'd planned. Her swords couldn't stop mine, and mine didn't break hers; that Beysib steel is good. I guess we were both surprised. And then she figured she better talk to me, and listen. . . . But she never blinked while I talked to her—so this Harka Bey, whatever it is, really must be from the palace and around the Beysa, right? The closer they are to the Imperial blood the more fish-eyed they are, right? And while I was talking to her a *snake*, one of those damned red-mouthed vipers, crawled up out of her clothes and wound up around her neck, lookin' at me as if *its* opinion was the one that really mattered. And the other one—the one who came forward after the test— her face was shiny and purple!"

"Then she should be fairly easy to identify if she's the one who killed your sister."

Cythen froze on the stool, searching the past few days, the past few months for any slip of the tongue when she might have let him know what Bekin was to her; that she pursued the killer of a Red Lanterns courtesan out of anything more than outrage or simple compassion.

"Molin told me," Walegrin explained. "He was looking for a pattern."

"Molin Torchholder? Why in the name of a hundred stinking little gods should Vashanka's torch know anything about me or my sister?" The anxiety and guilt transformed themselves into anger; Cythen's rich voice filled the room.

"When Myrtis asks Lythande and Lythande asks Enas Yorl and they ask for a specific person to escort the corpse from pillar to post then, yes—somehow Molin Torchholder hears about it and gets his answers."

"And you're his errand boy? His messenger?"

She had touched a sore point between them in her anger, and by the darkening of his face she knew to regret it. Back in the first days of chaos after the Beysib fleet heaved over the horizon, Molin Torchholder had been everywhere. The archetypical bureaucrat had kept his beleaguered temple open for business; his Prince well-advised, the Beysib amused and, ultimately, Walegrin and his band employed in the service of the city. In return, Walegrin had begun to hand back a portion of the garrison's wages for Molin's speculations. It was not such a bad partnership. Walegrin's duties kept him apprised of the merchants' activity anyway, and Molin seldom lost money. But for Cythen, whose family, when she'd had a family, had been rich in land, not gold, the rabid pursuit of more gold than you needed was degrading. And, though she would never admit it directly, she did not want Walegrin degraded.

"He told me," Walegrin replied after an uncomfortable silence, his voice carefully even, "because you are still part of this garrison and if something is going to make you act rashly he would want me to know about it. Bekin's death isn't the only one that's got us edgy. Each night since she died at least two Beysib have been found dead, mutilated, and the lord-high muckety-mucks are thinking about showing some muscle around here. We're all under close watch."

"If he was so damned all-fired concerned about how rashly I might act, then why in his departed god's name didn't he keep Bekin from getting killed in the first place?"

"You hid her too well. He didn't know who she was until she was dead, Cythen. You bought Myrtis's silence; she was the only one beside you who knew—and maybe Jubal, I guess. But, did you know she was working the Beysib traffic on the Street?" Walegrin paused and let Cythen absorb the information she obviously had not had before. "Most of the women won't, you know. I guess it's not just their eyes that're different. But she was killed by a Beysib serpent—a jealous wife maybe? And, now that Beysibs are getting killed by an ordinary rip-and-slash artist in numbers and places that can't all be written off to carelessness, you are a suspect, you know."

The anger had burned itself out, leaving Cythen with gaping holes in her defenses; the grief slipped out. "Walegrin, she was mad. Every man looked the same to her—so of course she'd work the Beysib, or Jubal. She didn't live *here*. She couldn't have known anything, or done anything to make someone kill her. Damn, if Molin cares who services the Beysib stallions he could have protected her anyway." A few tears escaped and, shamed by them, Cythen hid her face behind her hands.

"You should tell him that yourself. You're not going to be any use to me until you do." Walegrin rolled the parchment, then stood up to fasten his sword-belt over his hips. "You won't be needing anything—let's go."

Too surprised to object, Cythen followed him into

the palace forecourt. A handful of gaudy Beysib youths, brash young men and lithe, bold women, pushed loudly past them, the exposed, painted breasts of the women flashing from beneath their capelets in the sunlight. Walegrin affected not to notice; no man in Sanctuary would notice the flaunted flesh—not if he valued his life. The Beysib had made that very clear in the first, and—thus far—only, wave of executions. Cythen stared, though not as well as the Beysib could stare, at their faces and finally looked away, unable to find any individuality in the barbaric features. Prism could have walked beside her and she would not have known it.

One of the Beysib lords strode by, magenta pantaloons billowing around him, a glittering fez perched atop his shaved head, and a well-scrubbed Sanctuary urchin struggling with a great silk parasol behind him. Both Walegrin and Cythen halted and saluted as he passed. That was the way now, if you accepted their gold.

She was grateful for the shadows of the lower palace and the familiar sound of servants shouting in Rankene at each other as they approached the much-reduced quarters of Kadakithis and his retainers. In truth, though, she no longer wanted to see the priest, if indeed she had ever wanted to see him. Her anger had escaped and now she only wanted to return to her tiny room. But Walegrin pounded on the heavy door and forced it open before the Torch's pet mute could lift the latch.

Molin set down his goblet and stared at Cythen in the old-fashioned way that said: What has the cat dragged in this time? Cythen tugged at her tunic, well aware that the clothes of a garrison soldier, no matter how clean or cared for, were unseemly attire for a woman—especially one who had been an earling's daughter. And if he knew about Bekin, then he might have known the rest as well. She would have run from the chamber, had that been an option, but since it wasn't, she squared her shoulders and matched his appraising look with one of her own.

The priest was Rankan and he'd managed to retain all
the implied power and majesty that that word had ever
carried, despite the low ceilings and the laundry-women
battling outside his window. Bands of gold decorated
the hems of his robes, adorned his boots, and circled his
fingers. His midnight hair was combed to surround his
face like a lion's mane—yet it was not so dark or shiny
as his eyes. If the Torch's god had been vanquished, as
some claimed; if the Prince was simply a puppet in the
hands of the Beysa; if his prospects for wealth and
honor had been reduced, then none of it showed in his
appearance or demeanor. Cythen looked away first.

"Cythen has some questions I can't answer for her,"
Walegrin said boldly as he laid the parchment on the
priest's table. "She wonders why you didn't protect
Bekin when you first suspected there might be danger in
dealing with the Beysib, as she did."

The Torch calmly unrolled the parchment. "Ah,
three caravans yesterday; seventy-five soldats. We've
almost enough. *They* agree the first boat should be
bought with Rankan gold, you know. The longer we can
keep the capitol ignorant of our situation here, the better it will be for all of us. If they knew how much gold
was floating in our harbor, they'd bring half the army
down here to take it from us—and neither we nor *they*
want that." He looked up from the parchment.

"Have you found me a man to take the gold north
yet? I'll have other messages for him to carry as well.
The war's not going well; I think we can lure Tempus
back to his Prince. We're going to need that man's
unique and nasty talents before this is over." He
rerolled the parchment and handed it over to the mute.

Walegrin scowled. He had no desire to have Tempus
back in the town. Molin sipped at his wine and seemed
to notice Cythen for the first time again. "Now then,
for your companion's questions. I was not aware of the
unfortunate woman's relationship to Cythen until after
she was dead. And I certainly did not know there was

danger in bedding a Beysib until it was too late."

"But you were watching her. You must have suspected something," Cythen snarled, grinding her heel into the lush wool-and-silk carpet and banging her fist on the priest's fine parquet table.

"She was, I believe, a half-mad—or totally mad, you'd know better than I—harlot at the Aphrodisia. I can not imagine the dangers or delights of such a life. She entertained a variety of Beysib men, one of the few who would, and as the welfare of the Beysib is important to me, I kept tabs on them, and therefore her. It is a pity she was murdered—that is what happened, isn't it? But, mad as she was—sleeping with the Beysib—isn't it better that she's departed? Her spirit is free now to be reborn on a higher, happier level."

Theology came easily and sincerely to the priest. And Cythen, who knew her own sins well enough, was tempted to believe the resonant phrases.

"You knew something," she said pleadingly, clutching her resolve. "Just like the Harka Bey suspected something when I told them."

Torchholder swallowed his pious words and looked to Walegrin for confirmation. The blond, ice-eyed man simply nodded his head slightly and said: "It had been suggested by Yorl. Cythen seemed the most appropriate one for the task; she volunteered anyway."

"Harka Bey," the priest repeated, mulling over the words. "Vengeance of Bey, I believe, in their language. I've heard rumors, legends, whatever about them, but everybody's denied that there's anything to the legends. Poison-blooded female assassins? And real enough that Cythen met with them? Very interesting, but not at all what I'd expected."

"I believe, your Grace, that Yorl only suggested contacting the Harka Bey. It seems unlikely that they would have killed the girl: Indeed they deny it," Walegrin corrected, clenching Cythen's upper arm in a bruising grip to keep her quiet.

"What *did* you expect?" Cythen demanded of Molin,
wrenching free of Walegrin and raising her voice. "Why
is it so important that she slept with the Beysib men?
Which one of them do you suspect of murder?"

"Not so loudly, child," the priest pleaded. "Remember, we survive on sufferance; we can have no suspicions." He gestured to the mute, who went to the
window and began playing a loud folktune on his pipes.
"We have no rights." Taking Cythen's arm, he ushered
her into a cramped, windowless alcove, hidden behind
one of his tapestries.

Molin began to speak in a hoarse whisper. "And keep
quiet about this," he warned her. "The Aphrodisia is
the favorite gaming place of our new lords and masters,
especially the younger, hot-headed ones. There's an ele-
ment among them that does not appreciate the current
policy of restraint. Remember, these people are exiles;
they've just lost a war at home; they've got something to
prove to themselves. Sure, the older men say 'Bide your
time,' 'We'll go home next year, or the year after that,
or the one after that.' They weren't the ones on the
battlefields getting their asses kicked.

"The Beysa Shupansea listens to the old men, but
now, with the murders of their own people, she is
becoming nervous herself. The clamor for a stronger
hand is rising . . ."

Molin was interrupted by the sound of someone
banging on the outer door. "The palace is a sponge," he
complained, and he was in a position to know the truth.
"Wait here and stay quiet, for god's sake."

Walegrin and Cythen pressed back into the shadows
and listened to a loud, unintelligible conversation between Molin and one of the Beysib lords. They did not
need to understand the words; the shouts told them
enough. The Beysib was angry and upset. Molin was
having small success at calming him down. Then the
Beysib stormed out of the room, slamming the door
behind him, and Molin rushed back into the alcove.

"They want results." He rubbed his hands together nervously, releasing the scent of the oils he used on his skin. "Turghurt's out there calling for vengeance and his people are listening. After all, no Beysib would kill another Beysib in such a crude manner!" Molin's voice spewed sarcasm. "I've got no great love for the natives of this town but one thing they are not, to a man, woman or child of them—stupid enough to taunt the Beysib like this!"

Walegrin frowned. "So they believe it's a Sanctuary man, or woman, behind it. But at least one of the bodies was found on the rooftops, right here, in the palace compound. This place is guarded, Molin. We guard it; they guard it. We'd have seen him, at least."

"Exactly what I've told them. Exactly why I'm sure it isn't one of us. But no; they've been frightened. They're convinced the town is smouldering against them—they don't intend to be pushed any further and they're not about to listen to me.

"I figure it works this way: there are malcontents in this court just like anywhere else. I knew the bulk of the hotheads congregated at the Aphrodisia. I didn't think there was danger to it; I just meant to keep those young men watched. Their leader is the eldest son of Terrai Burek, the Beysa's prime minister. And a child more unlike the father you can't imagine. It's no secret the boy hates his father and would do anything to spite the old man—though I expect bullying the townspeople would come naturally to him anyway. Yet, the father protects his son and the common laws of Sanctuary can't reach him."

"You're talking about Turghurt, aren't you?" Walegrin asked, obviously recognizing the name, though Cythen didn't recall having heard it before. "Still, Cythen's sister was killed by venom—and the Harka Bey are all women."

"True enough, but if the Harka Bey is real then it's likely a number of other things are—like the rings with

reservoirs for venom and razor-sharp blades to simulate
the fangs. They've told me the venom can't be isolated,
but I don't believe them now—''

"Who is this Terket Buger?" Cythen inquired, her
thoughts warming to the idea of a name and face she
could blame and take vengeance upon. "Would I recognize him?''

"Turghurt Burek," Walegrin corrected. "Yeah,
you've probably seen him. He's a big man, a trouble-
maker. Taller than most of the Beysib men here by a
head or more. He's a coward, I'm sure, because we can
never find him alone. He's always got a handful of
cronies around. We can't lay a hand on him anyway—
though this time we're talking about killing." He
looked hopefully to the priest.

"Not this time, either."

They were once again interrupted by a hammering on
the outside door and the sounds of masculine voices
shouting in the Beysib language. Molin left the alcove to
deal with the intrusion and fared worse this time than
before. He was roundly berated by two men who, it appeared, had made up their minds about something.
The priest returned to the alcove, visibly shaken.

"It fits together now," he said slowly. "The boy has
boxed us all. Another Beysib woman has been found
dead—and mutilated, I might add—down by the wharf.
Young Burek has played his hand masterfully. That was
him, and his father, to tell me that the populace must be
controlled or wholesale slaughter of the townsfolk will
be on my conscience. The men of Bey will not see their
women defiled.''

"Turghurt Burek was here?" Cythen asked, her
hands moving instinctively to her hip, where she usually
wore her sword. She cursed herself for not having dared
to lift the tapestry a fraction to see his face.

"The same, and he's convinced his father now as
well. Walegrin, I don't know how you'll do it, but
you've got to keep the peace until I can get the old man

to see reason—or catch the murderers bloody-handed."
The priest paused, as if an idea had just occurred to
him. He looked hard at Cythen and she fairly cringed
from the plotting she saw in his face. "Catch them
bloody-handed! You—Cythen; how much do you want
your revenge? What will you sacrifice to get it?
Turghurt is full of himself, and he'll likely go back to
the Aphrodisia to celebrate this victory. He hasn't been
back since your sister died, but I doubt he'll wait much
longer. If not tonight, then tomorrow night. He'll go
back because he has to gloat—and because his kind get
no satisfaction from these high-handed Beysib women.

"Now, somehow your sister learned something she
shouldn't have and died for it. Could you lure him into
the same mistake and survive to let me know of it? I'll
need proof absolute if I'm going to confront his father.
Not a corpse, you understand; that will only fan the
flames. What I'll need is Turghurt and the proof. Can
you get it for me?"

Cythen found herself nodding, promising the Rankan
priest that she would get her vengeance as she got him
his proof; as she spoke another hidden part of herself
froze into numb paralysis. The meeting had become a
dream from which she could not seem to awaken: a con-
tinuation of all the nightmares that made her past so un-
pleasant to remember. Bekin was dead—but not gone.

She stood mute while the priest and Walegrin made
their plans. Her silence was taken for attentiveness,
though she heard nothing above the screaming of her
own thoughts. The priest patted her on the shoulder as
she left his rooms, following Walegrin into the forecourt again. Knots of Beysibs had gathered there, talking among themselves with their backs to the Sanctuary
pair as they walked back to the garrison. One of the men
did turn to stare at her. He wasn't tall so he wasn't
Turghurt, but all the same, the feel of the cold fish-eyes
regarding her finally loosened her tongue.

"Sabellia preserve me! I know nothing of Bekin's

trade. I'm still a virgin!" It was as much of a prayer as she had muttered since her father went down with an arrow in his throat.

Walegrin stopped short, appraising her in surprise. "You told me you'd worked on the Street of Red Lanterns?"

"I told you that I'd tried to work on the Street of Red Lanterns and that I couldn't. Don't look at me like that; it's not that unreasonable. Don't I have my own quarters now, and no one who'd dare to bother me there? A woman who lives with the garrison is safe from all other men, and a woman who is part of that garrison is safe from her cohorts as well."

"Then you've got more courage than I thought," he replied, shaking his head, "or you're an utter fool. You'd better let Myrtis know when you get there; she'll know how to turn it to our advantage."

Cythen grimaced and tried not to think of that evening, or the next evening. She left her sword in Walegrin's care and made her way to the Street. It was nearing dusk by the time she got there and some of the poorer, more worn women, who did not dwell in any of the major establishments, were already on the prowl, though the Aphrodisia was not yet open for business. One of them jeered at her as she climbed the steps to the carved doors: "They won't take your type there, soldier-girl."

She stood there uncomfortably, ignoring the comments from the street below and remembering why she always came in the morning. The doorman recognized her, however, and at length the doors swung open to her. The downstairs was beginning to come to life with music and women dressed in brilliant, flower-colored dresses. Cythen watched them as the doorman guided her to the little room where Myrtis was getting ready for the evening herself.

"I had not expected to see you again," Myrtis said softly, rising from her dressing table and discreetly closing the account book, which crowded out the cosmetic bottles. "Your note said your meeting did not go well. You had not mentioned returning here."

"The meeting didn't go well." Cythen eyed Myrtis's smooth, clenched white hands as she spoke. There was a barely perceptible nervousness in the madam's voice and a barely perceptible rippling to the edge of the table rug beneath the account books. Both could have any number of benign explanations, but Cythen had brought Bekin here expecting, and paying for, her sister's safety. Myrtis had not provided the services she had been paid for and Cythen's vengeance could be expected in several different ways.

"I've seen the priest, Molin Torchholder, and he's made a plan; a way to snare the one he suspects. I thought he would have sent you a message by now," Cythen said quickly.

Myrtis shrugged, but without unclenching her fists. "Since Bekin there have been other deaths: gruesome murders, many of them Beysib women. All the reliable couriers have been kept busy. There isn't time for the death of a Sanctuary girl. Perhaps you can tell me who Molin Torchholder suspects of using beynit venom when the Harka Bey denies all knowledge of it."

"He suspects a man, a Beysib man. He suspects that the death of my sister is not so different from the Beysib deaths."

"Has he given you a name?"

"Yes, Turghurt Burek."

"The son of the prime minister?"

"Yes, but the Torch suspects him anyway. He comes here, doesn't he?"

"That man has spies everywhere!" Myrtis grimaced as she relaxed and raised her fist toward the smouldering hearth. Cythen heard a small click; then watched as the flames leapt high and crimson. "Once primed, it must be shot," Myrtis explained, while Cythen shuddered. "We called him *Voyce* here; and he was always a

gentleman—for all that he's fish-folk. Bekin was special
to him; such childlike innocence is not at all common
among their women. He grieved over her death and
hasn't been back since she died.

"But he was also the second person to suggest the
Harka Bey to us." Myrtis paused, and just when Cythen
despaired of being believed at all, the starkly beautiful
woman continued: "I like him very much; he reminds
me of a love I once had. I was blinded. I have not been
blinded for . . . for a long time. The signs were there; my
suspicions should have been roused. Does Molin Torchholder have some notion of how we're to bring the
son of the Beysib prime minister to justice before there
is war in the town and we turn to Ranke for help?"

"Molin believes that since Bekin was the only Sanctuary woman who has been slain, she must have learned
something dangerous to him. Molin thinks that Turghurt will make the same mistake again, now that he's
convinced his father to see everything his way. But I will
be less easy to kill than she was, and snare him instead."

"You play a dangerous game between the priest and
this Beysib, Cythen. Molin is no less ruthless than the
fish-folk. And, here Burek is *Voyce*; none of my women
knows the true names of the men here, and if you value
your life you'll remember that. The Aphrodisia is a
place apart; a man need not be himself here—and they
expect me to protect them.

"Now Voyce is clever, strong and cruel, yet it would
be a simple matter to be rid of him, if that would serve
our purposes. The Harka Bey are not the only women
who understand killing. But he must be exposed, not
slain, and that will be all the more dangerous."

"I've come for my vengeance," Cythen warned.

"He will not expose himself to a garrison soldier, my
dear, neither figuratively nor literally." Myrtis gave
Cythen a slightly condescending smile. "His tastes do
not run towards strong-willed women, such as he was
raised with and his father serves. You do not have the

yielding nature that madness gave your sister."

"I'll become whatever I must be to trap him."

As she spoke, Cythen yanked loose the cord that bound her hair, shaking her head until the brown strands rose like an untidy aura around her face.

"Good intentions will not deceive him, either." Myrtis had become kind-voiced again. "Your need for vengeance will not make you a courtesan. There are others here who can bell our cat."

"No," Cythen protested. "He'll come here again and make his mistake again, and he might kill another of your courtesans. Isn't it to your advantage to let me risk my life rather than sacrificing one of those who belong to you?"

"Of course it would be to my advantage child, if I owned anyone. But just because I keep account books on love and pleasure, do not think I am completely without conscience. If Voyce is all he is suspected of being, I would be as guilty of your death, or anyone's death, as he would be."

Cythen shook her head and took a step closer to Myrtis, resting her fists on the table. "Don't lecture me about death or guilt. For five years since those bandits swept down and attacked us, I traveled with Bekin, protecting her, bringing her men, and killing them if I had to. It would have been better if she had died that first night. I'm not sorry she's dead, only sorry that she was murdered by a man she trusted, as she trusted all men. I don't blame you, or me, but I can't get her out of my memory until I've avenged her. Do you understand that? Do you understand that I must close the circle completely, myself, if I'm to have peace, if I'm to be free of her?"

Myrtis met Cythen's rabid stare and, whether she understood the dark emotions and memories that drove the younger woman or not, she finally nodded. "Still, if you are to have a chance at all, you must abide by what I tell you to do, Cythen. If he does not find you attractive, he will search elsewhere. I will give you her chambers and her clothes; that will give you an advantage. I will send Ambutta to bathe you, to help you dress and to arrange your hair.

"When he returns again, if he returns again, he will be yours. You may stay as long as you please, but he is not to be harmed in this house! Now then, you must also seem to belong here, and it will rouse suspicion if you take no others while you wait. I will set aside your portion—"

"I'm a virgin," Cythen interrupted in a far from steady voice. When her mind was focused on the fish-eyed murderer of her sister, she could manage to ignore the implications of the plan she had agreed to; but faced with the pragmatic logic of the madam, she began to realize that vengeance and determination might not be enough.

Myrtis nodded, "I had suspected as much. You would not want your sister's slayer, then, to be the first—"

"It won't matter. Just tell everyone that I'm being saved for just the right man. That's often the way of it anyway, isn't it? A special prize for a special customer?"

Myrtis hardened. "In those places where courtesan and slave are the same that may be so. But my women are here because they wish to be here; I do not own them. Many leave for other lives after they've grown tired of a life of love and earned a healthy portion of gold. But pleasure is not your talent, Cythen; you wouldn't understand. Men have nothing you desire and you have nothing to give them in return."

"I have a talent for deceit, Myrtis, or neither Bekin nor I would have survived at all. Honor your promise. Give him to me for one night."

With a gesture of worried resignation, Myrtis consented to the arrangement. She summoned Ambutta, who some said was her daughter, and had Cythen led into the private sections of the house where, for a night and a day she was fussed over and transformed. Before sundown of the next day she was ensconced in the plush seraglio where Bekin had lived, and died. Her garrison clothes and knife had been hidden in the dark paneled walls and she herself was now draped in lengths of diaphanous rose-colored silk—a gift to Bekin from the man who had slain her.

Staring into the mirror as the sun set, Cythen saw a woman she had never known before: the self she might have become if tragedy had not intervened. She was beautiful, as Bekin had been, and she preferred the feel of silk to the chafing of the linen and wools she normally wore. Ambutta had skillfully wound beads through Cythen's hair, binding it into a fanciful shape that left Cythen afraid to turn quickly, lest the whole affair come tumbling down into her face.

"There was a message for you earlier," Ambutta, a disturbingly wise woman no older than thirteen, said as she daubed a line of kohl under Cythen's eyes.

"What?" Cythen jerked away in anger, her stance becoming that of a fighter, despite the silk.

"You were bathing," the child-woman explained, twirling the brush in the inky powder, "and men do not come upstairs by day."

"All right, then, give it to me now." She held out her hand.

"It was spoken only, from your friend Walegrin. He says two more fish-folk have been found murdered: Actually it's three—another was found at low tide—but the message came before that. One of them was a cousin to the Beysa herself. The garrison is ordered to produce the culprit, or any culprit, by dawn or the executions will begin. They will kill as many each noon as fish-folk who have already died. Tomorrow they'll kill thirteen —by venom."

Though the room was warm and draftless, Cythen felt a chill. "Was that all?"

"No, Walegrin said Turghurt is horny."

The chill became a finger of ice along her spine. She did not resist as Ambutta moved closer to finish applying the kohl. She saw her face in the mirror and recognized herself as the frightened girl beside the wise Ambutta.

The hours wore on after Ambutta left her. Two knobs had burnt off the hour candle and none had come to her door. The music and laughter that were the normal sounds of an evening at the Aphrodisia House grated on her ears as she listened for the telltale accent that would betray the presence of the fish-folk, whatever common Ilsigi or Rankan name Myrtis gave them.

Couples walked noisily past her closed door; women already settled for the night. The smells of love-incense grew strong enough to make her head ache. She stood on a pile of pillows to open the room's only window and to look out on the jumble of the Bazaar stalls and the dark roofs of the Maze beyond them. Absorbed by the panorama of the town, she did not hear the latch lift nor the door open, but she felt someone staring at her.

"They told me that they had given you her room."

She knew, before she turned, that he had finally come. He spoke the local dialect well, but without any attempt to conceal his heavy accent. Her heart was fluttering against her ribs as she turned to face him.

He had left his cloak downstairs and stood before her in fish-folk finery, filling the doorway with his bulk. It was no wonder Bekin had adored him—she'd had a child's delight in color and shine. His pantaloons were a deep turquoise, embroidered with silver. His tunic was a lighter shade, slashed open to the navel, with sleeves that shone and rippled like the rose silk she wore. His fez was encrusted with glittery stones; he removed it with a smile; his shaved scalp glistened in the candlelight. Despite herself, Cythen flattened against the wall and regarded him with a mixture of fear and awe. His eyes shone as he watched her without blinking, and after a moment she looked away.

"There is no need to be frightened, Little Flower."

His arms circled the rose silk and drew her tightly against him. Strong blunt fingers pressed around her neck, digging in behind her ears so she could not resist as he forced her lips apart. She willed herself to numbness when he found the knots that bound the silk around her and undid them. Screams of outrage echoed in her mind, but she clung silently, unprotestingly, to his powerful arms.

"You are still frightened?" He asked after a while, running a finger over the curve of her hip as she lay limp on the pillows beside him. He was strong, as Walegrin had said he would be, but she did not quite have the nerve to find out if he was a coward as well.

She shook her head when he asked if she was afraid, but could not stop her hands from coming to rest on top of his, stopping his incessant motion. He bent over her, caressing her breast with his lips, tongue and teeth. With a strangled whimper, she stiffened away from him.

"You will see. There's nothing to be fightened of. Just relax."

He was staring at her: cold fish-eyes peering into her body and soul. All the warnings that Myrtis, Walegrin, and even Ambutta had given her chorused out of her memory and she wished she was Bekin: either dead or willing to love any man. Her confidence went out like a guttered candle. She felt him loosening the heavy belt that bound his pantaloons and knew she could not stifle the next screams that would rise from her throat.

There would be no second chance. She would fall, and probably die here in this room with her sister's ghost hovering in her thoughts. But she was a master of deceit, as she had claimed, which was much more than simple lying or pretending.

"Yes, I'm frightened," she whispered in a coy, little girl's voice she had just discovered, using the truth to buy a few more moments. She shivered and clutched the

discarded silk against her as he let her slide away from
him. "Do you know what happened to the girl who
lived in this room? While she slept, someone let a serpent into here and it bit her. She died horribly. Sometimes I think I hear it on the pillows, but they won't let
me have another room."

"There are no snakes in this room, Little Flower."

In the shadows, she could not be certain of his expression, and his accent made it difficult to read the
sound of his voice. Recklessly, she continued.

"That's what they tell me. The only snakes in Sanctuary which are so poisonous are the Beysa's holy
snakes—and those never go far from her in the palace.
But she was killed by snake venom. Someone had to
have put it in here. But she was only a mad girl from the
Street of Red Lanterns, so no one will search for her
killer."

"I'm sure your Prince will do all that he can. It would
be a crime among us, as well, if someone had stolen the
Beysa's serpent."

"I'm afraid. Suppose they didn't need to steal the serpent, suppose they only needed the venom. Suppose the
Harka Bey are angry because men like you come here to
women like me."

He took her in his arms again, brushing the sweat-
dampened hair back from her face. "The Harka Bey is a
tale for children."

She caught his hand in hers and felt the design of the
ring on his hand: a serpent, with fangs that rasped on
the ridges of her fingertips. He pulled his hand quickly
away.

"I'm afraid, Turghurt, of what will become of me—"

He struck like a snake, grabbing at her throat and
wrenching her head around into the candlelight. Her
right arm was hopelessly twisted in the silk and her left
bent backwards into agony.

"So Myrtis thinks it's me, does she?"

"No," Cythen gasped, aware now that she had used

his real name, as she had been warned not to do. "She knows it could not have been you who killed Bekin. Only women handle the serpents . . ." but they were both staring at the serpent ring shining in the candle-light.

"What are you?" he demanded, shaking her jaw until something ripped loose in her neck and she could not have answered him if she had wanted to. "Who sent you? What do you know?" He bent her wrist back until it was in the candle flame. "Who told you about our plans?"

Tears flowed through the kohl, washing the black powder into her eyes—but that was the least of her pain. She screamed, finally, though wrenching her jaw free of him was almost enough to make her faint. He caught her again, but it was too late. Even as he beat her head against the wall, someone was banging on the door. She fell back on the candle, extinguishing it with her body, and they struggled against each other in the darkness.

She broke free more than once, digging her filed nails into whatever vulnerable skin she could grab. But she did not have the strength to break his bones with her hands and could not find, in the darkness, the panel that concealed her knife. Someone was using an axe on the door now, and she thought perhaps it would not all have been in vain if they caught him for her death.

He caught her by the shoulder and brought his fist crashing into her weakened jaw. The force and the pain stunned her. She hung limp in his grip, defenseless against his second punch. He heaved her body into a corner, where it hit with a dead-weight thud; then he began moving frantically through the darkness as the axe continued to bite against the door.

Cythen had not lost consciousness, though she wished she had. Her mouth and jaw were on fire, although, ironically, one or another of his punches had undone the dislocation, along with loosening a few of her teeth. She could have screamed freely now, as she heard his

glittery clothing dropping to the floor, but the anguish
of her failure was too great.

A piece of wood had splintered away from the door.
Light from the lanterns in the hallway glinted off the
serpent ring which he held before his eyes. She realized
that he must think her dead or unconscious, and she
thought she might survive if she continued to be silent,
but he came at her as a second, larger piece of wood
came loose. The glistening serpent's head rose above his
fist.

She lunged away from him and felt something strike
her shoulder. In the swirl of pain and panic she did not
know if the fangs had pierced her; she knew only that
she was still alive, still wrapped around his legs and
trying to bite him with her already battered and bloody
teeth. He kicked free of her with little difficulty and
made a leap for the window as a hand reached around
into the darkness and worked the latch.

Though the door was open almost at once, Turghurt
had heaved himself clear of the window before they
reached him. And though Cythen protested her health
and survival, they made more of a fuss over her and the
ruined silk than they did over the escaping Beysib.

"He won't get far. Not without any clothes," Myrtis
assured her, holding up the discarded turquoise pantaloons.

"He'll be bleedin' naked!" one of the other women
tittered.

Cythen had already learned that the pain was bear-
able so long as she didn't try to talk, so she ignored the
chaos of conversation and searched for the panel that
concealed her proper clothes and knife. The Beysib
wasn't naked, she was sure of that. Somehow he'd
managed to exchange his bright silks for dark clothes
such as the Harka Bey had worn. He hadn't been able to
change his boots, though, and the light leather should
be easy to spot—if he wasn't already safe at the palace

by now. She shoved Ambutta aside and pulled on her own boots.

"You aren't going after him, are you? The garrison has men at both ends of the Street. They'll have him by now. I've already sent for a physician to see you." Myrtis reached gently toward Cythen's battered face, and Cythen warned her away with an animal growl.

With her hair still loose and glittering, she shoved her way to the door. Maybe Walegrin really was out there; it would be the first good thing that had happened. Maybe they had already caught Turghurt. She'd rather have Thrusher tend her wounds than some cathouse doctor. She kicked at the doorman when he tried to stop her and burst out into the Street.

Although the walls of the Palace were closer, they were more dangerous. She guessed Turghurt would have gone south past the Bazaar and into the Maze before heading back to the palace. It had not occurred to her that he might still be on the Street until a hand loomed out of the shadows and closed over her mouth. Her throat tore with an almost soundless shriek and she lashed back with her heels and fists before hearing a familiar voice.

"Damn you, bitch! We've got him cornered in a loft not a hundred steps from here."

She pried Walegrin's fingers from her face and stood before him, tears streaming down her cheeks and her whole body trembling.

"What happened to you?"

"I . . . got . . . hit," she said slowly, moving her mouth as little as possible.

"Did you get the proof?"

She shrugged. Was the ring and his attempt to kill her proof he had killed Bekin or the Beysib men and women?

"C'mon, Cythen. He broke out of there like a bull. He didn't punch you out 'cause you're ugly—"

She shook her head and tried to explain what had happened, but her mouth was too sore for so many words and he could make no sense of her gestures.

"Well, all right, anyway. Maybe we can pry something out of him now. We think he's found a regular hideout behind some of the older Houses." Walegrin led the way off the street to a dark jumble of buildings where two of his men waited.

"It's as quiet as a tomb up there," the soldier informed his captain; then, noticing Cythen, added: "What happened to you?"

"She got hit. Don't ask questions. Now, you're sure he's still up there?"

"There's only two ways out and he ain't used either of them."

"Okay." Walegrin turned back to Cythen. "You get him at all?" She shook her head to say no and he looked away. "Okay, Thrush, you come with me. Jore, you bellow if you see something. And Cythen," he tossed her a scabbard. "Here's your sword; redeem yourself."

They dashed across an open space and flattened themselves against the rough stucco walls of the building. It had been abandoned for some time. Chunks of stonework broke loose as they made their way to the gaping doorway. The central column of stairs to the upper room was only wide enough for one person and missing a good third of its boards as well. Walegrin drew his Enlibrite sword and started up them, motioning for the others to remain behind.

He moved smoothly and silently until, while he was raising his leg over two missing steps, the lower board gave way. The blond man lurched forward, using his sword for balance, not defense, and another sword swished through the air above him and bit deep into his arm. Metal began to sing loudly against metal; green sparks danced in the air. By their faint light it was clear that Walegrin, with a cut in his shoulder and his legs entangled in the ruins of the stairs, was taking a beating.

Thrusher shouted outside for help, though with Walegrin wedged in the stairway, there was no easy way to reach Burek, nor to protect their captain—but there was one way. While Thrusher watched in surprise, Cythen drew her own sword and prepared to get up to the second floor by running up and over Walegrin. With a handful of his hair and one foot planted hard on his thigh, she propelled herself over him, hoping that the sheer audacity of her move would keep Burek guessing for the moment it would take for her to regain her balance. She raised her sword just as his blade arced toward her—and Walegrin reached out to parry it aside.

The Beysib circled away from the stairwell, and Cythen edged along the walls. This room was not the dusty wreckage the lower parts of the building had been. Someone had been using it recently. Knives littered an otherwise clean table and a crude map of the town hung on the wall. There was another curved Beysib sword on the wall as well, but Turghurt hadn't taken it. The room was too small for the swirling double-sword style the Harka Bey had used. His stance was not that much different from her own, though his reach was substantially longer.

Walegrin, still struggling to free himself from the stairs, broke through another board and fell from sight, shaking the entire structure as he landed. From the commotion, Cythen knew they were trying to improvise a human ladder, but at that moment Turghurt was easily parrying her best cuts and she doubted they'd reach her in time.

She wouldn't have the strength to ward off many of his thunderous attacks. She could stall and hope they'd get something together in time, or she could charge him and hope for the same sort of clear shot as she'd gotten at the Harka Bey—though that would kill him and might make everything worse.

He guessed her intention to attack and back-pedaled across the room, laughing to himself. He was silhou-

etted by a hole in the walls where a window might once
have been and he seemed very large, but perhaps his
laughing had made him drop his guard just a fraction.
She sprang at him.

His eyes went wide with disbelief. He was falling
towards her before she touched him, the disbelief becoming a fixed, deathlike stare. His momentum pushed
her backwards and off balance, knocking her sword
aside. But he was no longer attacking, only falling. They
both went crashing to the floor and through it, as the
old wood gave way beneath them. Cythen heard a
scream—her own—then nothing.

III

The sun was bright in the courtyard of the palace.
Cythen, the swelling still apparent in her face, and
Walegrin, his arm in a sling, stood with the Hell Hounds
in the places of honor. There were, as yet, no Beysibs in
sight. Enas Yorl let the curtain fall from his hand and
sat back in the shadowed privacy of his study. It seemed
the whole population of the town had crammed around
the high platform whereupon the Beysa would pronounce judgment.

"Would you have stopped him for the courtesan's
sake alone?" he asked the darkness beside him.

"The girl-soldier has conquered her fears and her
past. We have made her a part of our sisterhood. We,
too, must adapt. Her vengeance is ours," the voice of a
Beysib woman replied.

"Ah, but that wasn't the question. If all you knew
was that the Blood of Bey, as you call it, had been used
to slay an innocent courtesan, and that it had been done
to make the suspicion fall on you; if there had been no
other crimes, would you have stopped him?"

"No. We have always been blamed for crimes we do

not commit. It is part of the balance we have with the Empire. One insignificant life would have made no difference."

Trumpets blared out a fanfare. Yorl lifted the curtain again. Sunlight fell on a four-fingered, ebony hand. The Beysa had arrived at the platform, her breasts so heavily painted they scarcely seemed naked. Her long golden hair swirled plumelike in the light breeze. The moment had arrived and the crowd grew quiet. Terrai Burek, the prime minister, ascended the platform and behind him, in chains, came his son, Turghurt.

The young man stumbled and the guards rushed forward to get him back on his feet. Even at this distance, it was plain that something had happened to the young man and that he had no clear idea why his aunt, the Beysa Shupansea, was standing in the sun, telling everyone that he was going to die for the deaths of his own people and for the death of a Sanctuary courtesan. Yorl let the curtain drop again.

"Then why did you use just enough venom on your dart to destroy his mind but not enough to kill him?"

The Beysib woman laughed melodically. "He overstepped himself. He thought to arouse Shupansea's rage by slaying Sharilar, her cousin, while they walked along the wharf. But he killed not only Sharilar, but Prism— and that we could not forgive."

"But you could have killed him outright. Wouldn't that have been the true vengeance of Bey?"

"Bey is a goddess of many moods; she is life as well as death. This is a lesson for everyone: for town and Beysib. They will respect each other a little more now. Shupansea, herself, needed to pronounce this judgment. She must rise to rule here or Turghurt will be only the first."

There was a collective gasp from the crowd and Yorl drew back the curtain for the third time. The Beysa was holding a small, bloody knife, while her serpent wound around her arm. Turghurt was already dead. The crowd broke into cheering, just as Yorl felt the sharp prick of fangs on his own neck.

Poison burned and gripped him in hands of red-hot iron. The sunlit courtyard grew dim, then black. The horned gateway to the seventh level of paradise shone before him. The ancient magician's spirit stumbled forward and fell, with the gate just beyond his reach.

Failure—and with the land of death almost within his grasp. He wept and brushed the tears away with a shaggy paw. The room was dark and filled with the odor from the pyre on which they'd immolated the criminal, depriving his spirit of eternal life within the goddess Bey. And Yorl was left with only the memory of death to sustain him.

VOTARY

David Drake

"Hai!" called the Beysib executioner as his left blade struck. The tip of his victim's index finger spun thirty feet across the Bazaar and pattered against Samlor's boot. "Hai!" and the right sword lopped the ends off the fourth and middle fingers together, so that the victim's right hand ended in a straight line, the four fingers all the length of the least, the only one to which a fingernail remained for the moment. "Hai!"

The auction block in the center of the Bazaar had been used for punishment before, but this particular technique was new to Samlor hil Samt. It was new as well to many of the longer-term residents of Sanctuary, judging from the expressions on their faces as they watched. The victim had been spread-eagled, belly against a vertical wooden barrier. That gave the audience a view of the executioner's artistry, which an ordinary horizontal chopping block would have hidden.

And the Beysib—Lord Tudhaliya, if Samlor had understood the crier—was an artist, no doubt about that.

Tudhaliya held his swords each at its balance and twirled them as he himself pirouetted. The blades glittered like lightning in the rain. The Beysib bowed to the onlookers before he spun in another flurry of cuts. The gesture was a sardonic one, an acknowledgment of the audience's privilege of watching him work. Tudhaliya was not nodding to the locals as peers or even as humans. For his performance, the executioner had stripped to a clout that kept his genitals out of the way when he moved. His arrival had been in a palanquin, however, and the richly brocaded Beysib who stood by as a respectful backdrop to the activity were clearly subordinates. And at the moment, his lordship was slicing off the fingers of a screaming victim like so many bits of carrot.

Well, the governance of Sanctuary had never been Samlor's concern. Blood and balls! How the Cirdonian caravan-master wished that he had no other concern with this cursed city either.

The first link of the information he needed had come from an urchin for a copper piece, sold as blithely as the boy would have sold a stale bread twist from the tray balanced on his head. The name of a fortune-teller, a S'danzo whose protector was a blacksmith? Oh yes, Illyra was still in Sanctuary . . . and Dubro the smith, too, if the foreign master's business was with him.

Samlor's intended business was in no way with the blacksmith, but the information was none the less good to know. Before entering the booth, the Cirdonian set his thumbs on his waist belt and tugged the broad leather a fraction to the side. That was less obtrusive than adjusting the belt-sheathed fighting knife directly.

"Welcome, master," said the woman who had been reading the cards to herself on a stool. Samlor looped the sash across the doorway hangings. There were the usual paraphernalia and a table that could be slid between the S'danzo and the lower, cushioned seat for clients. The young woman's eyes were very sharp, however. The Cirdonian knew that her quick appraisal of him as he slid aside the curtain of pierced shells gave often as much information as a reading would require, when retailed back to the sitter over cards or his palms or through "images" quivering in a dish of water.

"You came about the luck of your return—" and Samlor would have said that his face was impassive, but it was not, not to her. "No, not a journey but a woman. Come, sit. The cards, I think?" Her left hand fanned the deck, the brilliant, complex signs that some said reflected the universe in a subtlety equal to that of the icy stars overhead.

"Lady," said Samlor. He turned up his left palm and the silver in it. It was uncoined bullion, stamped each time it was assayed in a Beysib market. "You gave a man I met true readings. I need a truth that you won't find in my face."

The S'danzo looked at the caravan-master again, her smile still professional, but something new behind her eyes. Samlor's boot heels were high enough to grip stirrups, low enough for walking, and worn more by flints than by pavements. He was stocky and no longer young; but his waist still made a straight line with his rib cage, with none of the bulge that time brings to easy living. Samlor's tunic was of dull red cloth, nearly the shade of his face. His skin never seemed to tan in the sun and wind that beat it daily. His only touch of ornament was a silver medallion, its face hidden until the man moved to show the bullion in his calloused palm. Then toad-faced Heqt flashed upward, goddess of Cirdon and the Spring rains—and the S'danzo gasped, "Samlor hil Samt!"

"No!" the man said sharply in answer to the way

Illyra's eyes flicked toward the doorway, toward the ringing of hot iron heard through it. "Only information, lady. I wish you no harm." And he did not touch the hilt of his belt knife, because if she remembered Samlor, she remembered the tale of his first visit to Sanctuary. No need to threaten what his reputation had already promised, wish it or not. "I want to find a little girl, my niece. Nothing more."

"Sit, then," the S'danzo said in a guarded voice. This time the visitor obeyed. He held the silver out to her between thumb and forefinger, but she opened his palm and held it for her gaze a moment before taking her payment. "There's blood on them," she said abruptly.

"There's an execution in the square," Samlor said, glancing at his cuff. But it was unmarked, and even his boot had been too dusty for overt sign where the severed fingertip had touched it. "Oh," he said in embarrassment. "Oh." He raised his eyes to the S'danzo's. "Life can be hard, lady . . . and there are matters of honor. Not my honor since I went into trade—" his lip quirked in a wormwood grimace— "but of the family, of the House of Kodrix, yes. I've found little enough that brings me pleasure. But not that, not slaughter. Life is hard, that's all."

Illyra released his palm. The silver clung to her fingers in what was almost a sleight of hand, professional in that, though the reading was no longer simply professional or simple at all. "Tell me about the child," the S'danzo said.

"Yes," the stocky man agreed slowly. Little enough of pleasure, and none at all in some memories. "My sister Samlane was . . ." he said, and he paused, "not a slut, I suppose, because she didn't bed just anybody, and the decision was always hers. And not a whore, except as a lark, as little coin as there was to be had in our House. . . . She had a disdain for trade that did credit to the noble House of Kodrix. Our parents were

proud of her, I think, as they never were of me after I
found an honest way to buy their food—and replenish
their wine cellar.'' The grimace again, calling attention
to a joke that bit the teller like a shark.

The woman was quiet, as cool as the shells that
whispered in the door curtain.

"But she was very—experimental. So we shouldn't
have been surprised," Samlor continued, "that she'd
whelped a bastard before her marriage, while she still
lived in Cirdon. Samlane's personal effects were sent
back after she, she died—" Six inches of steel, her
brother's boot knife, were buried in her womb, and the
vision as clear in Samlor's mind as the edge of the knife
with which he had replaced that one. "I think Regli
wanted to pretend she'd never been born. Alum won't
hide stretch marks, but she'd passed for a virgin with
Regli. I guess Rankan nobles are even stupider than I'd
thought. The tramp! Gods! The *worthless* tramp!''

"Go on," Illyra said with unexpected gentleness, as if
she heard the pain and tortured love beneath the curses.

"The story was there in a diary, enough of it,"
Samlor continued. He was deliberately opening his
hands, which had clenched in fury at nothing material.
"The child was a girl, fostered with a maid of
Samlane's, Reia. I probably saw her myself—" he
swallowed "—playing in the halls with the other servants' brats. You could get lost in the house, a whole
wing could crumble over you and you'd never be
found." The hands clenched again. "My parents tell me
they never knew about the child, about Samlane, in that
big house. Pray god I never learn otherwise, or I'll have
their hearts out though they *are* my parents."

The S'danzo touched his hands, relaxing them again.
He continued, "She's four years old by now. She has a
birthmark on the front of her scalp, so the hair is
streaked white on the black curls. They called her Star,
my sister did and the maid. And I came back to Sanc-

tuary—'' Samlor raised his eyes and his voice, neither angry but as hard and certain as a sword's edge ''—to this hell-hole, to find my niece. Reia had married here, a guardsman, and she'd stayed after the—after what happened when my sister died. And she'd kept Star like one of her own, she told me, until a month ago, and the child disappeared, no one to say where.

"That's how late I was, lady," the Cirdonian went on in a wondering voice. "Just a month. But I *will* find Star. And I'll find any one or any thing that's harmed the child before then."

"You've brought something of the girl's for me to touch, then?" said Illyra. Professional calm had reasserted itself in her voice as she approached her task. This was the crystalline core on which all the mummery, all the "dark strangers" and "far journeys" were based.

"Yes," said Samlor, calm again himself. With his right hand, his knife hand, he held out a medallion like the one around his own neck. "It's a custom with us in Cirdon, the birth-token consecrating the newborn to Heqt's bounty. This was Star's. It was found in the mews of the barracks where she lived. Another child picked it up, a friend, so she brought it to Reia instead of keeping it herself."

Illyra's hand cupped the grinning face of Heqt, but her eyes glanced over the ends of the thong that had suspended the medallion. The surface of the leather was dark with years of sweat and body oils, but its core at the ends was a clear yellow. "Yes," Samlor said, "it had been cut off her, not stretched and broken. Help me find Star, lady."

The S'danzo nodded. Her eyes had slipped off into a waking trance already.

Illyra's gaze stayed empty for seconds that seemed minutes. Her fingers were brown and capable and heavy with rings. They worked the surface of the medallion they held, reporting the sensations not to the woman's mind but to her soul.

Then, like a castaway flailing herself up from the sea, the S'danzo spluttered again to conscious alertness. Her thin lips formed a brief rictus, not a smile, at the memory of things she had just seen. Samlor had let his own breath out in a rush that reminded him that he had not breathed since Illyra entered her trance.

"I wish," said the woman softly, "that I had better news for you, or at least more. No—" for Samlor's face had stiffened to the preternatural calmness of a grave stele "—not dead. And I can't tell you who, master—" the honorific professional as habit reasserted itself "—or even where. But I think I *have* seen why."

With one hand Illyra returned the medal as carefully as if it were the child herself. With the fingers of the other hand, she touched her own kerchief-bound hair. "The mark that you call the 'star' is the 'porta' to some of the Beysib. A sea-beast with tentacles . . . a god, to some of them."

Samlor turned his eyes toward the curtain that hid the execution, as within him his heart turned to murder. "That one?" Nodding, his voice as neutral as if all the fury at Lord Tudhaliya were not foaming over his mind as he spoke.

"No, not the rulers," Illyra said positively. "Not the Burek clan at all, the horsemen. But the fisher-folk and boatwrights who brought the Burek here, the Set-mur—and not all of them." The woman smiled at the trace of a memory so grim that its fullness wiped her face with loathing an instant later. "There was," she explained, looking away from the caravan-master, "a cult of Dyareela in Sanctuary in the—recent past. The Porta cult is like that. Only a few, and those hidden because it's sacrilege and treason to worship other than the Imperial gods."

"The Beysib have closed the temples here?" Samlor

asked. Her last statement had jarred him into the interjection.

"Only to human beings," Illyra said. "And the Setmur are human, even to the Burek." She smiled again and this time held the expression. "We S'danzo are accustomed to being animals, master. Even in cities Ranke conquered as long ago as she did Cirdon."

"Go on," said Samlor evenly. "Do these Beysib think to sacrifice Star to their—" he shrugged "—octopus, their squid?"

The S'danzo woman laughed. "Master—Samlor," she demanded, "is Heqt a giant toad that you might find near the right pond?" The man touched his medallion, and his eyes narrowed at the blasphemy. Illyra went on, "Porta is a god, or an idea—if there's a difference. A fisher-folk idea. Some of them have always had images, little carvings on stone or shells, hidden deep in their ships where the nobles never venture for the stink. . . . And now they have something else to bring them closer to their god. They have—" and she looked from the child's medal, which had told her much, to the Cirdonian's eyes, which in this had told her even more "—the girl you call your niece."

Samlor hil Samt stood with the controlled power of a derrick shifting a cargo of swords. The booth was suddenly very cold. "Lady," he said as he paused in the doorway. "I thank you for your service. But one thing. I know that the Rankans say their storm-god bedded his sister. But we don't talk about that in Cirdon. We don't even think about it!"

Except when we're drunk, the stocky man's mind whispered as his hand flung down the sash. His legs thrust him through the pattering curtain and again into the square. *Except when we're very drunk, but not incapable . . . may Samlane burn in the Hell she earned so richly!*

Amazingly, the execution was still going on. Lord

Tudhaliya's breechclout was black with sweat. His body gleamed as it moved through its intricate dance. His swords shone as they spun, and the air was jeweled with garnet drops of blood.

The victim's forearm was gone. Tudhaliya's blades were sharp, but they were too light to shear with a single blow the thick bone of a human upper arm. Right sword, left sword—placing cuts only, notching . . . Tudhaliya pivoted, his back to his victim, and the blades lashed out behind him, perfectly directed. The stump of the victim's elbow bounded away from the block. She moaned, a bestial sound . . . but she had never been human to Tudhaliya, had she? The Beysib entourage gave well-bred applause to the pass. Their left fingertips pattered on their right palms.

Samlor strode out of the Bazaar. He was thinking about a child. And he was thinking that murder might not always be without pleasure, even for him.

In the years since Samlor's first visit to Sanctuary, the tavern's sign had been refurbished. The unicorn's horn had been gilded, and his engorged penis was picked out with red paint, lest any passerby miss the joke. The common room stank as before, though it was too early to add the smoky reek of lamp flames. There were a few soldiers present, throwing knucklebones and wrangling over who owed for the next round. There were also two women who would have looked slatternly even by worse light than what now streamed through the grimy windows; and, by the wall, a man who watched them, and watched the soldiers, and—very sharply—watched Samlor as he entered the tavern.

No one was paying any attention to the fellow in the corner with the sword, the lute, and a sneer of disgust at the empty tankard before him. "Ho, friend," Samlor called to the slope-shouldered bartender. "Wine for me, and whatever my friend with the lute is drinking." The instrument had inlays of ivory and mother-of-pearl, but Samlor had noticed the empty sockets, which must recently have been garnished with gems.

The women were already in motion, lurching from their stools—remoras thrashing toward the shark they hoped would find their next meal. It was to the pimp against the wall that Samlor turned with a bright smile, however. "And for you, sir—" he said. His thumb spun a coin through the air. Its arc would have dropped it in the pimp's lap if the fellow had not snatched it in with fingers like eagle's talons. The coin was silver, minted in Ranke, a day's wage for a man and as much as these blowsy whores together could expect for a night. "If you keep them away from me. Otherwise, I take back the coin, even if you've swallowed it." Samlor wore a smile again, but it was not the same smile. The women were backing off even before the pimp snarled at them.

The minstrel had risen to take the cup Samlor handed him from the bar. It was wine, though poverty had drunk ale on the previous round. "I thank you, good sir," the man said as he took the cup. "And how may Cappen Varra serve you?"

Samlor passed his left hand over the sound box of the lute. The coin he dropped sang on the strings as it passed. "A copper for a song from home," he said. He knew, and from the sound the minstrel knew also, that the coin had not been copper or even silver. "And another like it if you'll sing to me out on the bench, where the air has less—sawdust in it."

Cappen Varra followed with a careful expression. He gave the lute a gentle toss in his hand, just enough to make the gold whisper again in the sound chamber. "So, what sort of a song did you have in mind, good sir?" he asked as he seated himself facing Samlor. The minstrel had set his wine cup down. His left leg was cocked under him on the bench; and his right hand, on the lute's belly, was not far from the serviceable hilt of his dagger.

"A little girl's missing," said Samlor. "I need a name, or the name of someone who might know a name."

"And how little a girl?" asked Varra, even more guarded. He set down the lute, ostensibly to take the cup in his left hand. "Sixteen, would she be?"

"Four," said Samlor.

Cappen Varra spit out the wine as he stood. "It shouldn't offend me, good sir," said the minstrel as he up-ended the lute, "there's folk enough in this city who traffic in such goods. But I do not, and I'll leave your 'copper' here in the gutter with your suggestion!"

"Friend," said Samlor. His hand shot out and caught the falling coin in the air before the sun winked on the metal. "Not you, but the name of a name. For the child's sake. *Please*."

Cappen Varra took a deep breath and seated himself again. "Your pardon," he said simply. "One lives in Sanctuary, and one assumes that everyone takes one for a thief and worse . . . because everyone else *is* a thief and worse, I sometimes fear. So. You want the name of someone who might buy and sell young children? Not a short list in this city, sir."

"That's not quite what I want," the Cirdonian explained. "There is—reason to think that she was taken by the Beysib."

The minstrel blinked. "Then I really can't help you, much as I'd like to, good sir. My songs give me no entree to those folk."

Samlor nodded. "Yes," he agreed. "But it might be that you knew who in the—local community—fenced goods for Beysib thieves. Somebody must, they can't deal among themselves, a closed group like theirs."

"Oh," said Cappen Varra. "Oh," and his right hand drummed a nervous riff on the belly of his instrument.

When he looked up again, his face was troubled. "This could be very dangerous," he said. "For you, and for anyone who sent you to this man, if he took it amiss."

"I was serious about the payment," Samlor said. He thumbed a second crown of Rankan gold from his left hand into the right to join the piece already there.

"No, not that," said the minstrel, "not for this. But . . . I'll give you directions. Go after dark. And if I thought you might mention my name, I wouldn't tell you a thing. Even for a child."

Samlor smiled wanly. "It's possible," the caravan-master said, "that there are two honorable men in Sanctuary this day. Though I wouldn't expect anyone to believe it, even the two of us."

Cappen Varra began fingering an intricate sequence of chords from his lute. "There's a temple of Ils in the Mercer's Quarter," he began in a rhythmic delivery. It would have suited the love lyrics his face was miming. "Just a neighborhood chapel. Go through it and turn right in the alley behind. . . ."

It had been three hours to sundown when Samlor left the Vulgar Unicorn, but it took him most of the remaining daylight to shop for what he would require during the interview. Nothing illicit, but the city was unfamiliar; and the major purchase was uncommon enough to take some searching. He found what he needed at last at an apothecary's.

The streets of Sanctuary had a different smell after dark, a serpent-cage miasma that was more of the psychic atmosphere than the physical. Under the circumstances, Samlor did not feel it would be politic to carry his dagger free in his hand as he might otherwise have done. He kept a careful watch, however, for the casual footpads who might waylay him for his purse, or even for the wine bottle whose neck projected from his scrip.

The chapel of Ils had once had a gate. It had been
stolen for the weight of its wrought iron. There was
nothing pertaining to the cult in the sanctuary except a
niche in which the deity was painted. There might at one
time have been a statue in the niche instead; but if so, it
had gone the way of the gate. Samlor slipped through
unobtrusively, though he was by no means sure that the
drunk asleep in the corner was only what he seemed.

The alley behind the chapel was black as a politician's
soul, but by now the Cirdonian was close enough to
operate by feel. A set of rickety stairs against the left
wall. A second staircase. The things that squelched and
crunched underfoot did not matter. There were other,
stealthy sounds; but the guards Samlor expected would
not attack without orders, and they would fend away
less-organized criminals as the Watch could not dream
of doing.

A ladder was pinned against the wall. It had ten
rungs, straight up into a trap door in the overhanging
story. Samlor climbed two rungs up and rapped on the
door. He was well aware of how extended his body was
if he had misjudged the guard's instructions.

"Yes?" grunted a voice from above.

"Tarragon," Samlor whispered. If the password had
been changed, the next sound would be steel grating
through his ribs.

The door flopped open. A pair of men reached down
and heaved Samlor inside with scant ceremony. Both of
them were masked, as was the third man in the room.
The third was the obvious leader, seated behind the oil
lamp and the account books on a desk. The men who
held Samlor were bravos; more perhaps than their
muscles alone, but certainly there for their muscles in
part. The leader was a black. The mask obscuring his
face was battered from age and neglect, but the eyes that
glittered behind it were as bright as those of the hawk it
counterfeited.

The black watched during the silent, expert search. Samlor held himself relaxed in the double grip as the guards' free hands twitched away his knife, his purse, his scrip; snatched off his boots, the sheath in the left one empty already but noted; ran along his arms, his torso, his groin. The only weapon Samlor carried this night was the openly sheathed dagger. To leave it behind as well would in this city have been more suspicious than the weapon.

When the guards were finished, they stepped back a pace to either side. Samlor's gear lay in a pile at his feet, save for the dagger, slipped now through the belt of one of the burly men who watched him.

Unconcerned, the Cirdonian knelt and pulled on his left boot. The man behind the desk waited for the stranger to speak. Then, as Samlor reached for his other boot, the masked leader snarled, "Well? You're from Balustrus, aren't you? What's his answer?"

"No, I'm not from Balustrus," Samlor said. He straightened up, holding the wine bottle. He pulled the cork with his teeth and spat it onto the floor before he went on. "I came to buy information from you," Samlor said, and he slurped a mouthful from the bottle.

The mask did not move. An index finger lifted minusculely for the chopping motion that would have ended the interview. Samlor spat the fluid in his mouth across the desk, splattering the topmost ledger and the lap of the seated man.

The hawk-masked leader lunged upward, then froze as his motion made the lamp flame gutter. There was a dagger aimed at Samlor's ribs from one side and a long-bladed razor an inch from his throat on the other; but the Cirdonian knew, and the guards knew . . . and the man across the desk most certainly knew that, dying or not, Samlor could not be prevented from hurling the bottle into the lamp past which he had spat so nearly.

"That's right," said Samlor with the bottle poised. "Naphtha. And all I want to do is talk to you nicely, sir, so send your men away."

While the leader hesitated, Samlor hawked and spat. It would take days to clear the petroleum foulness from his mouth, and the fumes rising into his sinuses were already giving him a headache.

"All right," said the leader at last. "You can wait below, boys." He settled himself carefully back on his stool, well aware of the stain on his tunic and the way the ink ran where the clear fluid splashed his ledgers.

"The knife," said Samlor when the guard who had disarmed him started to follow his fellow through the trap. An exchange of eyes behind masks; a nod from the leader; and the weapon dropped on the floor before the guard slipped into the alley. When the door closed above the men, Samlor set the potential firebomb in a corner where it was not likely to be bumped.

"Sorry," said the caravan-master with a nod toward the leader and the blotted page. "I needed to talk to you, and there wasn't much choice. My niece was stolen last month, not by you, but by Beysibs. Some screwball cult of them, fishermen."

"Who told you where I was?" asked the black man in a voice whose mildness would not have deceived a child.

"A fellow in Ranke, one eye, limps," Samlor lied with a shrug. "He'd worked for you but ran when the roof fell in."

The leader's fists clenched. "The password—he didn't tell you that!"

"I just mumbled my name. Your boys heard what they expected." Samlor deliberately turned his back on the outlaw to end the line of discussion. "You won't have contacts with their religious loonies, not directly. But you'll know their thieves, and a thief will've heard something, know something. Sell me a Beysib thief, leader. Sell me a thief from the Setmur clan."

The other man laughed. "Sell? What are you offering to pay?"

Samlor turned, shrugging. "The price of a four year old girl? That'd run to about four coronations in Ranke, but you know the local market better. Or the profit on the thief you give me. Figure what he'll bring you in a lifetime. . . . Name a figure, leader. I don't expect you to realize what this girl means to me, but —name a figure."

"I won't give you a thief," said the masked man. He paused deliberately and raised a restraining finger, though the Cirdonian had not moved. "And I won't charge you a copper. I'll give you a name: Hort."

Samlor frowned. "A Beysib?"

The mask trembled negation. "Local boy. A fisherman's son. He and his father got picked up by Beysib patrols at sea before the invasion. He speaks their language pretty well—better than any of them I know speaks ours. And I think he'll help you if he can." The mask hid the speaker's face, but the smile was in his voice as well as he added, "You needn't tell him who sent you. He's not one of mine, you see."

Samlor bowed. "I couldn't tell him," he said. "I don't know who you are." He reached for the latch of the trap door. "I thank you, sir."

"Wait a minute," called the man behind the desk. Samlor straightened and met the hooded eyes. "Why are you so sure I won't call down to have you spitted the moment you're through this door?"

The Cirdonian shrugged again. "Business reasons," he said. "I'm a businessman too. I understand risks. You'll be out of this place—" he waved at the dingy room—"before I'm clear of the alley. No need to kill me to save a bolt-hole that you've written off already. And there's not one chance in a thousand that I could get past what you have waiting below, but—" calloused palm up, another shrug—"in the dark. . . . You have people looking for you, sir, that's obvious. But none of them so far would be willing to burn this city down block by block to flush you, if he had to."

Samlor reached again for the latch, paused again. "Sir," he said earnestly, "you may think I've lied to you tonight . . . and perhaps I have. But I'm not lying to you now. On the honor of my House." He clenched his fist over the medallion of Heqt on his breast.

The mask nodded. As Samlor dropped through the trap into darkness, the harsh voice called from above, "Let him go! Let him go, this time!"

There was nothing ugly about the harbor water with the noon sun on it. The froth was pearly, the fish-guts iridescent; and the water itself, whatever its admixture of sewage, was faceted into diamond and topaz across its surface. Samlor sipped his ale in the dockside cantina as he had done at noon on the past three days. As before, he was waiting for Hort to return with information or the certain lack of it. The Cirdonian wondered what Star saw when she looked around her; and whether she found beauty in it.

There was commotion on one of the quays, easily visible through the cantina's open front. A trio of Beysib had been stepping a new mast into a trawler. As they worked, a squad of cavalry—Beysib also, but richly caparisoned in metals and brocades—had clattered along the quay. The squad halted alongside the boat. The men on the trawler had seemed as surprised as other onlookers when the troopers dismounted and leaped aboard, waggling their long swords in visual emphasis of the orders they shouted.

Nine of the horsemen were involved either in trussing the startled fishermen or acting as horseholders for the rest. The tenth man watched coldly as the others worked. He wore a helmet, gilded or gold, with a feather-tipped triple crest. When he turned as if in disdain for the proceedings, Samlor saw and recognized his profile. The man was Lord Tudhaliya, the swordsman who had been demonstrating his skill on an Ilsig animal the other day.

The fishermen continued to babble until ropes with slip knots were dropped over their throats. Then they needed all their breath to scramble after the cavalrymen.

The troopers remounted with a burst of chirruping cross-chat which sounded undisciplined to the caravan-master, but which detracted nothing from the efficiency of the process. Three of the men tied off the nooses to their saddle pommels. Tudhaliya gave a sharp order and the squad rode at a canter back the way it had come. Citizens with business on the quay dodged hooves as best they might. The fishermen blubbered in terror as they tried to run with the horses. They knew that a misstep meant death, unless the rider to whom they were tethered reined up in time. Nothing Samlor had seen of Lord Tudhaliya suggested his lordship would permit such mercy.

There were half a dozen regulars in the bar, fishermen and fish-merchants. When Samlor looked away from the spectacle, he found the local men staring at him. He gave a scowl of surprise when he noticed them; but even as the locals retreated into their mugs in confusion, Samlor understood why they had looked at him the way they had. The Cirdonian had nothing to do with the arrests on the docks just now; but he had nothing to do with this tavern, either. He had sat here during three noons and drunk ale . . . and on the third day, the Beysibs made an arrest on the dock below. To the vulnerable, no coincidence is chance. These fishermen were unusually vulnerable to all the powers of the physical world as well as those of the political one. No wonder the Beysib counterparts of these men had turned to a god their overlords would not recognize; a per-sonification, perhaps, of mystery and of the typhoons that could sweep the ocean clear of small boats and simple sailors.

Hort slipped into the cantina. He was dressed a little on the gaudy side. Still, he wore his clothes with the self-assurance of a young man instead of a boy's nervous gibing at the world. He raised a finger. The bartender chalked the slate above him and began drawing a mug of ale for the newcomer.

"I'm not sure you want to be seen with me," Hort muttered to Samlor as he took his ale. "The fellows they just carried off—" he nodded as he slurped the brew, toward the trawler bobbing high on its lines with the mast still swinging above it from the sheer legs. "Kummanni, Anbarbi, Arnuwanda. I talked to them just last night. About what you needed to know."

"That's why they were arrested?" the caravan-master asked. He tried to keep his voice as calm as if he were asking which tailor had sewn the younger man's jerkin.

"I would to god I knew," Hort said with feeling. "It could be anything. Tudhaliya is—Minister of Security, I suppose. But he likes to stay close to things. To keep his hand in."

"And his swords," Samlor agreed softly. His eyes traced the path the horsemen had taken as they rode off, toward the palace and the dungeons beneath it. "Would enough money to let you travel be a help?"

Hort shrugged, shuddered. "I don't know." He drained his mug and slid it to the bartender for a refill.

"I'm not afraid to be seen with *you*," Samlor said "But I'm not sure you want to tell me about the—cult—with so many other people around." He smiled about the cantina. The men there had just furnished him with a tactful way to prod the frightened youth into his story.

Hort drank and shuddered again. He said, "Oh, I was raised with everyone here. Omat's my godfather. They won't tell tales to the Beysib."

It wasn't the time for Samlor to comment. He assumed it was obvious anyway. Anyone will talk if the questions are put with sufficient forcefulness. But Hort must have known that too. The local man was not a coward, and he was not the worse for never having asked questions the way Lord Tudhaliya would. The way Samlor hil Samt had done, when need arose, might Heqt wash him with mercy when she gathered him in. . . .

"There's a boat went out last month at the new moon," Hort said beneath a moustache of beer foam. "A trawler, but not fishing. Do you know what Death's Harbor is?"

"No." Samlor had poled a skiff as a boy, when he hunted ducks in the marshes south of Cirdon. He knew little of the sea, however, and nothing at all of the seas around Sanctuary.

"Two currents meet," Hort explained. "Any flotsam in the sea gets swept into the eye of it. Wrecks, sometimes. And sometimes men on rafts, until the sun dries their skin to parchment shrouding their bones." He laughed. "Sorry," he said. "I forget what sort of story I meant to tell you." The smile faded. "Nobody fishes in Death's Harbor. The bottom is deeper than anyone here ever set a line. Scooped out by the currents, I suppose. The fish won't shoal there, so it's no use to us. But a Beysib trawler went there last month, and it's coming back now slower than there's any reason for. Except that it's going to arrive tonight, and the moon is new again tonight."

"Star's aboard her, then?" Samlor asked and sipped more ale. The brew was bitter, but less bitter than the gall that flooded his mouth at the thought of Star in Beysib hands.

"I think so," Hort agreed. "Anbarbi didn't approve. Of any of it, I think, though none of them said what was really going on. We'd seen the boat at sea, my father, all of us from Sanctuary that go to sea ourselves. That's what we talked about, though they didn't much want to talk. But from what Anbarbi let drop, I think there was a child on the trawler. At least when it put out.''

"And it'll dock here this evening?'' the Cirdonian said. He had set down his mug and was flexing his hands, open and shut, as if to work the stiffness out of them.

"Oh—'' said Hort. He was embarrassed not to be telling his story more in the fashion of an intelligence summary then of an entertainment with the discursions which added body to the tale and coin to the teller's purse. "No, not here. There's a cove west a league of Downwind. Smugglers used it until the Beysib came. There are ruins there, older than anybody's sure. A temple, some other buildings. Nobody much uses them now, though the smugglers'll be back when things settle down, I suppose. But the boat from Death's Harbor will put in there at midnight. I *think*, sir. I tell stories for a living, and I've learned to sew them together from this word and that word I hear. But it doesn't usually matter if my pattern is the same one that the gods wove to begin with.''

"Well,'' Samlor said after consideration, "I don't think my first look at this place had better be after dark. There'll be a watchman or the like, I suppose . . . but we'll deal with that when we find it. I—'' he paused and looked straight at the younger man instead of continuing to eye the harbor. "We agreed that your pay would be the full story when I had it to tell . . . and you'll have that. But it may be I won't be talking much after tonight, so take this,'' his clenched hand brushed Hort's, flexed to empty into the other's palm, "and take my friendship. You've—acted as a man in this thing, and you have neither blood nor honor to drive you to it.''

"One thing more,'' said the youth. "The Beysib—the

Setmur clan, I mean—are real sailors, and they know
their fishing, too. . . . But there are things they don't
know about the harborages here, around Sanctuary. I
don't think they know that there's a tunnel through the
east headland of the cove they've chosen for—whatever
they're going to do." Hort managed a tight smile. Sweat
beaded on his forehead. The risk he was taking by getting involved with the stranger was very real, though
most of the specific dangers were more nebulous to him
than they were to Samlor. "One end of the tunnel opens
under the corniche of the headland. You can row right
into it at high tide. And when you lift the slab at the
other end, you're in the temple itself."

Hort's coda had drawn from his listener all the awed
pleasure that a story well told could bring. The local
man stood up, strengthened by the respect of a strong
man. "May your gods lead you well, sir," Hort said,
squeezing the Cirdonian's hand in leave-taking. "I look
forward to hearing your story."

The youth strode out of the cantina with a flourish
and a nod to the other patrons. Samlor shook his head.
In a world that seemed filled with sharks and stonefish,
Hort's bright courage was as admirable as it was rare.

To say that Samlor felt like an idiot was to understate
matters. It was the only choice he could come up with at
short notice, however, and which did not involve others.
At this juncture, the Cirdonian was not willing to involve others.

He had rented a mule cart. It had provided a less
noticeable method of scouting the cove than a horse
would have done. The cart had also transported the
punt he had bought to the nearest launching place to the
headland that he could find. The roadstead on which
Sanctuary was built was edged mostly by swamps, but
the less-sheltered shore to the west had been carved
away by storms. The limestone corniche rose ten to fifty

feet above the sea, either sheer or with an outward batter. A lookout on the upper rim could often not see a vessel inshore but beneath him. That was to Samlor's advantage; but the punt, the only craft the Cirdonian felt competent to navigate, was utterly unsuited to the ocean.

Needs must when the devil drives. Samlor's great shoulders braced the pole against the cliff face, not the shelving bottom. Foam echoed back from the rocks and balanced the surge that had tried to sweep him inward with it. In that moment of stasis, Samlor shot the punt forward another twenty feet. Then the surf was on him again, his muscles flexing on the ten-foot pole as they transferred the sea's power to the rock, again and again.

Samlor had launched the punt at sunset. By now, he had no feeling for time nor for the distance he had yet to struggle across to his once-glimpsed goal. He had a pair of short oars lashed to the forward thwart, but they would have been totally useless for keeping him off this hungry shore. Samlor was a strong man, and determined; but the sea was stronger, and the fire in Samlor's shoulders was beginning to make him fear that the sea was more determined as well.

Instead of spewing back at him, the next wave continued to be drawn into the rock. It became a long tongue, glowing with microörganisms. Samlor had reached the tunnel mouth while he had barely enough consciousness to be aware of the fact.

Even that was not the end of the struggle. The softer parts of the rock had been worn away into edges that could have gobbled the skiff like a duckling caught by a turtle. Samlor let the next surge carry him in to the depth of his pole. The phosphorescence limned a line of bronze hand-holds set into the stone. The powerful Cirdonian dropped his pole into the boat to snatch a grip with both hands. He held it for three racking breaths before he could find the strength to drag the punt fully aground, further up the tunnel.

The tunnel was unlighted. Even the plankton cast up
by the spray illuminated little more than the surfaces to
which it clung. Samlor spent his first several minutes
ashore striking a spark from flint and steel into the
tinder he carried in a wax-plugged tube. At first his
fingers seemed as little under his control as the fibers of
the wooden pole they had clutched so fiercely. Conscious direction returned to them the fine motor control
they would need later in the night.

By the time a spark brightened with yellow flame instead of cooling into oblivion, Samlor's mind was at
work again as well. His shoulders still ached while the
blood leached fatigue poisons out of his muscles. He
had been more tired than this before, however. The very
respite from wave-battering increased the Cirdonian's
strength.

With the tinder aflame, Samlor lighted the candle of
his dark lantern. Then, carrying a ten-gallon cask under
one arm and the lantern in the other hand, he began to
walk up the gently rising tunnel. The lantern's shutter
was open, and its horn lens threw an oval of light before
him.

The tunnel was not spacious, but a man of Samlor's
modest height could walk safely in it by hunching only a
little in his strides. He could not imagine who had cut
the passage through the rock, or why. Scraps—a buckle,
a broken knife; a boot even—suggested that the smugglers used it. Samlor could imagine few circumstances,
however, in which it would pay smugglers to off-load
beneath the surf-hammered corniche rather than in the
shelter of the cove. For them, the tunnel might be useful
storage; but the smugglers had not built it, and in all
likelihood they had as little knowledge of its intended
purpose as Samlor did, or Hort.

Samlor set down the cask at what he estimated was
the halfway point along the tunnel. The cask had been

an awkward burden in the narrow confines, and its weight of a talent or more was as much as a porter would be expected to carry for even a moderate distance. Because it used muscles in a way that the punt had not, however, the hundred yards Samlor had carried the cask were almost relaxing.

The only thing certain about the escape he hoped to make in a few hours was that he would have very little time. Now the Cirdonian set the cask on end and drew his fighting knife. The blade was double-edged and a foot long. It was stout enough at the cross-hilt to take the shock of a sword and was sharpened to edges that would hold as they cut bronze, rather than something that its owner could shave with. Samlor had razors for shaving. The knife was a different sort of tool.

He set the point at the center of one of the end-staves, using his left hand to keep the weapon upright. The butt cap was bronze, flat on top, and a perfect surface for Samlor to hammer with the heel of his right hand. The blade hummed. The beechwood cracked and sagged away from the point. Working the knife loose, Samlor then punched across the grain of the other four end-staves as well. The line of perforations did not quite open the cask, but they would permit him to smash his heel through the weakened boards quickly when the need arose.

He was more aware than before of the lantern's hot shell as he paced the rest of the tunnel's length. He could hear someone above him when he reached the end of the tunnel. The susurrus could have been anything, wind-driven twigs as easily as the slippers of a guard on the floor above. There was a sharper sound to punctuate that whispering, however; a spear grounded as the man paused, or the tip of a bow. The stone conducted sounds very well, but it conducted them *so* well that Samlor could not get a precise fix on where the guard was in relation to the trap door. For that matter, the caravan-

master had no idea of how well the upward-pivoting
door was concealed. It might very well flop open in the
center of the room above.

The good news was that the sounds did not include
speech. Either the guard was alone, or the party was
more stolid than the random pacing seemed to suggest.

Samlor needed more information than he could get in
the tunnel. There would be no better time to learn more.
He shuttered his lantern and slid the worn bronze bolt
from its socket in the door jamb. There were stone pegs
set into the end wall as a sort of one-railed ladder.
Samlor set his right foot on the midmost, where his leg
was flexed just enough to give him its greatest thrust.
His right hand held the dagger while his left readied itself on the trap door. Then the Cirdonian exploded upward like a spring toy.

As it chanced, the door was quite well hidden in an
alcove, though the hangings that would once have completed the camouflage were long gone. There was no
time to consider might-have-beens, no time for anything
but the pantalooned Beysib who turned, membranes
flicking in shock across his eyes. He was trying to raise
his bow, but there was no time to fend Samlor away
with the staff, much less to nock one of the bone-tipped
arrows. Samlor punched the smaller man in the pit of
the stomach, a rising blow, and the point of the long
dagger grated on the Beysib's spine in exiting between
his fourth and third ribs.

The Beysib collapsed backward, his motion helping
Samlor free the knife for another victim if one presented
himself. None did. The nictitating membrane quivered
over the Beysib's eyes. In better light, it would have
shown colors like those on the skin of a dying albacore.
The blow had paralyzed the man's lungs, so that the
only sound the guard made as he died was the scraping
of his nails on the stone floor.

Samlor slid the body back through the trap door,
from whence its death had sprung. He hoped the victim

was not a friend of Hort; he sympathized with simple
folk looking for solace apart from the establishment of
such as Lord Tudhaliya. But they had made their bed
when they stole a child from the House of Kodrix.

The temple had been a single, circular room. It was
roofless now, and its girdle of fluted columns had
fallen; but the curtain wall within those columns still
stood to shoulder height or above. That wall had been
constructed around only three-quarters of the cir-
cumference, however. A 90° arc looked out unimpeded
on the waters of the cove, which lapped almost to the
building's foundations.

And out at the mouth of the cove, its hull black upon
the phosphorescence through which sweeps drove it
languidly, was a trawler. The vessel's sail was furled
because of the breeze that began to push against the
rising ride when the land cooled faster than the sea.

There were sounds outside the temple. Mice, perhaps,
or dogs; or even tramps looking for at least the sem-
blance of shelter.

More likely not. Nothing Hort had said suggested
that the ceremony planned for tonight would be limited
to the boatload who had carried Star to Death's Harbor. Not all the Setmur would be involved, but at least a
few others would slip in from the greater community.
The tunnel was as good a hiding place as could be
found; and if the guard had been placed in the temple, it
was at least probable that Star would be brought to it by
her captors.

Samlor slipped back the way he had come. He set the
tip of the Beysib bow between the edge of the trap door
and its jamb. That wedged the door open a crack,
through which Samlor could hear better and see; and be
seen, but the lights would be dim against discovery, and
the alcove was some protection as well. Then Samlor
waited, with a reptile's patience, and the chill certainty
of a reptile as well.

The firstcomers were blurs bringing no illumination

at all. Shawls, pantaloons like those the guard had
worn, sweeping nervously through Samlor's field of
vision. They chattered in undertones. Occasionally
someone raised a voice to call what might have been a
name: "Shaushga!" The corpse stiffening at Samlor's
feet made no reply.

Then a hull grated on the strand. There were more
voices, and more of the voices were male. Water
slopped between shore and hull as at least a dozen
persons dropped over the trawler's gunwale. Then the
temple floor rasped beneath the horn-hard soles of
barefooted fishermen. A tiny oil lamp gleamed like the
sun to light-starved eyes.

In the center of the open room, a Beysib in red robes
set down the burden he carried. It was Star, had to be
Star. She was dressed also in red. Her hair had been
plaited into short tendrils so that the blaze above her
forehead seemed to have eight white arms.

"I don't *want* to," the child cried distinctly. "I want
to go to *bed*." She refused to support herself with her
legs, curling to the pavement when the Beysib set her
down.

The man in red and a woman as nondescript as the
others in a brown and black shawl bent to the child.
They spoke urgently and simultaneously in Beysib and a
melange of local dialects. The latter were almost equally
unintelligible to Samlor for the accent and poor acous-
tics. The man in red held Star by the shoulders, but he
was coaxing rather than trying to force her to rise.

The trawler had been crabbed further into the cove so
that Samlor could no longer see it from his vantage
point. The Cirdonian held his body in a state of readi-
ness, but at not quite the bowstring tautness of the
instant before slaughter. There would be slaughter,
nothing could be more certain than that; but for the
moment, Samlor continued to wait. There were ten,
perhaps twenty, Beysib within the temple wall at the

moment. Some of them were between Star and the hidden door. That would not keep Samlor from striking if the need arose, but there was at least a chance that some of those now milling in the room would spread out if the ceremony began.

Star had gotten to her feet. She was pouting in the brief glimpse Samlor had of her face as she turned. He could not imagine how anyone had taken Star for the maid's daughter. Even the set of her lips was a mirror of Samlane's.

The Beysib chattering ceased. Their feet brushed quickly to positions flanking the temple opening. It was much as Samlor had hoped. Star stretched her hands out, palms forward, toward the cove. The man in red was still with her, but the woman had joined the others just outside the building. Star began chanting in a bored voice. The syllables were not in any language with which Samlor was familiar. From the regularity of the sounds, it was possible that they were from no language at all, merely forming a pattern to concentrate nonverbal portions of the brain.

Samlor tensed. He had already chosen the spot through which his dagger would enter the kidneys of the man in red. Then, suddenly, Lord Tudhaliya's troopers swept into the gathering with cries of bloody triumph.

The security forces might have intended to take a few prisoners, but as Samlor bolted from his hiding place, he saw a woman cut in half. The trooper who killed her had a sword almost four feet long in the blade. His horizontal, two-handed cut took her in the small of the back and bisected her navel on the way out.

The troopers had approached dismounted, of course. Even so, they had shown abnormal skill for cavalrymen in creeping up among the ruins. There was no way of telling how many of them there were, but it was certainly more than the squad that had made the arrests that morning. Lights began to flare, dark lanterns like

Samlor's own still hissing in the tunnel below.

The red-garbed Beysib bawled in horror and tried to enfold Star in his cloak, as if that would serve as any protection from what was about to happen. Samlor smashed the Beysib down with the dagger's hilt to his forehead, not from mercy, but because the point might have caught and held the weapon for moments the Cirdonian did not have to lose. Samlor grabbed the screaming child by the shoulder and spun for the tunnel mouth.

A Beysib cavalryman leaped from the crumbling wall. He was aiming a kick at Samlor's head.

The angle was different, but too many camels had launched feet at the caravan-master for Samlor to be caught unprepared. The boot slashed by his ear as he pivoted. The Beysib's sword was cocked for a blow that the fellow had to hold until he landed, or he risked lopping off his own feet. The long weapon did nothing to keep the Beysib's momentum from impaling him on the Cirdonian dagger. Samlor slipped the hilt as it punched home. He tossed Star to the trap door and rammed her through as he jumped in himself.

When Samlor tried to bang the stone door to, a Beysib sword shot through the gap and kept the edges from meeting. Instead of tugging against the springy steel, Samlor let the Beysib's own pull open the trap again. Samlor lunged upward through the opening. Before the sword could be transformed once more from a pry bar into a weapon, the Cirdonian had buried his boot knife in the trooper's throat.

The sword dropped into the tunnel as Samlor shot the bolt which closed the door. The last thing the caravan-master had seen before stone met stone was the face of Lord Tudhaliya turned to a fright mask by fury and speckles of blood. The Beysib noble was lunging to take the place of his dying trooper. His outstretched sword sang against the marble even as the bolt snicked home.

"Come on, Star, I'm your uncle!" Samlor shouted as
he grabbed the nearest handful of the child. He did not
particularly care whether she obeyed or even understood, for there was no time now to wait on a four-
year-old's legs. He let the Beysib sword lie, because he
needed his right hand for the lantern. Its unshuttered
light seemed shockingly bright in the closeness. Samlor
ran bent over, the girl under his arm as the cask had
been when he came from the punt.

Even as Samlor's heels hit the floor on his second
stride, hands and sword blades wrenched the bronze
latch into fragments. A file of Beysib troopers with
lamps and swords plunged into the tunnel behind Lord
Tudhaliya.

Samlor's plan had been based on the assumption
that his sudden assault would startle the gathering of
fisher-folk and give him the thirty seconds or so that he
needed to block his escape route. This security troop
was as well-trained as any force the Cirdonian had encountered, and they were already primed to rip open
hiding places. Presumably Tudhaliya thought he was
after fugitives from the ceremony, but that mattered as
little to him as it did to Samlor.

The Cirdonian smashed open the cask and kicked it
over. The naphtha gushed across the stone, darkening
it, and began to flow sluggishly back in the direction
Samlor was fleeing. Samlor dared not ignite the fluid
until he was clear of it. He took a stride and another
stride, ignoring Star's wailing as her shoulder brushed
the tunnel wall. The Cirdonian turned and flung his lantern toward the naphtha. Lord Tudhaliya batted the
light back past the fugitives with the flat of his sword.

Then the second Beysib trooper stumbled over the
cask and banged his own lamp down into the naphtha.
The tunnel boomed into red life. It singed Samlor's
eyebrows, even though Lord Tudhaliya shielded the Cirdonian from the worst of it.

The Beysib noble pitched forward. Samlor ran for the boat, clutching the child now in both arms. The capering fire threw their shadows down the tunnel ahead of them.

Samlor set Star in the stern of the punt and began shoving the vessel back toward the water. The sea had retreated since he dragged the punt out of it. While Samlor thrust at the boat, he glanced back over his shoulder. The blazing petroleum was creeping down the slope of the tunnel. Just ahead of it, his clothes afire but a sword gripped still in either hand, came Lord Tudhaliya. The swordsman's hair and flesh stank as they burned, but there are men whom no degree of pain will turn from a task. Samlor recognized the mind-set very well.

The Cirdonian still had a push dagger sheathed on his left wrist, but it was as useless against this opponent as the knives he had left in bodies cooling on the temple floor. Samlor snatched up the punt pole, sliding it forward in his grip. As Tudhaliya feinted with his left sword, Samlor thrust the pole into the center of the Beysib's chest.

With enough room to maneuver, Tudhaliya would have avoided the clumsy attack. Instead, his sluggish reflexes bounced him against the tunnel wall, and the end of the pole knocked him back into the spreading flames.

The Beysib stood up. Samlor poked at his groin, missed, but caught his opponent in the ribs with enough force to topple him again. Tudhaliya's swords snicked from either side, inches short of where Samlor gripped the pole. Chips flew, but the pole was seasoned ash and as thick as a man's wrist. Samlor thrust himself away, and the Beysib recoiled onto his back in the fire.

The naphtha sucked a fierce breeze from the tunnel to feed its flames. The glare flickered now around Tudhaliya's face, as instinct forced him to breathe. There was no help in that influx, only red tendrils that shrank lung tissues and blazed back out of Tudhaliya's mouth as he finally screamed.

"My sweet, my love," Samlor whispered as he turned back to the girl. "I'm going to take you home, now." The punt's flat bottom jounced easily over the stone as if the executioner's death had doubled the rescuer's strength.

"Are you taking me back to Mama Reia?" Star asked. She had watched Tudhaliya die with great eyes, which she now focused on Samlor.

The man splashed beside the boat for a few paces while the shingle foamed. Then he hopped aboard and thrust outward for the length of the pole. Since the tide had turned, there was no longer need to fend off from the corniche. When they were thirty feet out, the Cirdonian set down the pole and worried loose the lashings of his oars with his spike-bladed push dagger. "Star," he said, now that he had leisure for an answer, "Maybe we'll send for Reia. But we're going back to your real home—Cirdon. Do you remember Cirdon?" Inexpertly, the caravan-master began to fit the looms through the rope bights that served the punt for oarlocks.

Star nodded with solemn enthusiasm. She said, "Are you really my uncle?"

Poling had raised and burst blisters on both Samlor's hands. The salt-crusted oar handles ground like acid-tipped glass as he began the unfamiliar task of rowing. "Yes," he said. "I promised your mother—your real mother, Star, my sister. . . . I promised her—" and this was true, though Samlane was two years dead when her brother shouted the words to the sky—"that I'd take care of—oh. Oh, Mother Heqt. Oh, to have brought us so close."

Lord Tudhaliya had not trusted his men on the shore to sweep up the cultists. Someone in the boat Tudhaliya had stationed off the headland had seen the man and child. The Beysib craft was a ten-oared cutter. It began to close the distance from the first strokes that roiled the phosphorescence and brought the cutter to Samlor's attention.

An archer stood upright in the cutter's bow. His first shot was wobbly and short by fifty of the two hundred yards. He nocked another shaft, and the cutter pulled closer.

Samlor dropped his oars. He knelt and raised his hands. He did not trust his balance to standing up. "Star," he said, "I'm afraid that these men have caught us after all. If I try to get away, something bad may happen to you by accident. And I can't fight them, I don't have any way to fight so many."

Star peered over her shoulder at the Beysib cutter, then turned back to Samlor. "I don't want to go with them, Uncle," she said pettishly. "I want to go back to Cirdon. I want to play in the *big* house."

"Honey," Samlor said, "sweetest . . . I'm sorry. But we can't do that now, because of that boat." The cutter was too big to overturn, the caravan-master was thinking. But perhaps if he jumped into the larger boat with his push dagger, in the confusion they might—

The Beysib archer pitched into the water.

It was a moment before Samlor realized that the man had fallen forward because the cutter had come to an abrupt halt beneath him. The swift craft had thrown up a bone of glowing spray. Now the spray's remnant curled forward and away from the cutwater as a diminishing furrow on the sea.

"Now can we go to Cirdon, Uncle?" the little girl asked. She lowered the hands she had turned toward the cutter. Either her voice had dropped an octave, or the caravan-master's mind was freezing down in sudden terror. The white tendrils of Star's hair blazed and seemed to writhe.

The cutter's bow lifted. The boat disappeared stern-first with a rush and a roar and the screams of her crew. A huge, sucker-blotched tentacle uncoiled a hundred feet skyward, then plunged back into the glowing sea.

Samlor's hands found the oars again. His mind was ice, and his muscles moved like flows of ice. "Yes, Star," he heard his voice say. "We can go back to Cirdon now."

MIRROR IMAGE

Diana L. Paxson

The big mirror glimmered balefully from the wall, challenging him.

Even from across the room, Lalo could see himself reflected—a short man with thinning, gingery hair, tending to put on weight around the middle though his legs were thin; a man with haunted eyes and stubby, paint-stained hands. But it was not his reflection empty-handed that frightened him. The thing he feared was his own image copied onto a canvas, if he should dare to face the mirror with paintbrush in hand.

A shout from the street startled him and he went softly to the window, but it was only someone chasing a cutpurse who had mistaken their cul-de-sac for a short-cut between Slippery Street and the Bazaar. The strangeness of life in Sanctuary since the Beysib invasion, or infestation, or whatever it should be called, gave simple theft an almost nostalgic charm.

Lalo gazed out over the jumble of roofs to the blue

shimmer of the harbor and an occasional flash where the sun caught the gilding on a Beysib mast. Ils knew the Beysib were colorful enough, with their embroidered velvets and jewels that put a sparkle in even Prince Kittycat's eye, but Lalo had not been asked to paint any of them so far. Or to paint anything else, for that matter —not for some time now. Until the good folk of Sanctuary figured out how to transfer some of their new neighbors' wealth into their own coffers, no one was going to have either the resources or the desire to hire Sanctuary's only notable native artist to paint new decorations in their halls. Lalo wondered if Enas Yorl's gift to him would work on a Beysib. Did the fish-eyes *have* souls to be revealed?

Without willing it, Lalo found himself turning toward the mirror again.

"Lalo!"

Gilla's voice broke the enchantment. She filled the doorway, frowning at him, and he flushed guiltily. His preoccupation with the mirror bothered her, but she would have been more than bothered if she had known why it fascinated him so.

"I'm going shopping," she said abruptly. "Anything you want me to get for you?"

He shook his head. "Am I supposed to be watching the baby while you're gone?"

Alfi thrust past her flowing skirts and looked up at his father with bright eyes.

"I'm t'ree years old!" said Alfi. "I a *big* boy now!"

Lalo laughed suddenly and bent to ruffle the mop of fair curls. "Of course you are."

Gilla towered above him like the statue of Shipri All-Mother in the old temple. "I'll take him with me," she said. "The streets have been quiet lately, and he needs the exercise."

Lalo nodded and, as he straightened, Gilla touched his cheek, and he understood what she could so rarely manage to put into words, and smiled.

"Don't let the fish-eyes gobble you up!" he replied.

Gilla snorted. "In broad daylight? I'd like to see them try! Besides, our Vanda says they're only people like ourselves, for all their funny looks, and serving that Lady Kurrekai, she should know. Will you trust Bazaar tales or your own daughter's word?" She backed out of the doorway, hoisted the child onto one broad haunch, and scooped up the market basket.

The building shook beneath Gilla's heavy tread as she went down the stairs, and Lalo moved back to the window to see her down the street. The hot sunlight gilded her fading hair until it was as bright as the child's.

Then she was gone, and he was alone with the mirror and his fear.

A man called Zanderei had asked Lalo if he had ever painted a self-portrait—whether he had ever dared to find out if the gift the sorcerer Enas Yorl had given him of painting the truth of a man would enable him to make a portrait of his own soul. In return, Lalo had given Zanderei his life, and at first he had been so glad to be alive himself that he did not worry about Zanderei's words. Then the Beysib fleet had appeared on the horizon, with the sun striking flame from their mastheads and their carven prows, and no one had had leisure to worry about anything else for awhile. But now things were quiet and Lalo had no commissions to occupy him, and he could not keep his eyes from the mirror that hung on the wall.

Lalo heard a dog barking furiously in the street and two women squabbling in the courtyard below and, more faintly, the perpetual hubbub of the Bazaar; but here it was very still. A stretched canvas sat ready on his easel—he had been planning to spend this morning blocking out a scene of the marriage of Ils and Shipri. But there was no one else in the house now—no one to peer through his doorway and ask what he thought he was doing—no one to see.

Like a sleepwalker, Lalo lifted the easel to one side of

the mirror, positioned himself so that the light from the window fell full on his face, and picked up the paint-brush.

Then, like a lover losing himself for the first time in the body of his beloved, or an outmatched swordsman opening his guard to his enemy's final blow, Lalo began to paint what he saw.

Gilla heaved the basket of groceries onto the table, rescued the sack of flour from the child's exploring fingers, and poured it into the bin, then found a wooden spoon for Alfi and set him down, where he began to bang it merrily against the floor. She stood for a moment, still a little out of breath from the stairs, then began to put her other purchases away.

It did not take long. The influx of Beysib had strained Sanctuary's food supply, and their wealth had sent prices climbing, and though Gilla had hoarded a fair amount of silver, there was no telling how long it would be until Lalo was working regularly again. So it was back to rice and beans for the family, with an occasional fish in the stew. Now that so many new ships had been added to the local fleet, fish were the one item in ample supply.

Gilla sighed. She had enjoyed their affluence—enjoyed putting meat on the table and experimenting with the spices imported from the north. But they had subsisted on coppers for more years than she liked to remember, and few enough of those. She was an expert on feeding a family on peas and promises. They would survive the Beysib as they had survived everything else.

Alfi's short legs were carrying him determinedly toward the door to Lalo's studio. Gilla scooped him up and held him against her, still squirming, and kissed his plump cheek.

"No, love, not in there—Papa's working and we must leave him alone!"

But it was odd that Lalo had not at least called a welcome when he heard her come in. When he was painting a sitter, Vashanka could have blasted the house without his noticing, but there had been no commissions for some time, and when Lalo painted for pleasure he was usually glad for an excuse to break off for a cup of tea. She called to Latilla to take her little brother into the children's room to play, then coaxed a fire to life in the stove and put the kettle on.

Lalo still had not stirred.

"Lalo, love—I've got water heating; d'you want a cup of tea?" She stood for a moment, hands on hips, frowning at the shut, unresponsive door; then she marched across the floor and opened it.

"You could at least answer me!" Gilla stopped. Lalo was not at his easel. For a moment she thought he must have decided to go out, yet the door had not been locked. But there was something different about the room. Lalo was standing by the far wall, for all the world like a piece of furniture. It took another moment for her to realize that he had not moved when she came in. He had not even looked at her.

Swiftly she went to him. He stood as if he had backed across the room step by careful step until he ran into the wall. The paintbrush was still clenched in one hand; she tugged it free and set it down. And still he did not move. His eyes were fixed, unseeing, on the easel across the room. She glanced at it—a man's face, and at this distance she saw nothing remarkable—then turned to him again.

"Lalo, are you all right? Did you hear me? Shipri All-Mother have mercy—Lalo, what's wrong?" She shook his arm and still he did not respond to her, and a sick fear uncoiled itself beneath her heart and began to grow.

Gilla gathered him into her ample embrace and for a moment held him unresisting. His body was warm, and she could feel his heart beating very slowly against her own, but she knew with dreadful certainty that he was no longer there. Biting her lip, she guided him to the pallet and arranged him on it as one of the children might arrange a doll.

Fear's chill tentacles extended all the way to her fingertips now, and she remained kneeling before Lalo, chafing his hands less for his sake than for her own. His eyes were unfocused, the pupils darkly dilated. He was not looking at her. He had not been looking at the painting either, although his face had been turned toward it when she came in. These eyes were focused on something beyond their familiar walls, perhaps something even beyond Sanctuary—some inner darkness into which a man might fall forever and find no rest.

Shivering, Gilla tried to close his eyelids, but they slid open again upon that awful, sightless stare. She could feel a scream crouched in her breast, waiting for her to give way to horror and set it free, but she set her teeth painfully and heaved herself to her feet.

Hysterics would do neither of them any good now. Time enough to release the grief that was building in her when—if—there was no hope for him. Perhaps it was some strange seizure that would soon pass, or a new sickness that time and her strict nursing would cure. Or perhaps (her mind probed delicately at a darker thought and flinched away), perhaps it was sorcery.

"Lalo—" she said softly, as if her voice could still reach him somehow, "Lalo my darling, it's all right. I'll get you a doctor; I'll *make* you get well!" Already her mind was considering. If he did not wake of himself by tomorrow she would have to find a physician—perhaps Alten Stulwig—she had heard that his potions saved more lives than they took.

The teakettle began to wail, and as she hurried across the room, her hip set the easel teetering. Without stopping, she picked it up and set it in the corner with the picture facing the wall.

Lalo peered uneasily through murky clouds that roiled

about him like the mage-wind that had devastated Sanctuary the year before. But his life was still in him, though the stink was enough to drive the breath from a man's lungs. For a moment he thought himself back in the sewers of the Maze, but there was too much light. So where in the name of Shalpa Shadow-lord had he gotten to?

He took a step forward, then another, his feet finding their own way over the uneven ground. The colors that streaked the clouds nauseated him—sulfur yellow that shaded into a livid pink like an unhealed scar, and then to something else—an unnameable color that made his eyes hurt so that he had to look away.

Perhaps I am dead, he thought then. *Poor Gilla will grieve for me, but she has her hoard, and the older children are earning money of their own. She will do better without me than I would if she had left me alone.* . . . The thought was bitter, and he found himself weeping as he stumbled along. But the tears had no substance and after a little they disappeared. He returned to his probing, as a man will tongue the sore space where a tooth has gone.

All of the priests were wrong, both the ones who said that the gods take departed souls to paradise and those who are convinced one is condemned to Hell. Or perhaps I have such a spineless soul that I have deserved neither, and so they have sentenced me to wander here!

Lalo had spent half his life dreaming of escape from Sanctuary. But now he had lost Sanctuary, and he was astonished by the passion of his longing to see it again.

Something scurried by him and he jumped. Was it a rat? *Were* there rats here? And surely now he could see cobblestones beneath his feet. Trembling, Lalo stared around him as dim forms precipitated from the shadows —walls, perhaps, with arched doorways and the eaves of roofs peaking like broken teeth against a lurid sky. There—surely that was the broad façade of Jubal's place, but that was impossible—the Stepsons had

burned it, hadn't they? And then he was certain of the
wrongness, for next to it he saw the familiar skewed sign
of the Vulgar Unicorn, but the unicorn's eyes glowed
evilly, and blood dripped down its spiraled horn.

Abruptly he realized that he was beginning to hear
sounds, too—the kind of drunken laughter that comes
from men who watch a bully's fist smash a boy's face to
raw meat, or who take a woman one after another; the
kind of screaming he had heard once when he hurried
past Kurd's workshop, and the choked gurgle the
hanged men made as they died in the Palace Yard. He
had heard all those sounds in Sanctuary, and closed his
ears to them, but he could not ignore the sobbing that
seemed to come from somewhere just before him, the
hushed, incredulous whimpering of an abused child.

I was wrong, he thought, *I am in Hell after all!*

Lalo began to run forward, and suddenly figures were
all around him. Hawkmasks and Stepsons struggled as
lopped limbs flew like scythed wheat and drops of blood
splattered the cobbles like rain. A man staggered by him
and Lalo thought that it was Zanderei; then the figure
turned and he reeled back, for the face was gone.

Another came toward him—Sjekso Kinsan, with
whom he had shared a drink sometimes in the Vulgar
Unicorn, and behind him a woman with long amber
hair, Lord Regli's wife, Samlane, whom Lalo had
painted long ago, before he met Enas Yorl, before the
woman had died. There were others whom he thought
he recognized, thieves whose contorted features he had
seen on the gallows, Hell Hounds or mercenaries whom
he had seen in Sanctuary for awhile and then saw no
more.

They were looking at him, now, and closing around
him. Lalo began to run, burrowing through the dark
maze of this shadow Sanctuary like a maggot in an ancient corpse, seeking some unimaginable safety.

"Woman, you were fortunate to get me here at all!"

Alten Stulwig said stiffly. "My patients come to me, and I am certainly not accustomed to visiting this part of town!"

"But you know that my husband has influential friends who might object if you let their pet artist die unseen, don't you!" said Gilla nastily. "So you stop avoiding my eyes like a whore with her first customer and tell me what's wrong with him!" She lifted an arm as broad as Stulwig's thigh and he swallowed and glanced nervously down at the man on the pallet.

"It's a complex case, and there's no need to confuse you with medical terminology." He cleared his throat. "I am afraid—"

"Now that I *will* believe!" Gilla snatched his satchel and held it to her massive breast.

"What—what are you doing? Give me that!"

"I don't need your leech's twaddle, nor your evasions either, *Master* Alten. You just find something in this bag of yours that will make my man well!" She thrust it back at him and he shrugged, sighed, and opened it.

"This is a stimulant, *dograya*. You steep it into a tea and spoon-feed him four times a day. It will strengthen his heart, and who knows, it may bring him around." He tossed the little packet on the coverlet and rummaged around in the bag again, bringing out several yellowish cones wrapped in a twist of cloth. "And you can try burning these—if the smell doesn't rouse him I don't know what will." He straightened and held out his hand. "Two *sheboozim*—gold."

"Why Alten, I'm surprised—aren't you going to ask me to share your bed?" Gilla's laughter covered bitterness she had not allowed herself to feel for a long time as he blanched and looked away. She drew from between her breasts the thin chamois bag in which she kept her reserve of gold. There was more, hidden cunningly beneath floorboards or in the wall—even Lalo did not know where it was—but a house could burn. Better to keep something on her person against emergencies.

She slapped the coins into Stulwig's moist palm and watched, glaring, as he packed up his satchel and picked up the staff he had leaned against the door.

"The blessing of Heqt upon the healing—" he mumbled.

"And upon the hands of the healer," Gilla responded automatically, but she was thinking, *I have wasted my money. He doesn't believe his paltry herbs will do any good either.* She listened to the hurried clatter of Stulwig's sandals on the stairs as he hastened to reach his own lodging before darkness fell, but her eyes were on Lalo's still face.

And suddenly it seemed to her that his breathing had deepened and there was the suggestion of a crease between his brows. She stiffened, watching, while hope fluttered in her heart like a trapped moth, until his features grew smooth again. She thought of the great waves that sometimes slapped at the wharves though the sky was clear, that fishermen said were the last ripple from some great storm far out to sea.

Oh my beloved, she thought in anguish, *what bitter storms are raging in the far reaches where you wander now?*

The children were waiting for her when she came out of the studio, all of them except for her oldest, Wedemir, who was a junior master with the caravans. Her daughter Vanda had gotten leave from her Beysib lady when Gilla sent for her, and sat now with Alfi on her lap, looking at her mother with a fair approximation of the flat Beysib stare. Even her second boy, Ganner, had begged time from his apprenticeship with Herewick the Jeweler to come home. Only eight-year-old Latilla, playing with her doll on the floor, seemed oblivious of the tension in the room.

Gilla glared back at them, knowing they must have heard her argument with Alten Stulwig. What did they expect her to say?

"Well?" she snapped. "Stop looking at me like a

batch of gaffed cod! And somebody put the teakettle on!''

Lalo was following the scent, familiar as the stink of a man's own closestool, of sorcery.

He knew this much about the strange existence he was caught in now—even a dauber whose only magic had flowed through his fingers could smell sorcery here, and though in that other life Lalo had been wary of wizards, he had not been quite wary enough, and that was the start of the road that had led him here.

There, for instance, was the gaudy presence of the Mageguild, a mixture of odors from the faint aromas of the magelings to the full-blown, exotic outpourings of the Hazard-class wizards who were their masters—a potpourri with all the mixed fascination of Prince Kitty-cat's garbage bin. Here also was the alien tang of Beysib ritual, and the fuggy flavors produced by all the little hedge-wizards and crones, and the wavering scents of those who served in the temples of the gods.

But what he was seeking was not in the temples, though it came from a place that was close by—a house whose very foundations were sorcery. Someone was working a spell there even now, elegant magics that sent spirals of power smoking into the dim air. Lalo had known that flavor before, though he had not then recognized it—the unique atmosphere that surrounded Enas Yorl.

Focusing, he found that he could interpret what he was sensing as color, a line of light that snaked outward, another crossing it, and another, a net to capture any spirit that might be wandering there. And Lalo could feel the presence of those Others, beings less conscious than the ghosts he fled, but more active and aware.

A Symbol flickered into being in the center of the knot, pulsing lividly, color, shape, and flavor all combined to lure its intended prey. Lalo shuddered as something swept by him. The glowing lines distorted

and the Symbol in their midst dissolved and then re-
formed, imprisoning a roil of writhing energy and forc-
ing it into a form that human eyes could, however un-
willingly, see. But the Gateway that had opened for the
creature was still there, and Lalo, frantic for contact,
thrust himself through.

"*Ehas, barabarishti, azgeldui m'hai tsi!* Oh thou who
dost know the secrets of Life and Death, come to me!
Yevoi! Yevad!" The Voice snapped shut the gap and set
the imprisoned entity to whirling in a shower of nitrate
and sulfur-smelling sparks.

Lalo contracted like an upset snail, seeking to avoid
the touch of that light, the sound of those words. They
were the language of the plane from which the spirit had
come, and Lalo's present condition gave him the power
to directly apprehend them, and to realize that there
were worse places than the one in which he found himself now.

"*Evgolod sheremin, shinaz, shinaz, tiserra-neh,
yevoi!*" The Voice rolled on, conjuring the creature to
bring to him the knowledge of how to separate the soul
from a body to which it had been obscenely and in-
dissolubly fettered by sorcery, of a way, though the
price of it might be annihilation, to set such a soul
forever free. Lalo cowered from knowledge that was
never meant for his ears.

But presently the Voice stilled, the echoes died away,
and Lalo allowed himself to focus on the insubstantial
figure that stood within its own shimmering circle
beyond the triangle within which Lalo and the demon
shared an unwilling captivity. It was Enas Yorl—it
must be—yes, he would always know those glowing
eyes.

And at the same moment Enas Yorl appeared to
realize that his summoning had been more successful
than he intended. A wand rose, and power swirled and
eddied in the still air.

"Begone, oh ye intruding spirit, to thine own realm

where thou shalt wait until I do summon thee!''

Lalo was tumbled by a riptide of power and for a moment knew a desperate hope that the sorcerer's instinctive house-cleaning would send him home. But where was home, now?

Then the power ebbed, and Lalo sat up, still in the triangle. The demon in the sigil beside him spat and reached for him with flaming claws.

"Oh thou spirit who hast come to my summoning, I conjure thee to tell me thy name." Enas Yorl seemed unmoved by his first failure, and Lalo began to understand the patience and plain nerve required for wizardry.

He got to his feet and approached the edge of the triangle as closely as he dared. "It's me, Lalo the Limner. Enas Yorl, don't you recognize me?"

And as he waited for the sorcerer to reply, Lalo realized that he himself recognized Enas Yorl, and that was very strange, for the essence of the curse that tormented the sorcerer was that his form should never remain for long the same. With a kind of horrified fascination, Lalo looked into the true face of Enas Yorl.

He read there passions and evils at the limit of his comprehension, barely confined by lines of vision and tormented love. In that face all that was great and terrible were joined in an eternal conflict that only the slow erosion of hopeless years might ever hope to reconcile. And those years had already become so long. It was a face whose planes had been chiseled out by the relentless blade of power, ground down again by a kind of patient, painful despair. At last he understood why Enas Yorl had refused to let Lalo paint his portrait. He wondered which part of it the sorcerer feared most to see.

"Enas Yorl, I know *you*, but I don't know what I am, or why I am here!"

The sorcerer certainly saw him now, and he was laughing. "You're not dead, if that's what was worrying you, and there's no stink of magic about you. Were you fevered, or did that mountain you are married to knock you senseless at last?''

Lalo sputtered, denying it, while he tried to remember. "There was nothing—I was painting; I was alone, and—"

Abruptly the sorcerer grew grave. "You were painting? Yourself, perhaps? Now I understand. Poor little pond-fish—you have opened the forbidden weir and been swept through it into the great sea. Those whose portraits you have painted could reject the truth they saw, but *you* could not reject what you painted on the canvas without denying all you are!"

Lalo was silent, testing his memories. He had been painting a picture, and he had stepped back from the canvas when he was done, and he had seen. . . . Awareness lurched beneath him, dizzying—he glimpsed depths and distances, upwelling springs of light and darkness that could drown him equally, a universe of power that had been trapped beneath the façade that was the self he knew.

"And so you have run away from both the truth and its image, and your body lies abandoned somewhere. I can return you to it, if you truly desire—but don't you understand? Now you are free! Do you know what I would give to achieve what you have inadvertently—" the sorcerer stopped himself, "but I forgot. Your body is whole, and young. . . ."

Lalo scarcely heard. His first sight of the vastness within had been sufficient to send him in frantic retreat into the shadow-realm. But whence could he escape from here? The meaning of his vision hovered on the edge of comprehension, terrifying, tantalizing, beating at his awareness like mighty wings.

And then the wings were outside of him as well as within; the captive demon spiraled away in pinwheels of foul sparks like burning wool and the exquisite lattices of power within which Enas Yorl had imprisoned it were shattered by a rift between the worlds through which dark wings sliced like swords.

Pain dismemoried and dismembered him, and Lalo's consciousness was whirled away, trailed by the sorcerer's unavailing cry—

"Sikkintair, sikkintair!"

Gilla pulled her cloak more tightly around her and hurried over the worn cobblestones of Prytanis Street, hoping that the patter she had heard behind her was only wind-drifted leaves. The Jewelers' Quarter was supposed to be safer for foot travelers than the Bazaar, but everyone on her home ground knew that Gilla was not worth tackling.

But of course she was, today. Nervously she fingered the bag at her neck where the remainder of her little hoard of gold weighed so heavily. The services of wizards came high. Gilla cursed them all, cursed Alten Stulwig for his incompetence and Illyra the half-S'danzo who had been able to tell her only that wizardry was somehow involved, cursed Lalo for having gotten into this mess and most of all, cursed herself for her fear.

And the rustle behind her resolved into the thud of running feet, and Gilla wheeled, fear-fueled anger strengthening the massive arm that smacked into the first cutpurse as he came on. He buckled with a sound like a sliced bladder, and a knife glittered through the air to rebound with a tinny clatter from the nearest wall. Gilla brought her other fist down on the man's head and waded into his companion before he quite realized why his point man was down; she belabored his ears with all the obscenities that a lifetime on the edge of the Maze had taught her as she put her full weight into her blows.

The blood was singing in her veins and most of her fear had been washed away by adrenalin by the time

Gilla dusted herself off and resumed her progress. Behind her two battered figures stirred, groaned, and subsided again.

That martial energy carried her all the way past the last of the carpetmaker's shops and the stares of their owners, rolling up their wares now as the sun descended and painted the city with its fiery glow. It carried her all the way to the door of Enas Yorl.

But there she halted, her eye mazed by the sinuous swirl of brazen dragons that adorned it, her hand on the chill metal of the knocker, not quite daring to let it go. All the tales she had ever heard of the sorcerer yammered at her in the voices her children had used when she told them what she meant to do.

What am I doing here? Who am I to meddle with wizards? The voices were gentle, reasonable, and then, from some deeper part of her being came the thought: *Lalo passed through this door and came home to me. Where he has gone, I can go too.*

Gilla let the knocker fall.

The door opened silently. The blind servant of whom she had heard was standing there, with a silken blindfold in his hand. Licking lips that were suddenly dry, Gilla tied it around her head and let the servant take her hand.

At least she had the advantage of knowledge. Lalo had told her about Darous, and the blindfold, and the peculiar guardians that laired in the sorcerer's entry hall. But the sound of scales on stone and the sense of myriad bodies slithering about her nearly undid her, for snakes were her particular fear. *They're not snakes!* she told herself. *They're only basilisks!* But her fingers tightened on the cool hand of her guide and she was breathing hard when they emerged into another chamber in which some musky incense mingled sickeningly with the smell of sulfur.

The blindfold was taken away and Gilla looked around her with a sigh. The stone walls were stained with carbon, and a melted tangle of metal that had once been a brazier lay in the middle of the floor. A daybed was set into an embrasure in the marble walls, and after a moment Gilla realized that the huddle of rich fabrics upon it covered a man. She crossed her arms beneath her breasts and stared at him.

"After the bull, the cow," Enas Yorl said tiredly. "I might have known."

"Lalo?" Gilla saw the thin hand that lay upon the velvet quiver, shift, and become a more muscular member whose skin bore a thin dusting of bluish scales. Gilla swallowed and forced herself not to look away. "Lalo's been in some kind of trance for two weeks now. I want you to get him back into his body again." She reached for the bag at her neck.

"Keep your gold," the sorcerer said querulously. "Your husband already asked me that question and I agreed—it would be amusing to see what Sanctuary would make of a man who has faced his own soul—but Lalo is beyond my reach now."

"Beyond your reach?" Gilla's voice echoed painfully. "But they call you the greatest wizard in the Empire!" She met the red glow of the sorcerer's eyes, and after a moment it dimmed and he looked away.

"I am great enough to know the limits of my power," he answered bitterly. "I cannot speak for the Beysib, but no mage of Sanctuary will meddle with Sikkintair. The Flying Knives have taken your husband, woman. Go to the Temple of Ils and see if Gordonesh the priest will listen to you. Or better still, go home—Lalo is gods' business now."

The Sikkintair devoured Lalo's flesh and scoured his bones until the wind harped through his rib cage and drummed out a rhythm with the long bones of his thighs. His clever painter's hands, stripped of the muscle that had made their magic, rattled like winter-bared twigs against the sky.

And when they were done with the skeleton they let it fall, and mother earth laid down new flesh around his bones. He lay thus enwombed for a season or a century, and when his time was accomplished he found himself naked in a forest glade starred with flowers like jewels, his new body as supple and strong as a honed blade.

He jumped up and began to walk, content for the moment simply to enjoy the colors and the soft air and the singing power of this new body of his. And presently he heard music and turned his steps toward the sound.

Where the oak trees thinned, a grassy lawn sloped down to a pool fed by a gurgling waterfall. A table had been set there, covered with a cloth of crimson damask fringed with gold, and upon that cloth crystal flagons with wine of Carronne, platters of roasted meats and loaves of white bread and silver dishes heaped with oranges from Enlibar. *A feast fit for the gods*, thought Lalo. And indeed, the gods were feasting there.

"We have been expecting you," said a voice at his elbow. A maiden more beautiful than the fairest of Prince Kadakithis's concubines held out a robe of blue silk embroidered with dragons for him to put on, then knelt to ease his feet into sandals of gold. Her black hair curled to her hips, shimmering with blue lights in the sun, and when she looked up he recognized in her features the face of Valira, the little whore whom he had painted as Eshi, Lady of Love, and he trembled, understanding Who was serving him.

She led him to a seat at the end of the table and he began to eat, grateful that for the moment the other gods were continuing to talk among themselves. Next to Eshi sat one whom he could only suppose to be Anen—paunched and red-nosed like the bibbers who had been Lalo's companions in the days when he sought oblivion in the bottom of a mug of cheap wine. But the god's fat was opulence, and his flushed cheeks burned with a glow to lighten the hopeless heart. Remembering favors granted in times past, Lalo solemnly saluted him.

And the god saw, and looked at him, and meeting those deep eyes Lalo recognized a mute sorrow and remembered that this was the god who yearly dies and is reborn. Then Anen smiled, and as joy fountained in Lalo's heart, he saw that his goblet was filling with wine like the blood of a star.

The wine gave him courage to look at the others —gentle Theba the peace-bringer, and swift-footed Shalpa like a shadow beside her, whose face, when Lalo glimpsed it, reminded him strangely of someone he had seen often in the Vulgar Unicorn, though he could not for the moment think whom. But he saw the face of every mercenary he had ever known in the harsh features of Him-whom-we-do-not-name, armed and weaponed even here, and the sharp good humor of the women who haggled over fabric in the dyer's stalls in the face of bright-haired Thilli, until he began to realize that he recognized all of them—that he had painted all of them, that he had lived among them all in Sanctuary and never known.

"Father, you have disposed of Vashanka, at least for the present, but the priests of Savankala still hold a place of honor in Sanctuary!" Eshi was speaking to the blaze of light at the head of the table, whom Lalo had still not quite dared to look upon.

"Until a new body for Vashanka to use matures, his power is broken," the voice shimmered in Lalo's ears. "The Rankan gods do not trouble Me now. It is this new goddess, this Bey, that we must consider here."

"Her worshippers in Sanctuary are fugitives and the empire they fled from must still be Her first concern. How much power can She have in Sanctuary?" asked Thilli. For a moment her husband Thufir leaned forward to listen and Lalo flinched away from his eagle glance. The priests called Thufir the friend of the Sikkintair as Ils was their master. They had taught him their far-seeing. Had he ordered them to bring Lalo here?

"I am tired of all this quarreling," sighed Shipri. "I thought that when you had bested the Rankans we would have peace again. I have finally come to an understanding with Sabellia, and I suppose that this new goddess and I will have to do the same. At least She *is* a goddess, and therefore more likely than a god to be sensible about things."

Lalo sat back, relieved. He had painted his own wife as Sabellia, and in the past few minutes he had begun to fear Shipri's jealousy. But Gilla resembled the Sharp-Tongued One less and less these days, and he thought he would have portrayed her as the nurturing Mother of Ilsig now.

Then the splendor of the face of Ils was turned fully upon him, and, even in this remade body unable to gaze into that light, Lalo cried out and hid his eyes.

"Son of Ils, come here . . ." Sound was light, slivering painfully through Lalo's shut lids. He shook his head.

"Lord, I have served in the temple of your enemies, and I am afraid."

"But I have defeated those enemies. Stand on your feet and come to Me!"

I have already died, thought Lalo. *What else can He do to me?* He opened his eyes. Thufir Far-Seer was waiting to guide him to his Father, who masked his radiance with the face of the great marble statue in the Temple of Ils.

"You have painted many portraits since the Mage touched you, Limner—what did you see?"

Lalo fixed his eyes upon the silver necklace that glittered from beneath the god's dark beard. "Beasts . . ." he muttered, "and demons, sometimes, and sometimes . . . gods."

"And when you turned your sorcerer's gift upon yourself?" the implacable voice went on.

Lalo shuddered, but Thufir's grip held him to this reality. He had seen a pleasure in pettiness that shamed him and beyond that a longing for annihilation that terrified him and a capacity for love that terrified him even more. He had seen the depths of his own unguessed, untapped creative power.

"As you served Enas Yorl and the priests of Savankala, so now, my son, you shall serve Me," said the Voice of Ils.

Before him Lalo saw a white canvas, and brushes that surpassed his own as a Downwinder's donkey is surpassed by a horse of Trôs, and a palette with pigments for whose secret the color-grinders of Sanctuary would have given their souls. Lalo's right hand prickled with power that built, built—it must be grounded somehow —he groped for a paintbrush and dipped it into a color that was more than scarlet, touched it to the canvas and felt power surge through it in an explosive release like the climax of love.

His hand moved swiftly, splashing the canvas with scarlet, then down to the palette for a lambent gold, and lastly a shading of opalescent blue. Then he stepped back, the brush falling from his fingers, and the thing on the canvas stretched, flexed, and launched itself glittering into the air.

Eshi laughed and clapped her white hands, and Thufir smiled his slow, patient smile. Lalo stared as the miniature sikkintair that had come to life beneath his hands soared off through the trees.

"Before, you were able to paint the truth behind reality," the whisper of Ils echoed through the deepest chambers of Lalo's soul. "Now you will give Reality to the Truth you see. Do you not yet understand Who you are?"

> Oh Thou Blessed Mother of All Living,
> We wander, children who have lost our way—
> Guard us from all danger, and forgiving,
> Guide us homeward at the close of day.

"Holy Shipri, All-Mother, as Thou dost love Thine

own lord, hear me now!'' Gilla's murmur was lost in the hymn's sweet harmonies. ''Hear me and guide my own man back to me . . .''

Here in the chapel of the Mother, flickering candles struck sparks of color from the mosaics and one scarcely noticed the rough repairs where Vashanka's thunderbolt had cracked the wall. Gilla huddled in the shadows while the blue-robed priestesses passed back and forth before the marble image of the Goddess, continuing their song.

> *Whatever men destroy is for Thy mending,*
> *Forever feeding from Thy fruitful breast;*
> *Thou art the source of life, and at its ending,*
> *Once more within Thy holy womb we rest.*

And what if Lalo is already safe within Her arms? Gilla wondered then. *Perhaps the gods need a court painter, and what does Sanctuary have to offer that could compare?* She bowed her head, rocking back and forth while the chanting continued, sweetly counseling acceptance of life's eternal round of birth and death, and the tears she had so long suppressed fell like rain upon the marble floor.

The priestesses had finished and the chapel was silent when Gilla felt Vanda's touch on her shoulder and let her daughter lead her out into the harsh sunlight of Sanctuary.

''Don't tell me,'' said Vanda. ''Goronesh wouldn't even see you, and those hypocrites who serve Shipri told you that loss is part of the burden that women must bear.''

Gilla looked back at the golden dome of the Temple, still half-sheathed in scaffolding. ''Am I selfish to want Lalo back? I thought I was the strong one, but I need him!''

''Of course you do!'' said Vanda stoutly. ''And so do we!'' Her hair in the sunlight was the same bright copper Lalo's had been when he was young, but her gray eyes were troubled. Gillda swallowed the last of her tears and briskly wiped her eyes.

"You're right—I don't know what got into me!"

"And now will you come with me to see the Lady Kurrekai?"

For the first time since leaving the Temple, Gilla took note of her surroundings, and realized that instead of turning down the Avenue of Temples toward the town they were walking along the outer wall of the Palace Square. She sighed.

"Very well. Let us see what the foreigner can do, for it's certain I'll get no help from mage or god of Sanctuary!"

The Prince had obligingly offered rooms for the Beysa and her court in the Palace, though perhaps he was only making a virtue of necessity. Gilla wondered how they all managed to fit inside. Certainly the place seemed abustle with Beysib functionaries in laced breeks and loose doublets or the flared skirts and high collars they all affected. It seemed to her that they even outnumbered the silk-sashed Palace servants who went about their duties with such ostentatious solemnity.

Gilla looked at her daughter, already aping Beysib fashion in a gown cut down from an old petticoat of her lady's whose borders glittered with threads of gold. Whether this Beysib female was any help or no, certainly Gilla and Lalo had done a good piece of work when they used his Palace connections to get Vanda a position here.

The Lady Kurrekai occupied a chamber on the second floor of the Palace, close to the roomier apartments near the roof garden, which had been taken over by the Beysa. If Gilla understood what Vanda had told her of Beysib politics, Kurrekai was a cousin of Shupansea the Queen, not in direct line for the lost Imperial throne, but royal enough to keep one of the sacred serpents and to have been trained as a priestess.

Gilla shuddered, thinking of the beynit. Enas Yorl's basilisks had been bad enough, and now she must face this imported horror. *I must love that man,* she thought glumly, *or I would be running for home.*

And then they were at the door, and the choice was gone. She smelled some kind of incense, like bitter sandalwood.

"Ah, the mother of my little friend. You are welcome . . ." A voice rather deep and slightly accented greeted them. The figure that rose as they entered was tall and strongly built enough to make Gilla almost feel small. She blinked at the magnificence of the quilted petticoat, whose crimson brocade had been overlaid with goldwork until its original pattern could hardly be discerned, surmounted by panniers of deep blue cut velvet and a corset of the same material with long, tight sleeves. She had not realized before now that beneath the cloaks that Beysib noblewomen wore outside, their breasts were displayed. Kurrekai's breasts were large, firm, and bore nipples that had been intricately painted with a pattern in scarlet and gold.

"Do be seated. I will send for tea." Lady Kurrekai clapped her hands, subsiding back onto her couch in a rustle of silk. Vanda thrust a hassock behind her mother, and Gilla, who was finding that her knees had an alarming tendency to give way, sat down gratefully.

"Your daughter has been very helpful to me," the lady continued languidly. "She is quick, and oh, such pretty hair."

Vanda blushed and took the tea tray from the Beysib woman who had brought it to the door, set it on a low table of some intricately carven dark red wood, and began to pour. The tea service was made from a porcelain so fine it seemed translucent, and Gilla was abruptly conscious of the fact that she had not changed her gown since Lalo fell ill, and that her hair was coming down.

She wanted to get to the point of this visit and get out

of here, but the Beysib noblewoman was inhaling the fragrance of her tea as if nothing else in the universe mattered just now. Vanda remained kneeling before her, until Kurrekai nodded and finally took one ceremonial sip; then she swiveled around to pour tea into her mother's cup and her own. Gilla tasted the brew suspiciously and found it oddly pleasant. She drank it quickly and then held her cup awkwardly in her lap while the lady, with endless deliberation, absorbed her own.

Then, finally, she sighed and set the cup down.

"My Lady," said Vanda eagerly, "I told you about my father's strange illness. We have found no one in this city who can bring him back, but your people are wiser than we. Will you help us now?"

"Child, your sorrow is my own, but what do you suppose I could do?" Kurrekai's head turned within the stiff collar and her slow voice held concern.

"I have heard," Vanda swallowed and her voice went up a note, "I have heard that the venom of the beynit has many properties . . ."

"Ah, my companion," sighed Kurrekai. She leaned back, and from within one hollow pannier appeared a flicker of crimson, followed by a slim black body as the serpent slid slowly out of hiding and coiled itself lazily in the fold of her petticoat. Gilla stared, fascinated, at the darting scarlet tongue and the jeweled eyes.

"What you say is true. The venom can be a powerful stimulant if it is properly . . . changed. . . . But your father is not of my people. For him, only the venom's fatality would be sure."

"But there is a chance?" All the anguish of the past three weeks met in this moment and Gilla found her voice at last. This woman *must* agree to help them!

"I do not wish to kill a man of Sanctuary." The turn of Lady Kurrekai's head held finality.

But Gilla rose, and while Vanda still stared and the Beysib woman was just beginning to look around, launched herself across the room. When she stopped, the beynit was barely a foot from her outstretched hand. The crimson head darted upward like a flame and began to sway.

"Mother, don't *move!*" Vanda's shocked whisper hissed in the air.

Gilla remained still, now that she had reached her goal, looking for the first time directly into Lady Kurrekai's round eyes. "And a woman of Sanctuary?" she said hoarsely. "Why not? Lalo will die anyway and I will die too. Why not here?"

For an endless moment, Gilla held the other woman's unblinking stare. Then Lady Kurrekai shrugged, and with an almost careless movement interposed her fingers between Gilla and the red blur that was striking at her hand.

Stomach churning, Gilla sagged back on her heels. For perhaps the space of a minute the beynit hung with its fangs still embedded in the fleshy part of Lady Kurrekai's thumb. Then it began to wriggle, and the Beysib woman grasped it by the middle, with a little shake detached it, and encouraged it to slide back into the shelter of her pannier once more.

"In the name of Bey the Great Mother, the Holy One!" Kurrekai spoke suddenly, strongly, and then became very still, and though her eyes were open, they had become as lightless as Lalo's. Gilla watched, shivering with nightmares of what would happen if a woman of the Beysib died here. Vanda had crept to her side and was holding to her as she used to when she was a little girl.

There was a long sigh as the lady moved at last, and Gilla was not sure from which of the three of them it had come. A great drop of blood like a cabochon garnet was welling from Lady Kurrekai's thumb. She looked around, gesturing to Vanda with a movement of her head.

"Get me the little crystal vial from the cabinet—the

one with the dipper that used to hold perfume.''

Vanda got to her feet to obey as Lady Kurrekai faced Gilla again. ''I have attempted to transform the venom by altering the nature of my blood, but it must be used immediately. Scratch your husband's flesh so that the blood comes and touch a drop of this to the wound.'' She took the stopper from the vial Vanda was holding out to her, touched it to the drop of blood, and inserted it back in the vial with a little shake, squeezed her hand to produce a second drop, and a third.

''Go now as I have told you, and quickly.'' She thrust the stopper home firmly and handed it to Gilla, then delicately licked the smear of blood from her thumb. ''And remember I warned you—it may fail.''

''The blessing of the All-Mother be on you, Lady, and be you free of any blame.'' Gilla was already on her feet. ''At least you were willing to try!''

They hurried down the corridor, Vanda skipping to keep up with her mother's longer strides and trying to keep her voice down.

''Mother, how could you do that? I was terrified! Mother, you could have died!''

Gilla forged ahead silently, while those they encountered scattered from her path. It was not until they had crossed the Square and passed through the Westgate that opened out onto the familiar streets of Sanctuary that she paused for breath and turned to meet her daughter's wide eyes.

''Vanda, you are a woman now, old enough to take care of the younger ones if you must, and old enough, perhaps, to understand. If this works, you must promise never to tell your father what I have done for him.''

''And if it doesn't?'' Vanda said in a very small voice.

Gilla gazed at the teeming life around her, sunlight glaring harshly off browned faces, sounds of quarreling and laughter, the rich mixture of odors from the street, and for a moment felt as if she had lost her skin and had become a part of all of these.

"I have borne seven children and seen two die, and lived with the same contrary man for twenty-six years," she said slowly, "and I have just realized that I would sacrifice this whole city for one lock of his hair. If this stuff I am going to give him kills him," she shook the hand in which the crystal vial lay hidden, "I'm sorry, Vanda, but I will go after him."

Lalo the god was creating a woman, a goddess as beautiful as Eshi, as bountiful as Shipri, as wise as Sabellia, as dear to him as someone—he could not remember, but the brush splashed gold like sunlight across Her hair. There, the ripeness of breasts that could feed a dozen babes, and the opulence of haunch and thigh, and skin smoother than the silk of Sihan . . . Lalo smiled, and the brush moved as if of itself to suffuse that white flesh with a rosy glow like the inside of a shell.

And then he stepped back from the easel, smiling, and the figure he had been painting turned to him and took him by the hand.

He had expected that, and he reached with his other arm to embrace Her, but She continued to turn in his grasp, drawing him after her, faster and faster until the green meadow blurred around him.

"Wait! Where are we going? Beside the river there is a shady bower where we can lie, and—" Damn! If only She would stop and face him for a moment he would know Her name!

Clouds boiled around him with a roar of thunder. The difference between up and down was disappearing and the paintbrush was torn from his hand.

"Who are you?" he shouted. "Where are you taking me?"

And then he was hurtling through winds that tore away his awareness until he knew nothing but the implacable grip that held his hand. The world had disintegrated into pain and darkness, but through the clouds that whirled around him he glimpsed brief images—the pretentious splendors of a great city where a beleaguered emperor's banner flew; armies crawling like lines of ants across the plains; mountains that shuddered with the struggles of men and mages, and here and there a pocket of greater darkness where forces worse than human strove for mastery.

And then he saw below him a familiar curve of harbor and a tangle of houses and a tarnished golden dome, and pain clapped great hands around him and he fell.

Lalo's mouth tasted like the midden of the Vulgar Unicorn and he felt as if the Stepsons had been practicing maneuvers on the inside of his skull. Except for an annoying throbbing in his arm, he could hardly feel his body at all.

And Gilla was calling him.

Holy Anen blast me if I ever touch that wine again! he thought muzzily, and perhaps presently he would remember just what wine it had been. But now that he considered, he could not remember anything about what must have been an epic binge, and that worried him. Gilla would be furious if she had had to drag him home, and from the taste in his mouth he must have been sick, too. He groaned, wishing fervently that he could pass out again.

"Lalo! Lalo my darling, you've got to wake up! You wretched man, I heard you—open your eyes and look at me!"

Something wet ran down his neck and someone near him stifled a sob. Gilla? Gilla? But she would never weep over him after a drinking bout—a pail of cold water, maybe, but not tears. How long had he been unconscious, anyway?

As if he were trying to work an old lock with a rusty key, Lalo opened his eyes.

He was lying on the pallet in his studio. Alfi and

Latilla crouched at the foot of it, watching him with wide, awed eyes. Vanda was behind them, but her face held the look of one who has been suddenly released from fear. He turned his eyes—he did not yet trust himself to move his head—to the bedside, and saw Gilla. Her face was puffy and her eyes red from weeping, and as his gaze met hers they glistened with another tear.

Without thinking, he reached up and brushed it from her cheek; then he stared at his hand, pallid and veined and *thin*. And now that awareness of the rest of his body was returning, he realized that he felt curiously light, and his other hand clutched at the bedclothes as if to hold him there.

"Gilla, have I been ill?"

"Ill! You might call it that—and I'd rather not know what else it might be—" exploded Gilla, and Vanda got to her feet.

"Father, you've been lying in some kind of trance for almost three weeks now," Vanda added.

Three weeks? But just this afternoon he had been . . . painting. . . . He had looked in the mirror and then. . . . Lalo began to tremble as memory came back to him. His eyes filled with tears for the beauty of the other world, but Gilla's hands closed on his shoulders, and she shook him back to her own reality.

Lalo stared at her, and through the veil of her swollen features he saw the face of the goddess who had brought him home. It took a kind of inner focusing, and he found that now he could see another face beneath his daughter's familiar mask of cheerfulness too. Only the two younger children remained essentially the same.

So, he thought, *perhaps I will not need a paintbrush to do my seeing now*. He lay back, trying to assimilate the truth of what had happened to him into his memory of the man he used to be.

"So, how do you feel? Is there anything you want me to get you now?" Gilla finished wiping her eyes and resolutely blew her nose on a corner of her apron.

Lalo smiled. "Well, I haven't eaten for three whole weeks—"

"Vanda, there's soup on the stove," Gilla said sharply. "Go heat it up, and you little ones go with her. You've seen him, and Father doesn't need you underfoot here. Everything will be all right now."

Gilla bustled nervously about the room, smoothing the covers, heaping pillows behind Lalo so that he could sit, pushing a chair back against the wall. Lalo flexed his fingers, feeling them tingle as blood began to circulate freely once more, and wondered how he had gotten the scratch on his arm.

Beside the pallet were piled some scraps of paper and a piece of charcoal. *Can I still draw?* he wondered, and seeing that Gilla was not watching him, he pulled a piece of paper toward him, picked up the charcoal and drew a line, then another, then some shading, and the paper showed him a deftly drawn representation of a common Sanctuary dunghill fly. He stared at it for a moment with a question he dared not even put into words, but it remained unchanged before him—a drawing of a fly.

Lalo smiled a little wryly and set the charcoal down. *What did I expect, here?*

Gilla came back to him with the bowl of steaming soup in her hands, sat down beside the pallet, and dipped in the spoon. Lalo blew gently on his drawing to get rid of the charcoal dust and laid it aside. When Gilla held the spoon to his lips he opened his mouth obediently. *I could do this myself*, he thought, but he realized that feeding him fulfilled some need of Gilla's own. The hot liquid soothed his throat, and his body seemed to absorb the moisture like a sponge.

"That's enough for now," said Gilla, taking it away.

"It was very good." Lalo looked at her face, wondering how he had ever seen anything but the goddess there. Then he frowned. "I was painting a picture, Gilla. What happened to it?"

She nodded toward the corner. "It's over there. Do

you want to see?'' Before he could stop her she had gone to pick up the painting and brought it to him, leaning it against the wall.

He stared at it, reading it as he had read Gilla's face a moment ago, and knowing that he would never be able to forget the journey from which he had just returned. It would take some getting used to.

"A self-portrait,'' said Gilla meditatively. "Of course. I didn't really want to look at it before.''

After a moment he cleared his throat, knowing that in this knowledge, at least, they were equals now. "Well?''

"Well," she said slowly, "you must know that this is the way you always look to me.''

Her hand moved to enfold his, and feeling suddenly light-headed, Lalo lay back against the pillows again. His ears were buzzing—no—it was only a fly circling in the middle of the room. He thought a moment, then, feeling a little foolish, glanced down at the piece of paper that still lay on the coverlet.

It was blank. Lalo looked up quickly and saw the fly spiral across to the mirror, for a moment hover there, then buzz purposefully through the window and away.

MURDER, MAYHEM, SKULDUGGERY... AND A CAST OF CHARACTERS YOU'LL NEVER FORGET!

THIEVES' WORLD™

EDITED BY
ROBERT LYNN ASPRIN and LYNN ABBEY

FANTASTICAL ADVENTURES

One Thumb, the crooked bartender at the Vulgar Unicorn...
Enas Yorl, magician and shape changer...*Jubal*, ex-gladiator and
crime lord...*Lythande the Star-browed*, master swordsman
and would-be wizard...these are just a few of the players you will
meet in a mystical place called Sanctuary™. This is *Thieves' World*.
Enter with care.

__80584-1 THIEVES' WORLD	$2.95	
__80585-X TALES FROM THE VULGAR UNICORN	$2.95	
__80586-8 SHADOWS OF SANCTUARY	$2.95	
__78713-4 STORM SEASON	$2.95	
__80587-6 THE FACE OF CHAOS	$2.95	
__80588-4 WINGS OF OMEN	$2.95	
__14089-0 THE DEAD OF WINTER	$2.95	
__77581-0 SOUL OF THE CITY	$2.95	
__80595-7 BLOOD TIES	$2.95	
(On sale August '86)		

Stories
⊱ of ⊰
Swords and Sorcery